"I *can't* be Jake Monroe's parole officer."

Rachel could hear the tinge of desperation in her voice, but Harold seemed not to notice.

"Like it or not, Rachel, you're it," he said. "I can't just hire someone off the street. People around here will be looking to see how well we can keep Little Jake Monroe out of trouble."

Rachel's temper snapped. "He's not 'Little' Jake, damn it! He's twenty-nine years old and six foot three. I wish people would stop calling him that."

Harold cleared his throat. "You're a good social worker. You care about people. But you can't get sentimental about Lit—ah—Jake Monroe."

I'm not sentimental. I'm the mother of his child.

ABOUT THE AUTHOR

Linda Markowiak is a former trial lawyer who once argued a case before the Ohio Supreme Court before turning to writing romance. She likes incorporating courtroom drama into her books, and loves most of all to write a happy ending.

Linda and her husband, Jim, own a gifts and collectibles store in northern Ohio, and have a ten-year-old son, Stephen, a twenty-year-old cat and a ninety-four-pound dog. She writes about what she loves and values: families, small communities and good people determined to do the right thing despite the obstacles. In what passes these days for spare time, she enjoys traveling, reading and long walks.

Books by Linda Markowiak

HARLEQUIN SUPERROMANCE
629—COURTING VALERIE
717—FIRM COMMITMENT
755—MOTIVE FOR MARRIAGE
785—RELUCTANT WITNESS

Don't miss any of our special offers. Write to us at the following address for information on our newest releases.

Harlequin Reader Service
U.S.: 3010 Walden Ave., P.O. Box 1325, Buffalo, NY 14269
Canadian: P.O. Box 609, Fort Erie, Ont. L2A 5X3

LOVE, LIES & ALIBIS
Linda Markowiak

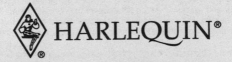

TORONTO • NEW YORK • LONDON
AMSTERDAM • PARIS • SYDNEY • HAMBURG
STOCKHOLM • ATHENS • TOKYO • MILAN • MADRID
PRAGUE • WARSAW • BUDAPEST • AUCKLAND

ISBN 0-373-70819-X

LOVE, LIES & ALIBIS

Thank you to Karen Nowak,
assistant prosecutor, terrific trial attorney,
colleague and friend, for patiently answering all my
odd questions about murder and the parole system.

PROLOGUE

Ten years ago

"THE JURY IS BACK with a verdict," the bailiff announced.

The jury is back. The jury is back. The one thought kept circling in Jake Monroe's mind. *Good, just think that one thought. Don't let them see how scared you are.* With the sheriff's deputy on one side and his court-appointed lawyer on the other, Jake walked into the courtroom. Judge Randall had taken his place on the bench. Jake's eyes flitted to the jury box. Still empty, but in five minutes—ten?—he'd discover if, at age nineteen, his life was over.

The jury is back.... God, it was useless to repeat the words because now he really couldn't shut out all the other thoughts. They kept coming through the fear, thoughts curling up from his toes, touching his damp palms to flash into his brain.

He was innocent. He didn't do it. Nobody would believe him because he was Little Jake Monroe, whose first sin was being born the son of Big Jake Monroe....

Jake panicked. The prosecutor had said Jake had motive and opportunity. Nobody believed that he hadn't done it—not even Rachel...and the jury was back....

Please, he thought, but it wasn't exactly a prayer. Jake Monroe had never learned how. He looked around, trying desperately to reorient himself. The jury hadn't entered the courtroom yet, but the spectators had. The Grange *Post Gazette* reporter, the guy from the Columbus paper, the good folk of tiny Grange, Ohio.

Get a grip, Jake. He straightened his spine and rubbed his palms on the thighs of his cheap khaki slacks. They were the pants his public defender had bought him so he wouldn't have to wear his prison jumpsuit in front of the jury, and freak them into a hasty judgment. It was about the only tangible thing Ben Kismer had done for him. Ben was only a year out of law school, and Jake was one of his first clients.

"Sit down," Ben said, looking almost as young and nearly as uptight as Jake.

From behind, he could hear more people coming into the gallery. Was Rachel here? He'd told her not to come. He'd shouted at her to stay away. But if she was here, maybe he wouldn't panic, or let them see him cry. Or beg.

Rachel wouldn't be here. She hadn't come for the whole trial. Even Rachel didn't believe in him.

He had loved her. He'd talked to her, told her things he'd never told anyone else. He'd held her in the back of the cab of the old farm pickup and touched her perfect body. And all the time, he hadn't quite been able to believe she loved him. He marveled that of all the girls he'd known, it was Rachel Penning, with her good-girl prissiness and high-class looks, who had seen some good in him.

He'd had so many plans. *They'd* had so many plans.

Until the police had come for him one night. He'd come home after he'd finished cleaning Joann Floutz's gutters. His father was drunk again, zonked out on the sofa. Jake was in the barn, trying to fix the cows' water tank. While Big Jake had been getting tanked, he'd let the cows' water run dry. The cows were restless, uncomfortable, milling around the receptacle, lapping at the dry, rusty metal of the tank bottom.

So first Jake had hauled water for the cows in buckets, two heavy buckets at a time, from the faucet on the porch along the slick path to the barn. By his side on every trip was Spook, his old white dog. When the police had come, they'd found Jake in the barn. He was on his knees, a pipe wrench in his hand, trying to unclog the waterline. He was caked with manure. Cow dung and Spook had been Jake's only alibis when they'd questioned him about the murder of Joann Floutz.

He was nineteen years old, and he didn't trust easily. Certainly he didn't trust the local cops. He'd been so very, very scared. So he'd lied. He'd said Rachel had been with him that night. He was with Rachel most of the time nowadays anyway, though they met in secret. Rachel would say he'd been with her. Of that, Jake had been certain. It was a certainty born of being loved for the first time in his life.

But Rachel hadn't lied. She'd said she was home alone all evening, while her father was at an insurance meeting in Columbus.

So, the cops said, why would Jake lie about where

he'd been if he didn't have something to hide? By that time, it was too late for the truth.

Now, a month later, his trial was over and the bailiffs were getting ready to close the doors to the courtroom. Jake turned around and scanned the crowd. No Rachel.

The jury filed in.

Late-afternoon sunlight in a million colors spilled into the room through the tall, stained-glass windows on either side of the jury box. One window depicted the scales of justice, perfectly balanced, the other a blindfolded woman in a toga. Jake knew what the blindfolded woman represented; he'd read about all of this in some book or other. *Justice is blind.*

He was innocent. He was *innocent,* and surely, somehow, somebody would realize that he was innocent, because there had to be justice, it couldn't go down this way....

"Jake!" It was a hiss from the visitor's gallery.

Jake half turned. It was Chris Drewer, Rachel's friend. He was standing in the front row, his hands on the railing that separated the spectators from the accused. "Remember, we can appeal if we have to."

Ben yanked on Jake's sleeve. Jake turned around again, facing the bench.

Of all the people in town, only Chris had tried to help Jake. When he was first in jail, Chris had brought six hundred dollars from Rachel and a thousand of his own. All he had, though he said he was trying to get more.

Jake had used the money to hire an attorney from outside Grange, but the money had run out too quickly. So now he had Ben. Chris had tried to help, though, and a small rush of gratitude crept into Jake's chest, mingling with the panicky fist.

"The defendant will rise."

Jake stood, willing his legs to be steady. Ben stood beside him.

The bailiff handed a paper from the jury foreman to the judge. Judge Randall read it, shot Jake a look he couldn't interpret.

The judge spoke. "Ladies and gentlemen of the jury, have you reached a verdict in the case of Jacob Monroe?"

"It's Jake." To his surprise, Jake realized it was he who had spoken, and that—more amazing still— his voice had come out loud, steady, clear. "It's not Jacob. It's just Jake." He'd always been ashamed of his family, of his father, of his very name. So why, here and now, when his whole life was at stake, did it seem so important that the judge say his name right?

"Jake Monroe," the judge corrected himself, a dull flush of red crossing his cheekbones.

The jury foreman squirmed uncomfortably. "We have reached a verdict, Your Honor."

"How do you find the defendant, Jake Monroe? Guilty or not guilty of involuntary manslaughter in the death of Joann Floutz?"

The foreman hesitated for a split second. "Guilty."

The panic in Jake's chest exploded into a red wall in front of his eyes. All around him there was noise, a yell of triumph from Joann's husband, a thrill of voices from the spectators, the thwack of the big door opening and closing. The judge was asking the jury for their verdict on the robbery count. Guilty.

Guilty. And he was innocent! Innocent, damn them!

He grabbed for control. Into the hubbub, he shouted. "Your Honor, I'm innocent! Let me take the stand, right now—"

"Mr. Monroe, your trial is over. The jury has found you guilty." Wearily, the judge stood and prepared to leave the courtroom.

The sheriff's deputy approached with handcuffs.

Rachel, he thought. *Please,* and then he went numb. Rachel had betrayed him, and Big Jake had always said his kid would come to a bad end. That was the way it was with the Monroes. Jake had nothing. Not even his freedom.

Only his pride. He thrust his chin up and held his hands out and let them snap the cuffs on him. No way was he going to be a spectacle for the people who had come to hear his fate.

Justice is blind, he repeated bitterly to himself.

Justice was also deaf and dumb.

CHAPTER ONE

RACHEL DREWER was late. The March morning was getting away from her. She hoisted her overflowing canvas tote onto her shoulder and opened the door to the garage. "Come on, Andy, let's go!" She tripped on the narrow step, but righted herself despite her high heels.

"I gotta feed the cats." Andy looked up at her plaintively.

The cats were circling Andy, begging, meowing. Okay, they were yowling. Rachel sighed. The cats had been fed last night, but the concept of scheduled meals had yet to sink in. All had been strays before finding their way to the Drewers.

Now they had quite a menagerie. Waldo was stone-deaf and blind in one eye. Carmen Sandiago was a scruffy, half-grown calico that had produced three kittens the day after she'd appeared on Rachel's doorstep. Added to those five were the Bookends, two old females that looked exactly alike, slept back-to-back and somehow never had acquired individual names.

Feeding the cats was one of Andy's chores, but heck, Rachel was going to be even later if she waited for her ten-year-old son to maneuver the bag of cat food. Grabbing the bag from the shelf in the garage,

Rachel leaned down to pour a goodly amount into a bowl.

"Waldo, stop it!" The big tom couldn't wait; he was starting to climb her leg. "Waldo!" It was useless; Waldo couldn't hear her. With the half-full bag, she swiped futilely at his paws. He squirmed and dodged her with ease. "Ouch! Now you've done it!" Three perfectly placed runs were skittering down the leg of her panty hose.

She really should wear slacks to work. The skirt-and-blazer routine was part of her old life; the stylishness that had been ingrained was hard to shake. But stockings and high-heeled pumps definitely didn't fit into her life as a widowed, working mom.

Andy was looking up at her with a grave expression. "Grandma says we have too many cats."

"We *do* have too many cats." The understatement of the year. Why would a woman with a kid to raise on her own and a job workload that had abruptly doubled in the last month still have this overwhelming urge to save the world's cast-off cats? Chris had indulged her in this, as he'd indulged her in so many things. He'd even let her take in Spook when the old dog had needed a home. Maybe he should have said "no" more often.

Opening the car door, she heaved her tote bag into the back seat, then held out her hand for Andy's book pack. "Does Peppy have food?" As if they didn't have enough animals, Andy's grandmother had presented him with a dachshund puppy for his last birthday. Everyone in the family, from her mother-in-law, Leora, to Rachel to Andy, was downright nuts about the little dog.

"Yep. I checked."

"Good job, Andy."

His dark eyes lit up and he grinned. She couldn't help a rueful smile of her own as she ruffled his hair. She was glad to see that Andy was smiling more often these days. The ten months since Chris's death in an automobile accident had been difficult. Andy missed his dad very much. They both did; Chris had been a good husband and father. A father in almost every way—no, a father in every way that counted.

Chris had been Rachel's companion and her help-mate. He'd always been the one to drive Andy to school if the boy missed the bus. Now it was up to her. If they left this minute, Andy wouldn't be marked tardy. She had an extra pair of panty hose stashed in her desk—or had she used them already? "Let's go, kiddo. No more delays. March on. Man the torpedoes, full speed ahead, don't stop for any-thing—"

"Uh, Mom? I did sort of forget to check Peppy's water dish."

Groaning, Rachel told her son to wait for her in the car while she hurried back into the house to check the dog dish and grab an extra pair of nylons.

In the kitchen, the telephone was ringing. Charg-ing up the stairs, she let the answering machine click on.

"Rachel? It's Harold."

She froze on the steps. Her boss hated answering machines and made it a point of pride not to talk into one. "I see here that you have an appointment at the high school. You're going to have to reschedule it."

She did have an appointment at ten. She had wall-to-wall appointments these days, ever since she'd been stuck with Charlie Malchek's adult parole work in addition to her own juvenile probation duties. Racing back downstairs, she snatched up the receiver and pressed it to her ear.

"Anyway," Harold was saying, "come into the office instead, and we'll talk about how you're going to deal with this. See you in a few minutes, I hope. Ah, goodbye, I guess."

"Harold? Harold!" she shouted into the receiver before he could hang up.

"Rachel?" His voice came back more strongly. "I knew you'd still be there," he added in an ah-*ha* voice. "That's why I hate talking into these machines. You just know the person's there and they won't talk to you. Anyway, you're late this morning."

"I know that," she said, but she resisted her first urge, which was to apologize like a guilty child. She might not have overslept this morning if she hadn't been up until after midnight last night writing reports.

As the county administrator, it had been Harold Sanderson's decision not to bring in a temporary replacement after Charlie Malchek had gone on extended sick leave a month ago. Harold simply expected Rachel to pick up the slack, to handle all the adult parole and probation work in addition to her own duties. Known throughout the county as a cheapskate, her boss simply refused to acknowledge that Grange wasn't such a small town any longer.

She was a social worker, Rachel thought with resentment, not a law enforcement type. For four years, ever since earning her degree, she'd handled only juvenile cases. It was a tough, rewarding job all on its own.

"I'll be in the office as soon as I drop Andy off at school," she promised. "But I'm out of there at a quarter to ten. I won't cancel my ten o'clock appointment."

"We'll see," Harold said with his typical zest for a little drama.

Sighing, Rachel put down the phone. Grange might be a growing town with growing pains in its criminal justice system, but she wasn't going to miss that appointment no matter what Harold thought he had in store for her.

"IT'S ABOUT TIME," Harold grumbled when Rachel made her appearance in his office fifteen minutes later.

"I had to take Andy to school," Rachel repeated patiently. "Chris isn't around to do that anymore."

Harold's expression immediately softened. He could be difficult to work for, but he was a kind man. He had liked Chris and had been concerned and helpful when Rachel had lost her husband. "Ah, hell." He got up and poured her a cup of coffee from the pot. "Take this. For once it's fresh, even if it's lukewarm." For good measure, he added a huge spoonful of the nondairy creamer that Rachel loathed.

Still, she took the cup gratefully and sipped. "Now, what's going on, anyway?" she asked with a smile.

Harold's eyes lit with excitement. "Jake Monroe's been paroled."

Ohmygod. The cup started to slip from her fingers. She plunked it down on the desk. Coffee sloshed over her hand, but she hardly noticed. A rush of memories enveloped her, followed quickly by a strange kind of thrill, and then the fear came. It was the fear most of all that settled in her belly.

Andy. *Andy.*

"Paroled?" she whispered.

"Paroled," Harold repeated in a voice that seemed overly loud. "After ten years, Jake Monroe's coming home."

It won't make any difference. For a second, Rachel thought she'd said the words out loud, but then she realized Harold was still waiting for her to speak. She was trembling, and she tried to force herself to calm down.

Everything would be all right. Jake knew nothing about Andy. That day in the county jail, right before his trial, he'd made it clear he wanted nothing more to do with her. She hadn't known it at the time, but she was pregnant. And when she'd discovered that she was going to have Jake's baby, he'd already been convicted and sent to the penitentiary. So she'd written him four desperate letters, as if from prison he could help her. As if somehow their love would survive it all....

But Jake had sent back her letters unopened. In a way, he'd chosen not to learn about their baby. That had left Rachel barely eighteen, pregnant and terrified. And alone.

So Jake didn't know about Andy. Andy knew nothing about Jake, either. Chris had wanted it that way, had insisted on it. Once Rachel had had no choice. And over the last ten years, she'd decided Chris had been right.

Now she had to protect her son. She lifted her chin. "Whether or not Jake Monroe is coming home has nothing to do with me." As soon as the words were out of her mouth, she knew that was not true. Because... Oh, God. Jake coming home had *every-thing* to do with her. A hot wash of fear rolled over her again. She'd have every reason in the world to spend time with Jake. Thanks to Charlie Malchek's heart attack and Harold's refusal to replace him, Rachel Drewer was now Jake's parole officer.

"No," she said, a tinge of desperation in her voice which she couldn't hide. "I can't be Jake's parole officer."

"Now, Rachel," Harold began. "I know you like working with the kids better, but you're good at your job." He puffed his chest out a little. "I have every confidence in your ability."

Confident? In her ability? What in God's name was he talking about? Surely Harold knew she had a conflict of interest, an insurmountable conflict of interest.

No, he didn't. He wouldn't know that Chris had been Andy's stepfather, not his father. Only two people in the world had ever known, and one of them was dead. But Harold wouldn't even know Rachel and Jake had been seeing each other so many years ago. They'd kept their secret well.

"I can't." She sought, then seized on a reason. "You know darn well this double job is undoable." She leaned forward. "I've gone along because I like my job and I know the county has budget problems. I've been coping—after a fashion—but this is too much. I've dealt with a couple of felons, a thief, that guy who embezzled from the bank. But we've never had a convicted murderer on the parole list before." She winced at her own words. She'd never believed Jake had killed anyone. He talked tough, but she'd known the boy inside, the gentle boy who'd said he loved her. He was innocent, of that she was sure—had *always* been sure—but he'd gone to prison for ten years for the crime. She shivered. Prison did things to people. Whatever gentleness Jake had hidden so deeply years ago would be long gone.

None of that mattered now. The sadness she hadn't been quite able to put aside, she'd buried deep within herself and never talked about. The fear for Jake's safety in the often brutal prison system could still wake her up nights, but she'd got used to staring at the night-washed ceiling and hearing the breathing of the husband beside her. She didn't love Jake anymore. His refusal to open her letters, the prospect of having a baby alone, had taken care of *that* emotion. She'd been content with Chris. Contentment, she'd discovered, beat the heck out of passionate love any day.

On her own, she could handle Jake. As Harold said, she was a professional. But with the complication of Andy... Well, it would be better if she just stayed away from Jake. Period.

She stood, but tried not to pace. "Jake's case will be complicated. He'd have to check in often, at least twice a week at first, in order to show we're protecting the community. I don't have time for that many check-ins." She took a deep breath, knowing her logic was irrefutable.

"You can handle it," Harold repeated. "Charlie's coming back in a couple of months, and then he'll take over Monroe's case. I expected Charlie back sooner, but getting pneumonia after his surgery... Well, I can't just hire somebody off the street at this late date, and people around here trust you. Like it or not, Rachel kid, you're it. People will be scared of Jake. The newspaper and everybody in town will be looking to see if we can keep Little Jake Monroe out of trouble.''

Rachel's temper snapped. ''He's not 'Little Jake,' damn it! He's twenty-nine years old and six foot three!'' Her fists balled. ''I wish everyone would just stop calling him that!''

Harold's coffee cup stopped halfway to his mouth as he stared at her. Her cheeks flushed hot.

''It's just that it's so unfair,'' she added lamely, wondering if she was as red as she felt.

Harold cleared his throat. ''You've always been tenderhearted. You're a good social worker, you care about people. But you can't get sentimental about Lit—ah, Jake Monroe.''

I'm not sentimental. I'm just the mother of his child.

Abruptly, she turned toward the window. Harold's office—like her own next door—was a high-ceilinged, square room in the ground floor of the courthouse annex. Long windows with panes of bubbly, wavy glass looked out over the courthouse lawn. The lawn itself was a sweep of new green grass, broken up by beds of pansies, a couple of fountains and a World War II soldiers' memorial. The sight was colorful, well tended, pleasantly familiar. What had Jake seen of the outdoors in these last ten years?

''Harold, I have a conflict of interest,'' she said quietly to the window. ''I have a...personal reason for not wanting to be Jake's parole officer.''

From behind her, she heard his chair squeak. ''What kind of personal? The guy's been gone ten years.''

"When we were kids, we were kind of involved."
Well, she thought with a bitter humor, as confessions
went, that was pretty lame.

"Involved," Harold repeated, sounding stunned.

She couldn't look at him. "In high school," she
added quietly. Harold was okay, but he was Harold.
Once she'd wished for a mother to confide in. She'd
started to tell her best friend, Cindy, once, and she'd
told Chris, who had listened but then insisted that
she never mention her relationship with Jake to anyone again. Now, it turned out, she was confessing an
old, forbidden love to her *boss*.

"Well, now," Harold said, and there was a long
pause. She knew if she turned she'd see the shock in
his eyes. Rachel Penning Drewer had never in her
whole life—as far as anyone knew—done anything
to damage her reputation as the town's golden girl.

The silence got long, but Rachel resisted the urge
to fill it. "So, it was a bit of a crush, wasn't it?"
Harold finally added in a hearty tone.

Rachel turned. "Yes, a crush." It had started out
that way, a sheltered girl's fascination with long hair
and faded jeans, an intense stare and a give-'em-hell
attitude. It had grown to something much, much
deeper as she'd taken walks with him and his dog,
had seen him tenderly bandage Spook's cut foot, always stop and rest when the old dog started to pant.
It had grown deeper when she found out he read
authors like Sinclair Lewis and John Updike on the
sly. It had grown to something deeper still when he
had kissed her and groaned and put aside a tough
boy's pride and told her he loved her.

"I loved him," she added, deciding to let Harold

think what he would. The emotion was private, but she wasn't ashamed of it.

"You were a kid," Harold said firmly.

"Yes, I was young."

"So, you're not, like, in love with him now or anything?"

Rachel looked into her boss's eyes and realized the man was completely out of his depth. "No," she said, and she meant it. "I'm not in love with him now, and I know for a fact that he's not in love with me."

"Well, then, that's all right." Harold picked up his coffee cup, then set it back on his desk. He got up and lumbered around the desk. For a second, she thought he was going to hug her. Instead, he patted her shoulder awkwardly. "Unless you can give me something better than a story about puppy love, I don't think we should talk about this again."

She couldn't tell him about Andy. She just couldn't. "All right," she said, feeling suddenly tired.

"Do your job, Rachel."

This *was* her job, like it or not. Could she do it and still be fair to everyone, to Jake and to the community of Grange? Actually, adult parole was very routine. There was a set of parole requirements. All she had to do was verify that Jake met those requirements. Objective criteria. Check the appropriate boxes on the forms, her judgment only really coming into play if there was a parole violation, at which time she'd have to weigh any mitigating circumstances. Surely, now that he was finally out of prison, Jake wouldn't do anything that might get his parole revoked.

If she had any questions—if any issue came up that required some judgment that might be clouded by the past—she'd talk it over with her boss. Or better yet, she'd write a memo. Document everything.

There was no reason in the world for her and Jake to have any personal relationship, no reason in the world that he should ever have to learn about Andy. After all, Jake had to concentrate on rebuilding his life. Who, under those circumstances, would want the complication of a kid he'd never seen, a kid who thought another man was his father?

"When's Jake being released?" she asked.

"Two weeks. Can you find him a place to stay?"

"Yes. I'll call Reverend Carson. He has that furnished apartment over the garage at the parsonage. Jake will need a job, so I'll see what I can come up with on that, too."

"Well, Lit—ah, Jake Monroe won't be a jailhouse lawyer anymore." Harold gave her a satisfied grin.

Over the last few years, Rachel had heard stories about Jake from the prosecutors. One or two prisoners at every facility learned to write briefs and act as self-taught "jailhouse lawyers" for other prisoners. Most of them were little more than nuisances, filing motions and generally causing trouble. She'd heard Jake was different. His briefs were well written and some had had good enough legal arguments to have caused the prosecutors quite a bit of work over the last two or three years.

"I can't imagine anyone in town hiring him," she said sadly. Jake had never had a chance. Probably wouldn't have a chance now, despite a fine mind. "Maybe at one of the dairies…"

It was hard to get help with the milking at most

dairies, and Jake had experience running his father's farm. He'd always liked animals, but she knew he'd hated the farmwork. But under the circumstances, she imagined he'd accept any job. She could talk to one of the farmers in the area. Most had bought their insurance from her father, and would do her a favor if she asked.

The professional side of her kicked in fully, her mind going over the details of arranging for the first few days of her new parolee's life. That was the key, she decided. Think of him as just another parolee. Bottom line was, she had two weeks to learn to think of Jake Monroe as just part of her job.

THE DAMN THING of it was, she could make all the resolutions she wanted, but Jake wasn't just another parolee. She knew it the moment she felt him standing in the open doorway. Rachel had pretended all morning that this wasn't *it,* the day she'd see Jake again after ten years. The effort had cost her. She'd tipped over her coffee mug. And her stomach was in knots as she'd struggled to concentrate on paperwork.

"Hello, Rachel. Mrs. Drewer."

Jake. Here. Her palms were suddenly, ridiculously damp, even before she looked up.

Then she *did* look up and her mouth went sand-dry. He was the same...and he was not the same. Her mind conjured one word: *more*. More of everything. Darker. Tall, as she remembered, but even more fit than the boy he'd been. Jake had shoulders that nearly spanned the narrow doorway, that strained the fabric of his new-looking chambray shirt. Thank God Andy looked more like her than his biological father. Jake's features were so distinctive and compelling that the whole town might have learned her secret otherwise.

In his hand was a small duffel bag. His once-long, wavy hair was razor-cut short, and the shorn, shining black strands served only to emphasize the stark regularity of his features—his dark eyes, set under straight, uncompromising eyebrows, his thin, straight nose, and the mouth that…the mouth that she had once loved. She swallowed hard and smiled. "Hello, Jake."

He didn't smile back. Ten years ago, he had seldom smiled—but he'd smiled at *her*.

How had she managed to forget how intently he stared? How that intensity had once intimidated her and then fascinated her? The silence grew long. With Jake Monroe, there never had been any social niceties. Anyway, what had she expected him to say? *How have you been, Rachel, old love? Have you had a nice life while I was on hiatus in the penitentiary?*

"Jake, how are you?"

He finally cracked a smile, one that had no warmth. "About how you'd expect, I'd guess."

His voice was different. Deeper. Grittier. That change rattled her, too. He didn't seem nervous, but maybe that was because he'd had a couple of weeks to get used to the idea of seeing her again. God knew, Rachel had needed the time. "Did you know I was going to be your parole officer?"

"They told me. Rachel Drewer. It didn't take much to figure out that my new parole officer was you, and that you'd married Chris, after all. That must've made your father and his mother very happy."

His bitterness came through loud and clear. Rachel had been a baby when her mother died. Her father loved her and had meant well, but had been overbearing. He'd plotted out a future for his daughter according to *his* values. She wished now she hadn't told Jake those stories about the constant matchmaking her father and Chris's mother had indulged in. Now he might get the wrong idea, that she hadn't cared for Chris, had just settled...

She'd been pregnant, with no way to support a baby and the certainty that her father wouldn't welcome Jake's child. She'd shed some bitter tears of her own before doing what had to be done. But Chris had deserved better than second best. His memory deserved better.

She sensed Jake watching her, and she struggled to fill the silence. "I'm just subbing in this job. I'm a social worker. Maybe they told you that, too. Anyway, I got my degree four years ago." Lord, he wouldn't think somehow she'd *planned* to supervise him when he came out, would he? "I was supposed to just be doing juvenile delinquency work. Believe me, I never thought I'd be your parole officer." She looked up suddenly, straight into his eyes. They met hers, but she couldn't read his expression.

"Just like old times," he said. "Rachel Penning watching out for Jake Monroe. There for him every time she's supposed to be."

And not there otherwise, he was implying. So, she hadn't imagined the sarcasm. He blamed her in part, she knew, for having to go to prison in the first place. She'd never forget that scene in the county jail ten years ago. *Why didn't you lie?* he'd shouted. *If you love me, why didn't you believe in me?* She would have been his alibi, if she'd only lied.

She'd tried to explain that, regardless of any issue of right or wrong, the thought had never even occurred to her. She'd tried to say that she'd lied maybe half a dozen times in her goody-goody life and been immediately caught by the expression on her face. He hadn't wanted to hear it. He hadn't wanted to hear from her a few months later when she'd desperately needed his support.

"Look, Jake," she said, her voice more crisp than she'd intended. "I don't like this any more than you do, okay?"

His gaze never left hers.

But Rachel was ten years older than the last time she'd seen him, and she'd been a married woman. She was immune these days to a handsome face and a tough-guy act.

And, hey, by this time it surely was no act. She had to remember that, for her son's sake if not her own. "Why don't you sit down. We have paperwork to go over." She gestured with her hand to the chair in front of her desk.

He eyed it for a moment, then settled in. The chair was old, and it squealed alarmingly as it took his weight. He sat up straight, big hands resting on lean thighs. Waiting.

"Comfortable?" she asked.

"No."

Belatedly, she decided it would have been a kind gesture, one of confidence in him, to have moved her own chair out from behind her desk so that she could sit beside him as she did with the kids she dealt with. But over this past month, she'd learned to sit behind her desk with new parolees in order to emphasize her authority. It was important for them to know who was in charge. But surely that didn't apply to the innocent.

Not to Jake.

"Would you like some coffee?" she asked quickly, trying to compensate for her blunder.

"No." He paused, and the smallest flash of some emotion flickered in his eyes. Weariness or wariness or pain—or all three; she couldn't decide. "Rachel, let's just get this over with. Or should I call you Mrs. Drewer?"

"Give it a rest." Stung, she pulled a stack of paperwork toward her. He wanted all business? She'd give him all business. She paged through the stack, though she knew the whole thing by heart. "Your prison record is exemplary. No disciplinary problems, a release for charity work that went without incident, a reputation for leadership among the other prisoners. That's all very good." She winced inwardly at her schoolteacher tone and hurried on. "You got a bachelor's degree in political science in less time than it took me to go to school for my own degree."

"I didn't have much else to do," he said.

Not like her, she thought. While he was studying in those early years, she'd been walking the floors with a colicky baby, redecorating an old house within walking distance of Main Street, budgeting carefully, cooking from scratch—in other words, trying very hard to be a good wife to a man who knew she didn't love him. School had taken a back seat for quite a few years.

She'd always wanted to go to college, and she and

Chris finally had saved enough for the tuition and child care. After earning her degree four years ago, she had wanted to go on for her master's degree. They hadn't been able to manage that. But she'd been lucky. She'd had part of her dream, and under her circumstances, how many women got an education?

He was watching her, waiting for her to speak. "Does it bother you that I'm your parole officer?" she asked abruptly.

"Yes."

Oh. Well, what did she expect? She was his former lover—the lover he thought had betrayed him. She knew for a fact that any feeling between them was dead. As for attraction—well, she was ten years older, a woman with too many freckles, a bit of a tummy that she tried to cover with a red blazer. The man oozed virility, always had. She oozed…mom. Woman with Too Many Cats.

He shifted. "Look. I'm a paroled murderer. Convicted of involuntary manslaughter, a killing done during a robbery. I'm lower than pond scum in this town."

There was no self-pity in his tone, only bleak truth, and it was a truth she suddenly couldn't bear. Impulsively, Rachel reached out, started to put a hand across the desk. He didn't move. For a second, her hand hovered in the air as it dawned on her that the worst thing she could offer was pity. Quickly, she reached for a pencil, but her fingertips hit it, instead. The pencil arced high over the desk, and Jake reached out and caught it deftly. She met his eyes. The tiniest glimmer of shared memories lurked there.

"I'm still kind of clumsy," she admitted. Confused by that tiny, tiny spark of warmth, she looked down.

He laid the pencil back on her desk. Finally, he spoke, and his voice was hard, impersonal again. "Your being my parole officer just rubs it in. But I've learned to accept quite a few things that aren't pleasant. So, just give me the drill, the full drill like you would anybody else sitting in this chair. What do I have to do to stay on this side of the law for a change?"

She'd prepared for this meeting. She hadn't prepared for the jolt of attraction that still seemed to be there...a one-sided jolt that embarrassed her thoroughly. But she'd see the rest of the interview through if it killed her.

She opened a drawer and found another pencil, which she used to check off an item on her list. "I've arranged for an apartment, if it's okay with you. Reverend Carson from the church has an apartment over the garage of the parsonage that he rents out very reasonably. It's fully furnished, not fancy, but comfortable. You don't know him, he came here after you went...had gone. He's a bit of a crusader."

"Willing to give a felon a chance." Jake actually smiled grimly.

She leaned forward. "The question is, will you give people a chance, Jake? He's a man who cares about people, and he's fair-minded. You might actually like this guy if you make the effort."

His smile died. "Right," he said with heavy sarcasm.

She knew perfectly well that very few people in the world had given Jake a chance, even before Joann Floutz was pushed from a balcony. "I've also found you a job if you want it,'' she continued doggedly. ''Over on Higer Road there's a hundred-and-fifty-cow dairy that needs a hand with the morning and evening milking.''

''I've got a job. Well, an interview, anyway.''

''Oh.'' She waited for him to say more. When he didn't, she asked, ''What kind of job?''

''With Judge Randall. He needs a law clerk. Usually, he takes only law students, but when he knew I was coming out of prison, he wrote and asked to see some of my briefs.''

The sudden yearning that he couldn't quite mask made his dark eyes glow. His whole body leaned forward ever so slightly, as though every muscle and sinew was hungering for this one chance. His expression, his stance was so like the boy she'd known—the secret dreamer, the one with big plans—that Rachel's heart squeezed painfully.

''Oh, Jake, that's wonderful.''

''I want that job.''

''Can I help?'' she asked. ''What can I do? Talk to the judge?''

He smiled then. Really smiled, under the garish, slightly flickering green light of the fluorescent ceiling fixture. That smile lit his whole face, showed teeth strong and white, the front two endearingly crooked, the only thing about Jake that had ever been boyish. That smile slammed her in the chest and took the wind right out of her.

''Rachel,'' he said, his voice a dark whisper.

''Rachel,'' said a loud voice from the doorway. Startled, guilty, she looked up to see Harold. He said, ''I thought I'd stop in and see how things were going.''

Jake turned toward the sound. Harold looked him over, his curiosity obvious.

Rachel spoke up quickly. "We're just discussing some of Jake's job prospects."

Harold managed—with one incredulous look Jake's way—to make it clear what he thought of Jake's job prospects. "Well, now, that's fine." He remained in the doorway.

"Come on in," Rachel said. Jake and Harold... Now *there* was a lousy combination. But her boss's presence would certainly keep her mind focused on business. And, she knew after that smile she'd just exchanged with Jake, she definitely needed to focus on business.

Harold came into the small room. Jake stood and turned. "Jake Monroe," he said evenly, holding out his hand.

Harold looked down at the outstretched hand for a long moment. Finally, he stuck out his own hand, shook Jake's vigorously. "Harold Sanderson. I'm the county administrator."

Rachel smiled in relief. Not that she'd expected Harold to refuse Jake's offer of politeness, but... well, you couldn't always count on Harold's sensitivity.

Without being invited, Harold came over to the desk and sat in the chair next to Jake. "Now, don't mind me. I'll just sit here a while."

Rachel gritted her teeth as Jake retook his own seat. The atmosphere in the room was suddenly tense again. She sifted through her paperwork. "Here are the regulations. You'll need to read them to yourself and sign them, but I'm required to read them out loud to you." She picked up the paper. She had dreaded

this part, and now Harold was watching her to see
how she was handling the interview.

"One. You are to report for work every day as
scheduled, and must notify both me and your employer if you're sick or otherwise unable to be at
work on time.

"Two. You must report in to me at my office on
a regular basis." She looked up. "At first, this will
have to be twice a week. We'll work around your
job schedule, no problem there. The purpose of these
meetings will be so that we can talk about whatever's
happening in your life, smooth your transition back
to Grange, and so that you can share any difficulties
that you might be having." God, this was awful.
"We want you to succeed in establishing yourself as
a law-abiding citizen," she read from the paper.

She hurried on, reading faster now, not adding any
encouragement or comments of her own, which she
would have done if he'd been any other parolee.
"You will be required to do six hours of community
service per week. Your parole officer—me, I mean—
will help you set that up. You must avoid all contact
with known criminals and felons. You may not take
illegal drugs or be in a room where anyone else is
using. You are not permitted to frequent any taverns
or establishments where liquor is sold." She couldn't
look at him, wondering if he was remembering his
father. Big Jake had died of liver disease five years
ago, the same year her own father had passed away.
Two hundred people had shown up for her father's
funeral. The county had paid for Big Jake's burial.
She swallowed and read on determinedly. "You
cannot leave the state of Ohio, and for the first six

months of your parole, you cannot leave Grange County without my permission.

"You must obey all laws. If you commit another felony, or if you violate the conditions of your parole which I have just read to you, and there are no mitigating circumstances, I may have to issue a warrant for your arrest. If the parole board finds you've violated your parole, you will be sent back to prison to serve the remainder of your sentence." She looked up finally.

Jake hadn't moved; he was back to that stiff pose, dwarfing the worn vinyl chair, his hands open, splayed fingers pressing on either thigh.

Harold spoke. "Do you understand the conditions of your parole?" He was asking the question that Rachel should have asked.

"Yes."

Rachel took a deep breath. "Then read this and sign it if you agree to abide by all the terms." She handed him the paper, and she and Harold waited while he read.

Finally, he reached for a pen and signed his name. Boldly, in black. "Now. Anything else?"

Rachel let out a breath. It was almost over. "Not really. Nothing formal, anyway. I can show you where your apartment is. You'll want to unpack your things." Her eyes went to the small duffel bag, and it struck her anew how difficult the last ten years must have been.

"It's over the garage of the parsonage, you said. I remember where the church is. Or do you have to go with me?"

"No, you're a free man now, Jake."

His eyes flickered. "Fine. Then I'll see you on Wednesday." He stood.

Resisting the urge to first swipe her palm along the fabric at her hip, she held out her hand and hoped he wouldn't notice how damp, how hot her palm was. "That's it, Jake. Good luck, and welcome home."

His hand touched then enfolded hers for the briefest instant. His palm was big, as hot as her own, hard, callused. He nodded and was gone.

Harold waited a moment, then stood and came around her desk. "Whew. That is one hard-ass— Sorry."

She waved off his apology.

"He doesn't seem like he's going to give you any trouble, though. Did he take the job at the dairy?"

"Judge Randall might hire him to write briefs instead."

Harold let out a long, low whistle. "Well, now, isn't that interesting. If he gets hired, we'll have a convicted murderer playing lawyer over at the courthouse. One thing I'll say, Rachel kid. Around you, life is surely more interesting than when Charlie had this job."

Harold was standing by the window. He stuck his thumb into the soil of one of Rachel's potted ivies. "You give this plant any more mothering and it's going to take over the walls next." He paused. "Hey, speaking of mothering, where's that picture of Andy, the one where he just got his haircut?"

"Oh. I was straightening up and, ah, just didn't get around to putting it back out on my desk."

She could feel herself flush scarlet at the almost-lie. She wasn't going to hide from Jake the fact that

she had a son. And though she knew she had been
right—*was* right—to keep the knowledge of who her
child's father was from both Andy and Jake, she felt
a wash of guilt. She wouldn't lie; she wouldn't have
to. Jake would have no reason to suspect that Chris
wasn't her son's biological father.

She just wasn't up to discussing her son with Jake,
not in this first meeting. There was absolutely no
reason for her to be feeling guilty, she told herself
firmly. She'd tried to tell Jake about Andy long, long
ago. Now it was simply too late.

Too late for everything.

CHAPTER TWO

A HOT SHOWER. One fantasy come true, anyway. Long after he'd soaped up and rinsed off, Jake tipped his face into the stream of water and let it run down his body. He'd thought he'd had it bad back there at that old dairy, but nothing compared to the cold showers and crummy food in the joint.

Forget it, he told himself, not wanting to spoil his first genuinely hot shower in ten years. He was never going back, not to the farm or the joint. He'd had plenty of time to think while he was locked up, and he'd made plans.

The basics of life first. This apartment was fine, good, actually the best place he'd ever lived. The reverend hadn't been here to greet him, but the guy had left the key and a note, a gesture of trust that had momentarily stunned Jake.

He'd put away his few clothes, then given some thought to groceries. He had a few bucks that he'd earned in jail, writing those briefs. The parole office had some initial start-up money for him; he'd read that on the form. He figured the county that had sent an innocent man to prison owed him, and he would have taken it. Except that it would have been Rachel handing him the check. She hadn't offered, and for that he was grateful.

As he'd told her, he'd had to accept a lot of things

these last ten years. Given that, it shouldn't have been so tough to sit there and look at Rachel and know she was real. To know that she'd once been his but never would be again.

But he'd handled it as he handled everything else. By focusing on the plan.

He was going to find the real killer of Joann Floutz. No matter what, he was going to clear his name. Thanks to Big Jake, it wasn't much of a name, but it was *his,* and one of his few possessions at the moment.

Then after he cleared his name, law school. And then the bar exam. It was a plan ten years in the making.

The water went lukewarm, then cool. Jake turned it off, stepped out of the shower and toweled himself. As he ran the towel down his thigh, he brushed over his scar, the remainder of his one prison fight. It had happened shortly after he'd arrived, and the other guy had had a knife. He'd had only his fists.

The other guy had lost.

Jake grimaced. He took no pleasure in the memory. The thought that every day of his sentence might be like this had scared the hell out of him. Lying in the prison infirmary, looking at the cracked plaster walls while a bored, half-competent technician stitched him up, Jake knew he had a choice. He'd proven himself with his fists. He could join the gang, the brutal elite of prison society, and survive. Or he could choose another way. That day, Jake had chosen to use his brain. Not merely to survive, but to live.

He'd kept his body fit, but he'd spent more time studying, and he'd discovered an aptitude for the law. He'd bartered those skills in the joint, writing appeals for prisoners. He'd bartered for a few dollars, but mostly for privacy and peace.

Yes, he'd found an aptitude for the law. But he'd also found pleasure in it, a sheer intellectual challenge that gave him something else to think about at night when he'd shut his eyes and see Rachel's face. Over the years, he'd built her up into a vivid fantasy. A fantasy of love and acceptance, things that were good and right and that other people took for granted. Sometimes, he'd almost convinced himself she'd never been a real woman at all. Surely he'd never expected to see her again.

Yet his first day back he'd seen her, and she was no fantasy. He'd prepared for their meeting, but actually standing there in that doorway—hell, he'd felt sucker punched, kicked in the gut just by the sight of her.

Those lost years had made her features more distinct. She'd gone from all-American girl next door to striking woman. Her honey-colored hair had lost none of its sheen, and was cut in a short bob that just scraped her chin. He imagined that her fine hazel eyes had lit at the sight of him, just as they had long ago. He hadn't just fantasized about the freckles, he knew now. If anything, she had more than he remembered, as if she'd spent her time outdoors in the sun and wind. Her breasts were lush and full, her figure rounded and feminine.

He remembered with groin-tightening detail how once they had lain together in tall, ripening grass, and he'd made love to those freckles of hers, teasing from one to another with his finger, then with the tip of his tongue...

Get a grip, Monroe. Rachel was his parole offi-

ccr—that was enough to cool any hormonal rush. It
was hard not to resent that she was in charge of his
life. If he'd needed any reminders that he'd been a
fool for dreaming ten years ago, he'd got it today in
that little office.

Rachel. Rachel *Drewer*. Another man's wife.

Coming out of the bathroom, Jake tossed the towel
to the floor next to the dresser and put on his dress
shirt with his jeans. Sticking a couple of twenties into
his worn wallet, he set out early for his interview
with Judge Randall.

He'd been gone ten years, but you'd never know
it by the appearance of downtown Grange. Yesterday, one of the wardens had told him the place was
growing a bit, becoming one of the outer bedroom
towns that fed into Columbus.

But Main Street itself was nearly the same as he
remembered. Dry cleaners and income tax preparers,
the Laundromat and the tiny convenience store, the
yarn-and-crafts store, with a display of afghans in the
front window. Along the sidewalks were half whiskey barrels filled with dirt and blooming pansies.

The chamber of commerce must still be around,
buying flowers to beautify the town. All the time he
was growing up, Rachel's father and old lady
Drewer—Chris's mother—had taken turns at the
presidency. As he passed the corner, he stopped, startled. Penning Insurance was now Smothers Insurance. Had Rachel's father died? Once, he and Rachel
had spent so much time hiding their love from her
rigid, overbearing father. It was hard to believe he
was just...gone.

Drewers Emporium was still there, though, right
across the street from the insurance office. In Jake's

early childhood, the place had just been Drewers
General, but old lady Drewer had changed the name
when she went all out trying to attract a classier cli-
entele.

He crossed the street. It still looked like the only
store downtown that carried clothing, but the place
had a subtle air of neglect about it that he didn't
remember from before. Heck, he remembered Drewers as *the* place, had once imagined how incredible
it would be to have a business with your name over
the door, a business that everybody recognized and
respected. Now the Easter decorations in the front
window looked a bit limp and faded by the sun.

He stood for a second at the doorway, not at all
sure what kind of reception he'd get inside. The good
feeling from his hot shower and the sensation of
clean, crisp clothes on his back was fading rapidly
as he realized how difficult it was going to be to get
through the next few days with his pride intact.
Squaring his shoulders, he pushed open the door.

A doorbell played some silly Easter song, on and
on. From behind a glass case a young woman
straightened. "Can I help you?"

She was maybe twenty, and he didn't recognize
her. Anyway, he barely glanced at her face; his gaze
was riveted by her ample chest. She looked as if
she'd literally poured herself into a top made of some
kind of shiny purple fabric.

"Well, hello," the woman drawled. "I don't think
I've seen *you* in here before."

He pulled his gaze up to her face. She had white
lipstick and long dark hair, and she had a row of
about fifteen silver hoops running up her ear. All
those holes punched in one ear. God, he *had* been

away for a long time, if this had become the fashion for women. This morning, Rachel had had on little pearl studs, one in each ear.

The salesclerk was smiling. A bold smile. "I'm Cathy. What can I do for you?" He'd swear she pushed her chest out even farther.

She was coming on to him, he realized with a start. He'd been worried about his reception, and this woman was coming on to him. A laugh—quickly suppressed—threatened to erupt out of his throat. It had been so long since a woman had approached him that he'd almost missed a very blatant signal.

She was still smiling, cracking her gum, in no real hurry to wait on him.

"I need a necktie," he said.

"Oh. Over here." The woman took him to a rack that held ten ties. He looked around, startled anew. There were a few suits on the rack over by the wall, a small stack of dress shirts. He remembered the place as being a lot better stocked than this.

The girl took a quick look around and lowered her voice. "If you want a really cool necktie, you have to go to the mall."

"The mall?" Grange had been the smallest of small towns. When Jake left, it had been an hour's drive to the nearest mall, and he'd never been there.

She looked at him as if he were a little dense. "The big mall, with Eddie Bauer. Actually, I'm going to get a job there as soon as my wheels are fixed." She cocked her head at him, assessing. "If I were you, I'd skip these and go for something like more in fashion, sexier, if you know what I mean. Heck, you're too cute to wear a necktie, anyhow. I'm strictly a tight-jeans-and-denim-shirt kind of woman.''

He smiled at her. "Well, I have a job interview, so I need a tie."

"Awesome! How about red?" She pulled a plain tie in sand-washed silk from the rack.

Jake took the tie and stood in front of the mirror. It took a few tries to get the tie right; he'd never had much practice, even before going to prison. Behind him, he could see a segment of the girl's smiling face. He straightened the knot.

"Cathy, see if the gentleman would like a sport coat to go with that tie." The voice was firm, full of authority. Familiar. His gut tightened.

The girl's face disappeared from the mirror and Jake turned slowly.

Leora Drewer stood a few feet away from him. Her steel-gray hair was shorter than he remembered, and she wore a pale lavender knit suit that Jake assumed was expensive. Her cheeks were painted with distinct circles of pink rouge. "We've just got in some new coats, some navy with brass buttons and some from the better designers." With a sweep of her hand, she indicated a short rack of suit coats. Surreptitiously, Cathy rolled her eyes at Jake.

"No, thanks, just the tie." Jake left the tie on and went over to the cash register to pay. She didn't recognize him, he realized. Fine. Good. He'd deal with Leora Drewer another day.

Mrs. Drewer followed him. "If you do decide you need a coat, don't forget our selection. Cathy could help you, or I'd be glad to help you myself, the next time you're in. A handsome fellow like you would be a pleasure to fit. A good advertisement for the Emporium.''

Cathy positioned herself behind the cash register, but Mrs. Drewer waved her away and took the younger woman's place. ''Cash or charge, sir?''

''Cash.''

She punched in a few numbers, looked up expectantly. He saw the exact moment she recognized him. Her faded blue eyes went wide and her mouth formed a little ''o'' of surprise. She drew in a deep, suddenly raspy breath. ''Lit—Little Jake?'' she whispered.

''Just Jake now,'' he said firmly. Try as he might, he couldn't get his lips to form the smile of greeting that he knew would be the polite thing to do. ''Hello, Mrs. Drewer.'' His voice sounded mocking, not at all what he'd intended.

''But...but you're—''

''I'm back,'' he interrupted. He handed her the money. She held the bills in a hand that shook.

He hadn't expected a welcome-home reception, not here. Big Jake had shoplifted in Drewers Emporium once too often. Jake had done it once too, when he'd been eight, and old man Drewer had scared the hell out of him, threatening to call the cops. He'd expected surprise, disapproval from Mrs. Drewer. But the sheer depth of her reaction puzzled him.

''You're back?'' Mrs. Drewer repeated, still staring at him. ''For good?''

''For good. I need my change, please.''

''Oh. Oh, yes.'' Slowly, she started to take a few bills from the cash drawer.

"Were you like, in the army or something?" Cathy asked Jake brightly.

"No." Jake was starting to sweat. He wanted out of here, right now. "Mrs. Drewer, my change, please," he repeated.

"Working overseas, like on some oil well somewhere?" This last was from Cathy again.

He had smiled at the girl a few minutes earlier, not really flirted. He'd had no intention of pursuing a relationship. And hell, by tonight, half the people in town would know he was back, and the other half—those who'd moved in since Jake had gone to prison—would know that he was a convicted murderer. Jake braced himself, telling himself he didn't care what Cathy-of-the-earrings thought of him.

Mrs. Drewer finally put some bills and a few coins in his hand. Jake shoved the lot into his pocket. Okay. Escape.

"He's been in prison!" Mrs. Drewer finally found her voice.

"Prison?" Cathy let out a little squeal. "Holy cow."

Jake steeled himself not to react.

"Jeez." She looked him over carefully. "Well, that's kind of cool."

What? Was everyone in this town flaming nuts?

Mrs. Drewer was short, but she drew herself up to her full five feet. "Cathy, you stay away from Jake Monroe." Her voice shook a little as she faced Jake. "We don't want your money."

It was obvious the Drewers had fewer customers these days. Maybe they shouldn't be so choosy about who they served. Jake felt his mouth tighten. He would not have come here, anyway, except that he needed a tie for his interview.

His interview. One step on a long road to respect.

"I don't plan to be back," he said, hearing a gruff note in his voice. He turned and walked out of the shop. The tinkling sounds of "Peter Cottontail" followed him out the door.

"WHY ON EARTH didn't you tell me that Little Jake is out of prison?"

Rachel, just home from work, stood in her doorway in her stocking feet and faced her mother-in-law.

Leora didn't give her a chance to reply. "Surely, Rachel, they must tell you things like that. Surely, they must tell all of you down at the courthouse when they let a murderer out of prison!"

"They let an innocent man out of prison. And I knew he was coming home," Rachel said quietly, holding the door open. "Come on in. Andy's outside in the backyard and I was just about to start dinner."

Leora marched past her. "And you didn't tell me?"

Rachel and her mother-in-law were close. It was the kind of news she'd usually share, one of the things they'd have talked over. If it had been anyone but Jake.

"The paper says he's been paroled." Leora held up a folded newspaper. "And besides, he came into the shop today, as bold as brass, buying clothes."

Ouch, Rachel thought. She'd forgotten to give him his check from the county. Fortunately, Jake seemed to have enough money for clothes. She took a deep breath. She'd known she'd have some explaining to do the minute she'd heard Jake was out of jail. In years past, the Drewers had had a lot of problems in the store with Big Jake Monroe. "Jake has served a good part of his sentence, and the parole board has decided to give him a chance now to rejoin society."

"Rachel, was that the right thing to do? I know you think he didn't do it, but he had a trial and everything…" Her voice took on a suddenly unsure quality that was not typical of her. "Even before, he was a juvenile delinquent."

Rachel flared. "Jake's juvenile offenses were minor. Very minor, considering that he got no supervision at home. And, yes, I think he's innocent. For one thing, it was supposed to be a robbery. Yet all the police found at Jake's house was an old tape player of Joann's. Where was her television, her VCR? Where was that amber necklace that was so valuable?"

Jake had said Joann had given him the tape player as payment for yard work. The items stolen in the robbery had never been found. Rachel had puzzled over that information. She'd believed instinctively in his innocence—she'd *known* him. But the missing items had reinforced her opinion, too. Rachel and her mother-in-law had had this discussion before. Leora knew how Rachel felt about Jake's conviction. Everyone knew.

Abruptly, Leora's shoulders sagged. She was a handsome, if sometimes overly made-up woman, in her mid-sixties. She usually put in a full day at Drewers without so much as a hair out of place. Today she looked more tired than usual. Well, Rachel thought ruefully, apparently she wasn't the only one who'd been unsettled by Jake today.

Rachel knew that a lot of people found Leora to be formal to the point of coolness. But she'd come to know another side of her mother-in-law. Leora had been supportive all these years, helped her with Andy. She'd commiserated with Rachel about the small problems of running a household and the bigger ones concerning Rachel's job. Over coffee, over meals together, she had listened and they'd laughed together. When Chris had been killed, they had held each other and cried. In some ways, Leora had become the mother Rachel had never had.

"Please don't be upset," Rachel said gently. "Jake just came in for some clothes, you said. I don't think he'll be back any time soon."

Leora closed her eyes for a second. "He behaved himself. But his father used to drive us crazy. There was hardly even any use calling the police on Big Jake. He'd come in all slobbery and think he was sneaky, when we could see that he was stealing the merchandise, right out from under us. All the sheriff ever did about it was make Big Jake return whatever he took and then put him in the drunk tank to sleep it off. It was so pathetic, but it made me so angry, just the same."

"Jake is not Big Jake."

"I *know* that. It's just that…"

Rachel shook her head. It was so hard for Leora to keep an open mind about people. Her mother-in-law had always had a strong belief in the importance of genes—what she called "good blood."

"I'm Jake's parole officer now."

Leora straightened and let out a long breath. "Oh, Rachel."

"There's nobody but me until Charlie comes

back," Rachel reminded her. "And I intend to give
Jake a fair chance. That's my job, after all."

Leora studied her for a minute, then nodded reluctantly. "You always see the good in people. Jake—
I know he never had a chance. I remember that kid
in those raggedy sneakers, stealing that new white
pair of high-tops. Part of me wanted to just give them
to him. But that was a long time ago and today is
today. No matter what you feel, Jake was convicted.
A jury said he killed Joann Floutz."

"They were wrong."

"You can't fix this. Some things have to be accepted."

She couldn't even convince her own mother-in-
law, Rachel thought in sudden weariness. Leora was
right. A person had to make the best of things, go
on with life no matter what. Hadn't she done exactly
that? She'd married Chris. Thanks to him, her son
would never have to face the harsh judgment of the
town, as Jake had. For a second, Rachel felt like
closing her own eyes, leaning her own back against
the wall.

The back door slammed. Rachel heard Andy calling to Peppy. Then, "M-o-o-m! When's dinner?"

The little dachshund exploded into the hall ahead
of her son. The dog's body was impossibly long and
low, and his silky ears flew out behind him like tiny
banners. His toenails scrabbling on the hardwood
floor, he made straight for Leora.

She bent and the puppy sailed into her. "Peppy,
how are you, little guy?" the older woman crooned,
stroking from his head along his backbone.

Rachel smiled at the ecstatic, wriggling puppy.
She would have rescued a mutt from the shelter, but

Leora had bought a purebred animal. It made Rachel feel warm inside to see her elegant, self-contained mother-in-law baby the pup.

Peppy rolled onto his back, his little tail going a hundred miles an hour.

"Grandma! Hey, when did you get here?" Andy appeared in the hall doorway, his usually serious face alight. Leora held out her arms and Andy came into them.

Leora hugged him tightly. Fiercely, and long.

"Hey, Grandma, let me go. You're squeezing my stomach." Andy squirmed just like Peppy. Smiling a smile that looked a little strained, Leora let him go but ruffled his hair.

She looked up at Rachel, the remnants of the smile—and the strain—still in her eyes. Meeting her mother-in-law's gaze, Rachel started, wondering suddenly if Leora knew. If that was why Jake had shaken her so…

Impossible. Chris was the one who had been so adamant that Andy's parentage be a secret. Surely he wouldn't have told a soul, even his mother. And from looking at Andy, Leora couldn't possibly have guessed. Her son's dark hair and eyes might have been inherited from Jake, but Chris had been dark, too.

She was imagining things, Rachel told herself firmly. It was natural that Jake's return had her imagining things, remembering. But she wasn't going to wallow in those memories.

"Why don't you stay for dinner?" she asked Leora. "I defrosted chicken."

"Aren't you tired? Why don't I take both you and Andy out for dinner?"

"Oh, Mom, let's go out for pizza. *Pul-ease,*" Andy said.

"Sure. That sounds really nice." Maybe what she needed tonight was her family and the distraction of a crowded, noisy pizza parlor. "I can always make chicken tomorrow night."

Andy stuck his thumb in the air. "All *right*. I'll get my quarters for the videos."

The video games at the pizza parlor were an even stronger lure than pizza with extra cheese. Rachel smiled. "Listen, kiddo, wash your hands before we go."

Andy headed for the bathroom, the puppy scampering at his heels.

"I'll drive," Leora offered.

On the way to the restaurant, Leora asked Andy what he'd been doing before her arrival.

"Playing baseball," he said.

"By yourself?" She sounded startled.

"Sure. I was just throwing the ball up and catching it. Getting my new mitt worn in."

From her seat next to her mother-in-law, Rachel listened. Andy loved playing baseball. Before his death, Chris had been working with Andy, throwing the ball around for their son in the backyard after dinner. Now Andy had signed up for the softball league at church this spring.

"I'll play catch with you after we get home, if it's not too dark," Rachel offered.

"Okay," Andy said, but with little enthusiasm. No matter how hard Rachel tried, she threw the ball like a girl, according to Andy. She'd corrected his sexism more than once, which was, she suspected, the only reason he didn't make the comment tonight. But it was true that Rachel wasn't good at sports.

Leora stopped for a traffic light, but there were few other cars at the intersection. "Rush hour" in Grange lasted from about five o'clock to five-fifteen.

Jake had been athletically inclined, Rachel remembered suddenly. His big body had moved with grace, his long legs efficient, his reach deft and sure. It was too bad he couldn't have played Little League as a kid, she thought with a stab of pain.

Then, as if her memories had conjured him, she saw Jake. He was waiting to cross the street, a six-pack of cola in his hand. His light jacket was cut full, but he still wore those formfitting jeans he'd had on earlier in the day.

God, he was so attractive. No wonder the young Rachel hadn't had a chance. It was a good thing she was older and wiser now.

Jake headed up the block and Rachel lost sight of him as Leora parked the car. Then, with a sinking sensation in her stomach, she saw where Jake was going. To the pizza parlor.

Leora apparently hadn't seen. "Come on, Andy," she urged when her grandson dawdled with his seat belt.

"Sure you guys don't want burgers?" Rachel asked quickly.

"Burgers? I thought we were going for pizza." Andy got out of the car. "I had a hamburger for lunch. Now I want pizza. You said we were getting it."

"Right. Grandma's treat. Pizza it is." Leora shooed him up the walk.

"Jake's in there," Rachel said quietly to her mother-in-law.

"Oh, Lord." Leora stopped on the sidewalk.

"Come on." Andy had reached the door and was motioning to them.

"Look," Rachel said finally. "We can't avoid Jake now that he's back. Downtown isn't that big."

Leora gave her a quick nod and followed her grandson. As soon as they'd hit the doorstep, Andy took off. The video games were in a room to the right of the main restaurant. His hand already in his pocket, Andy disappeared.

Then Rachel noticed Jake standing by the order counter. A couple of people stood in line, and about half the tables were filled. But there was only a low hum of conversation. Rachel frowned as she realized the place was too quiet. Then she noticed that a lot of people were staring toward the order counter... and suddenly she knew what was going on. They were watching Jake.

The realization made her sad. This pariah treatment was downright unfair. She knew most people in town believed in his guilt, and even the newcomers would be fascinated—and apprehensive—at the thought of a convicted murderer back in their midst. Rachel marched past the other waiting patrons straight toward Jake. Leora trailed behind her.

Jake turned and saw them, but made no gesture of greeting. He had to know everyone in the place was talking about him.

"Jake, how are you?" she asked a little too brightly, quite a bit too loud.

His expression didn't change, but she caught the slight narrowing of his eyes. He knew what she was up to, and he didn't look particularly grateful. "About the same as I was this afternoon." His gaze took in Leora. "Mrs. Drewer," he acknowledged.

Leora was standing next to her, and nodded stiffly.

"Ordering a pizza?" Rachel asked Jake, then winced at how inane the conversation was. Now that she was here, publicly standing up for Jake, she felt awkward. He wouldn't want her pity, that she knew instinctively. He didn't even seem pleased by her support. Leora shifted uncomfortably, forcing Rachel closer to Jake. From a step away, he seemed so big.

"I ordered takeout," Jake said. If her nearness affected him, he didn't show it. "I was going to take a stab at cooking, but decided I'd celebrate a little. I missed pizza."

At that moment, the clerk handed over a small pizza box to Jake. A celebration for one. Rachel's heart squeezed.

Jake held the box in one hand. "Chris out of town?" he asked.

Next to her, Leora sucked in her breath.

"Out of town?" Rachel echoed, feeling stupider than ever.

"Yes. He's not with you. Is he out of town?"

"Oh, Jake." Of course Jake couldn't have known of Chris's death. "He...died ten months ago."

Jake gazed at her a long moment. "Rachel. God, I'm sorry." He reached out then and touched her. Quickly on the forearm, a small gesture of comfort. The warmth of his touch seemed to penetrate all the way through the layers of her jacket and sweater to her skin.

"Chris was a good man," Leora said, her voice firm.

"Yes, he was," Jake agreed quietly. "A generous, good man."

Rachel felt her throat thicken. At her urging, Chris had given Jake money for a lawyer. Chris had not been a wealthy man; he'd just returned from college and was learning the family business. He'd given Jake his entire savings just because she'd believed in Jake's innocence and she'd asked for his help.

But, given their history, Jake's words were generous, too. She'd had *two* fundamentally good men in her life.

"Mom?" She felt a tug on her coat sleeve. "Can we get a pitcher of cola?" Andy had reappeared and was standing next to her. She froze.

Jake froze, too, staring down at her son. A stab of fear went through her middle, though she told herself for the hundredth time that he couldn't possibly guess....

She swallowed. How she had dreaded this moment! But she'd prepared for it, too, knowing that it was inevitable that Jake would one day meet Andy. "Jake, I'd like you to meet my son, Andy."

"Hello, Andy," Jake said in a voice that suddenly sounded husky.

"Hi," Andy said shyly, ducking his head a little.

"Andy is a fine boy," Leora said decisively. "A very good student. He looks like Rachel, don't you think?"

Jake hadn't taken his eyes off her son. "Yes, he looks a lot like Rachel. He's a handsome young man." He looked up, and for a second, his mouth went tight. "You must be very proud, Mrs. Drewer. And Rachel."

Andy had already lost interest in the adults, pulling

some change from his pocket and counting his money.

The cashier motioned for Jake. With a small nod, he turned away from them and pulled out his wallet.

Rachel felt relief course through her whole body. Jake had met Andy, and though he'd obviously been surprised that she had a son, he'd also apparently taken the situation at face value. Okay. She let out a breath. Thank you, God.

Jake turned, the pizza box in his hand. What she ought to do, Rachel knew, was let him pass, get this meeting over with as soon as possible. But that little pizza box... "What are your plans for your first night home?"

"Watch some television, I guess, or read. Then early to bed." He shrugged a little. "After all, I start work in the morning."

"Jake! You found out about the job already?"

His tone had been offhand, but at her words, he smiled, showing those white teeth. "Yes. The judge liked my work, he said."

Something inside her went warm and soft. "No wonder you're celebrating. You deserve to celebrate."

Why don't you join us? She almost said the words out loud. But she didn't dare, because she knew that—even a decade later—something about Jake affected her. Around him, she felt hot and jittery and aware. So Jake was dangerous. Not as a convicted felon. No, he was dangerous to her as a woman, to the woman he'd hurt deeply ten years ago. And he was dangerous to her family, to the life she'd made for herself and her son. She didn't dare let him get close to her again.

So she let him go out the door alone, carrying pizza for one.

CHAPTER THREE

"SO I SHOULD DENY the defendant's motion to suppress, huh?" Judge Randall smiled, gave a small shake of his head and leaned back in his chair.

Jake sat across from him at the big, old oak conference table in the judge's chambers. Judge Randall used the table as a desk, and it was piled high with legal briefs and law books. Jake paged through the memorandum he'd prepared, trying to find the citation he wanted.

"There's precedent that the police can use the results of a search under circumstances like those in our case," he said, glancing down at the paper as he talked. "There's a chain of court of appeals cases, supporting the state of Ohio's position, and..." Belatedly, he looked up. Judge Randall was sitting still, just watching him, that bemused smile still on his face. "What?" Jake asked.

The judge picked up a pen. "Some in the prosecutor's office were fit to be tied when I decided to hire you. Said you'd come down on the defendant's side all the time."

"Well, they were wrong."

"Yes."

"The law is clear on these issues you've asked me to research," Jake told him.

"So you've said." The judge indicated Jake's memorandum. "So it appears."

"And...?" In his two weeks on the job, Jake was coming to learn things about his boss. At his trial ten years ago, Judge Randall had seemed forbidding, larger than life. Now Jake was coming to see him as a man. A thoughtful man with a dry sense of humor.

The judge cracked a genuine smile. "I like being right, is all."

Now Jake's curiosity, which he'd held at bay for two weeks, prompted him to say, "I'm a convicted felon. I've been a jailhouse lawyer for seven years. Didn't *you* worry I'd give you bad advice, go for the defendant's position every time?"

Judge Randall put down his pen. "Of course I worried. But I decided to give you a chance. And in these two weeks, you've done research for me three times, and each time you've told me the prosecution is right."

Jake nodded. He'd assumed that people in the prosecutor's office were less than happy with the judge's choice.

In fact, Gerry Pendask, the county prosecutor, had yet to actually speak to Jake. Jake took perverse pleasure in passing the guy on the stairs and saying hello in the most casual way possible, as if they were colleagues. Now he said quietly, "I wouldn't take a chance on skewing results." He desperately needed this job. The judge had to know how much.

Judge Randall nodded thoughtfully. "I think there's a little more to it than that. I think you really love the law for its own sake."

Jake hadn't realized anyone had noticed his passion for the law. He'd figured everyone just assumed he'd been a jailhouse lawyer to survive in the joint, and that now he was making use of the only skill he had. He almost felt like smiling.

His life was going better than he'd dared to hope. But he still woke up nights, sweating, thinking he was back in a cell. He'd rise and go over to the window, and push it all the way up, letting the cool air of freedom wash over his bare skin. Sometimes, even that wasn't enough. Then he'd pull on a pair of jeans and walk in the dark garden of the parsonage and think *I can go outside any time I want.*

He couldn't go just anywhere, of course. He was stuck in Grange County until his parole was up. He was going to ask Rachel about permission to travel outside the county at their meeting today.

All his conversations with Rachel so far had been short and to the point. Yet there was something…she seemed nervous, very conscious of him. He was conscious of her, that was for sure.

Yes, as soon as the judge was done with him here, he had to check in with Rachel. See Rachel. Jake pushed back his own chair and rubbed the bridge of his nose. Freedom was an illusion as long as he had to keep checking in with Rachel.

He looked up to find the judge watching him again. "So which is it?" Judge Randall asked. "A passion for the law, or just keeping your nose out of trouble?"

"Both, I guess." Jake said it reluctantly. He'd learned long ago not to speak of things that were important to him. Suddenly, his curiosity wouldn't let him go until he asked a couple of questions. "Just why did you hire me, anyway? I gave you nothing but trouble, filing all those briefs from jail. You're an elected official, and you're going to take plenty of heat come election time for having a felon for a law clerk.''

The judge abruptly pushed back his chair. Rising, he went to one of the long windows and stood looking out, his face in profile. ''I wondered when you were going to ask that.'' He hesitated. ''I suppose it's just as well that the issue's out in the open.''

Jake waited.

''Ah, hell,'' Judge Randall said finally. ''You might as well know the truth. I was never sure you were guilty.''

A powerful surge of emotion shot through Jake. An odd, warm sensation—*someone believes in me.* And the coldest anger he'd ever felt in his life. The anger spilled over. ''You weren't sure I was guilty, but you let them send me to the joint for *ten years?*'' He was on his feet now too.

''Jake, it's not easy for a judge to set aside a jury verdict.''

Jake cursed. ''It's not usual practice, but it can be done. It can be done!''

Judge Randall turned to face him and said very evenly, ''It can't be done by judges who'd like to be reelected.''

Jake balled his fists by his sides as he struggled to control his anger. Moments passed.

The judge looked him straight in the eye. ''I'm telling you the truth now. Do you want to find another job?''

''Where? Milking cows?'' Jake didn't even try to hide the bitterness in his voice.

The judge nodded. Then he came back to the table. Across an expanse of old, gleaming gold wood, they

stared at each other. Randall put out a hand, then
withdrew it. Finally, he said quietly, "I've never felt
good about not setting aside that verdict. Over the
years, I was sure some of that stolen property would
turn up, but it never did. My wife told me I'd done
the right thing, that circumstantial evidence is as
good as any. They'd found your fingerprints all over
Joann Floutz's house."

"I'd been working for her." Jake tried not to
shout. "I'd cleaned her gutters that day. Of course
my fingerprints were there."

"You were the last to see her alive." The judge's
voice was weary. "They found her tape deck at your
house."

"And none of the stolen merchandise. Why would
I get rid of a fancy TV and VCR and keep an old
tape deck?"

The judge sighed. "Yes, I wondered about that.
But there was that false alibi—"

"I didn't do it," Jake interrupted. He didn't need
any reminders of that deliberately false alibi—and
his certainty that Rachel would back him up. An
overwhelming tiredness laced through his anger.
Would he be having to say he was innocent for the
rest of his life?

The judge said, "For a few months after that trial,
I waited for some hood to turn up, fencing Joann
Floutz's necklace. To have that necklace come up in
a raid on a pawnshop or something. But it never
did."

The missing amber pendant was distinctive. Joann
had worn it often, and once, she'd taken it in her
fingertips and held it a little way out from her chest
and shown Jake the piece of butterfly wing embedded

in it. She'd said it made the piece valuable. She'd leaned forward, inviting him to take a good look.

There was no way he was going to have his eyes that close to his employer's breasts, so he'd mumbled something about having to go back to work. He'd felt her looking at him that day, and he'd taken a push broom in his hand and turned his back on her and started sweeping out her garage.

Well, the judge might have thought about that pendant for months, but Jake had thought about it for *years*. Long after he'd gone to prison, Jake had waited for the same thing the judge had—that the necklace would show up in the hands of some punk. Proof of Jake's innocence.

And now Jake was going to find that stolen property if he could.

"I didn't kill Joann Floutz," he repeated.

There was a long moment of silence, and then the judge held out his hand.

Jake looked at that hand. When he'd hired him, Judge Randall had shaken his hand. It was the first sign of real respect Jake had been shown since getting out of prison. Hell, it was one of the few times in his life he'd been shown that kind of respect.

Yet the judge—by not exercising his option to set aside the verdict—had sent Jake to prison for ten years. Now Jake had a choice. He could take that proffered hand or he could refuse it. If he refused it, would he have a job?

He thought so. He looked away. .

Judge Randall cleared his throat. "It hasn't set well with me since I hired you that we didn't get this straight between us." The judge dropped his hand.

"I suppose it'll take you a while to see things from my perspective."

"I suppose it will." Maybe someday his anger would ease. Maybe clearing his name would help. He hoped so. Jake picked up his brief, and the galling bitterness hit him again, like a spasm. "If you're done with me, I've got to check in with my parole officer."

"Jake."

Jake waited.

"Jake…" The judge hesitated. "Hell, I don't have any more to say. I said it all, and it… It's not enough, is it?"

"No," Jake said. The judge had merely echoed Jake's own thoughts, and a sudden weariness swept him. He was tired of always being angry. But it seemed that anger would always be a part of his soul.

HE RAPPED on the door frame and Rachel motioned him in. She was already sitting at the little table she had over by the window. She was dressed in some kind of green jacket. A blazer, very tailored, and she had a silk scarf draped around her neck. As always, she looked beautiful…and classy. Jake sat down beside her. He was grateful that she chose to do things this way, instead of sitting behind her desk.

"How's it going?" she asked with a smile.

He shrugged. "About how it goes most days."

"Is everything all right at work?"

"Yes."

She gave him that Rachel-smile, that genuine one that lit up her whole face. But then she spoiled it by making some kind of note on her pad. Her professional concern was something else that rankled. That little notation made him sarcastic. "If you're concerned, why don't you check with Judge Randall?"

She put down her pen and gave him a level look. "I'm glad things are going well."

"As my parole officer?"

"Jake."

He was a little sorry for the sarcasm. He was still reeling from the judge's words a few minutes ago, but there was no reason to take it out on Rachel.

Kind and generous Rachel. She was a girl who'd invited all the shy kids to her birthday parties, the kind who would bring a kitten home even though it exasperated her father. Sometimes, Jake had felt like one of Rachel's strays.

Whenever he had that thought—and he'd had it plenty when he was a teenager—it had bothered the hell out of him. "Look," he said abruptly, "I want to travel out of town. My parole regulations say I can't go without your permission so I'm…" All of a sudden this was very hard. "I'm asking for your okay. I want to travel to Columbus."

"Why?"

"Because I want to." He couldn't tell her why. He was planning to violate about four conditions of his parole by poking around places where known felons hung out, in search of an amber necklace that had been missing for more than a decade. She'd have to say no.

"Jake, your parole conditions are just the same as every other parolee's. You can't leave the county."

"Not even for a…side trip?"

"A vacation?" She looked at him skeptically.

Ah, screw it. "Forget it. What more do I have to do for today's check-in?"

There was a long pause. Then without answering, Rachel got up and went to the coffeepot. "Do you want some coffee?"

"No, thanks."

"Well, I'm having some."

"Okay," he said. "Black, please." The smart thing to do would be to finish his check-in and be gone. There was no reason to stay and socialize with Rachel. It brought back too many memories.

She filled two mugs and came over to the table. She put one in front of him and then took her place. "I know we need to keep this about business," she began, and she bit her lip. "It's just that...I'm having a hard time with this situation."

"*You're* having a hard time?"

She sat up a little straighter. "As a matter of fact, I am."

"You could have fooled me. For two weeks, you ask me questions, like do I have all my utilities turned on yet, you ladle out some professional kindness and then out the door I go."

"It occurs to me..." She fiddled with her coffee cup, running a fingernail along the rim, a fussy gesture that had never been typical of her. "What I mean is, I've been thinking. I'd like us to be friends." She looked at him, a little blush on her cheeks.

Friends. They'd been lovers and sex had always been hot, immediate, like a flash fire. He'd held her and touched her skin; he knew where every freckle was, he knew how she moaned and quivered in his arms. She was still the prettiest woman in the world, she'd been turning him on for ten years, and it was always all he could do when he checked in not to look at her breasts and legs. But now she was in charge of his life, and she'd told him she wouldn't allow him to travel twenty miles from home. Friends? "Sure," he said. "Friends. Okay."

She looked relieved. "Good."

She wouldn't be so relieved if she knew that for two weeks he'd sat in this chair and lusted after his parole officer. She wouldn't be relieved if she knew he sat here sometimes and imagined kissing her—and more—right in her office. Imagined her lying back on the desk, her classy clothes rumpled, her skirt up, her eyes half-closed with passion. Or Jake sitting right where he was now, but pulling her down to straddle his lap...

Surely quite a few of the guys she'd supervised over the years must have lusted after her, too. But none had been her lover. None remembered how she felt, how she smelled, like some kind of flowers after a hot day's rain.

He hadn't been with a woman since Rachel, ten years ago. What he ought to do, Jake thought now, is go somewhere—anywhere there were nice, single women, and have a get-out-of-prison-free-at-last roll in the hay. Maybe then he could handle these meetings with the businesslike approach Rachel took. Maybe he wouldn't alternate between having to guard his pride and wanting to kiss her. Maybe he could handle his check-in as her friend.

He took a long swig of coffee.

Rachel was back to running her fingertip along the rim of her mug. Round and round. *Friends* should have an easier time making conversation than this. "How's Andy?" he asked.

She jumped. "Andy? He's fine. Just fine."

"Leora?"

"Oh, fine, too." She looked at him and blushed again. "Well," she said brightly, starting to push back her chair. "This has been—"

Almost without thinking, he reached out and grabbed her wrist.

She let out a little gasp. "Rachel, this isn't…" He didn't quite know what he wanted to say. "Maybe friends is an okay idea. You know a lot about me. But I don't know anything about what these last ten years have been like for you."

She bit her lip. "I know."

There was a curious tension in his spine, a thickness in his throat. "Andy, for example. I don't know anything about Andy."

Her eyes widened. With guilt, he supposed. After all, today he'd learned that Judge Randall—the man he'd been feeling warmly toward, the man who'd given him the first real chance he'd ever had—could have gotten him a new trial ten years ago. Somehow, in the wake of that news, Jake wanted to hear about Andy, about how soon Rachel had left Jake's arms for Chris's. He wanted to take it all on the chin, all at once.

He released her hand, but he held her gaze. "How old is Andy?" he asked softly. For two weeks he'd asked himself that question. While he'd been shuttled from one penitentiary to another in those early days, scared to death and longing to hold Rachel, she'd been with Chris. Somehow, like rubbing salt in a wound, he had to know exactly how long she'd missed him before finding herself a new lover. One that was acceptable to her father, to the community.

She said very quietly, "He's just finishing third grade."

One of the secretaries appeared in the doorway. "Rachel, can you come here for a minute?"

Rachel practically jumped out of her seat. "Coming." She closed her notebook with a snap. "We're all done here, Jake. No use you waiting for me. I'm sure you need to get back to work. I'll see you in a couple of days."

Just like that, she was gone.

On his way out a few minutes later, he saw her standing over in a corner, talking with some grubby, long-haired kid. Jake didn't acknowledge her little wave.

She was embarrassed, of course. There had been that awareness that had leaped between them for a second there. Added to that awareness was that Rachel had confirmed what Jake had already figured. If Andy was nine, she'd gotten together with Chris within months of Jake being sent to prison, and became pregnant almost immediately as well. No wonder she was embarrassed.

Jake had been careful to use protection. But Chris obviously hadn't. So what? Chris had something to offer her. Marriage. He was the town golden boy, after all, and who would be better for the town golden girl than the town golden boy?

All Jake had ever wanted was people's respect and to marry that golden girl. Those ordinary things other people seemed to take for granted.

His body had hurt in prison; it was cold there and the cold penetrated your bones, especially in the winter. But even in the summer it was dank.

Out of prison at last, his body was warm. But his

heart ached—an actual physical pain. When he'd
gone to prison he'd hoped Rachel would have a life,
but how quickly she'd gone after that life was what
made him sick at heart.

Rachel. The judge. *Rachel.*

For the first time in his life, he understood some
of what must have made Big Jake pick up a bottle
of whiskey.

But he'd vowed he'd never do that. If he did, they
would win, all those people who'd said Big Jake's
son would never amount to anything.

A WEEK LATER, Rachel took her notes out of the
drawer. She was not looking forward to Jake's scheduled visit today.

She'd been stunned earlier this morning when Al
Mortimer, one of Grange's uniformed officers, had
called. She worked closely with the police; they let
her know when one of her parolees was leaning toward trouble. But she'd never expected trouble from
Jake.

She scanned her notes, though she knew them by
heart. She'd written down everything Al had said, in
shock, not allowing herself to think until after she'd
murmured a thank-you and hung up.

But she was thinking now. Why would Jake jeop-
ardize his parole? It made no sense. He'd been on
his way to putting his life back together; he had a
fine job and a nice apartment. She knew only too
well that both were the best Jake had ever had.

Just then he knocked on the door frame, prompt
as always. The boy she'd known had worn blue jeans
as a kind of uniform. Jake the man wore trousers and
a crisp cotton shirt and a subtle tie. The formality of

his clothing was a sharp contrast to the man's rough edges. She liked the contrast, and she always reacted when she saw him. She always hid her reaction, too.

It was easier to hide it today because she had a lot to say to Jake. She forced herself to keep from blurting out her questions. She was a professional and this was a professional problem. So she rearranged her paperwork and invited him to sit at the table they used.

"How are things going?" she asked. The question was a kind of ritual with her parolees. Some said "okay," but for others the simple question was all they needed to get talking. She was part cop, part counselor, and with the kids she supervised, part mom.

"Okay." Jake was one of those who used the fewest words. He put his hands out on the table, palm down. Good-looking hands, dusted with gleaming black hair. Masculine hands.

She shook her head as if to clear it. Damn Jake for making this so complicated. "Things are going okay, are they? I know the job's going well, but I was wondering about your free time."

There was the slightest pause, so slight that if she hadn't been studying him closely, she would have missed it. "I do a lot of extra research in my free time," he said.

"What else?"

He looked away, and she felt a rush of fear and anger. When Al had called, her first reaction had been denial. Someone who looked like Jake must have gone to that pawnshop in the seediest part of Columbus. It must have been someone who looked like Jake who'd gone for a quick walk with Danny "the Duke" Duncan, the known criminal who ran the place.

But Al was certain that the person who'd met with Danny had been Jake Monroe. The Columbus police had been staking out the shop for weeks. They had a surveillance video, and Al had seen it.

Rachel hadn't been shown the tape, and she was reluctant to trust Al's judgment. She knew that some on the police force were just waiting for Jake to cause trouble.

So she'd done some checking of her own. What she'd found out disturbed her greatly. Danny "the Duke" Duncan had been in the penitentiary recently. In fact, he'd gotten out six months ago and was on parole himself in Columbus.

He'd been in the same cell block as Jake Monroe.

Her throat felt dry, painfully so. If she asked him a direct question now, would Jake take the typical parolee's way out and lie to her? She took a deep breath, but she found in the end that she couldn't be as direct as she wanted to be. Her heart was hammering too hard. "What else are you doing with your free time?"

"Taking notes, Rachel?" He still wasn't looking directly at her. Instead, he studied the walls, the curtains, the calendar picture on the wall—one of a little girl reading a storybook.

"Too much free time can get a parolee in trouble," she said. "It's perfectly within my bounds to ask what you do with yours."

"It's perfectly within bounds for you to know what I do every minute of every day."

She knew her power over him rankled, but she refused to respond to the sarcasm. This time he would not put her on the defensive. She picked up her pen. "Let's start with what you did yesterday."

"After work I went home, made a couple of grilled-cheese sandwiches and read a book."

"What did you do in the afternoon? Say, around two o'clock?"

He turned to look at her finally. Then he said very, very softly, "Damn."

She closed her eyes for a moment. "Did you really think I wouldn't find out?"

His hands fisted on the tabletop. "I'd hoped you wouldn't."

"What did you do?"

"I've been working so many hours I'd already earned some compensation time from the county. So I took the afternoon off and went to Columbus." He kept his eyes steady on her. "I went to see a guy I knew in prison. He was in the joint for grand theft and embezzlement. Now that he's out, he manages a pawnshop."

The breath whooshed out of her lungs. Even when caught, parolees tended to tell the most outlandish stories. Jake had done what few did: he'd told the truth. In that moment, she knew one of the reasons her throat had been so tight. She couldn't have stood it if he had lied to her, made excuses, tried to manipulate her as if he were a real criminal.

He said, "How did you find out?"

"A police officer spotted you coming out of the store." It was only half the truth. But she wasn't allowed to tell Jake Monroe, convicted felon, parole violator, about any police activities. She certainly couldn't tell him that the police were running a stake-out, complete with hidden camera and videotape.

"Why, Jake?" She heard the emotion in her voice; she wasn't quite able to control it. "You're an intelligent man, and I know you understood the conditions of your parole. You know one of the most important things is that you can't have contact with a known felon."

His eyes, so dark brown they were almost black, glittered with intensity. "I went because that guy was a friend of mine in the joint. I couldn't be too choosy about my friends there, you know. Oh, I avoided the child molesters and rapists. Instead, I hung out with the thieves. I made it my business to be friendly with the Duke, there in the joint. Because the Duke knows about every big-time fencing operation in Ohio." He paused. "I wanted him to tell me if an amber necklace had ever been fenced on the q.t. I wanted him to ask around and keep his eyes open."

"Oh, Jake."

"Are you going to report my parole violation? Have me arrested?" The words were still coming in that soft, level tone, but there was an underlying bitterness lacing them, too. Old hurts. New hurts.

Rachel's eyes suddenly filled with tears. She jumped up and turned away so he wouldn't see them. She had never been able to stand it when he was hurting. She couldn't stand it now. "I have to consider mitigating circumstances," she said as she turned.

"What more mitigating circumstances can there be than my trying to prove my innocence? An innocence you claimed to believe in once upon a time."

An innocence you wouldn't support by giving him his alibi. She picked up her watering can and saw through a kind of sheeny haze that it was almost

empty. She poured the trickle of water onto the dirt
of her big ivy plant while she thought. She did think
Jake was innocent. But encouraging him in this...this
scheme—''Jake, you're going to get in trouble. I'm
not going to report you this time because I can understand your motivation.''

She swallowed. He'd gone for a walk with Danny
''the Duke'' Duncan; the police knew about it although they hadn't been able to monitor Jake's conversation. So she had only his word that he'd talked
about a missing amber necklace....

She needed her job. She had a child to support.

But it was her call.

She took a deep breath. ''I can't just give you an
okay to travel. I can't encourage you in this venture.
It's been ten years. You aren't going to find any evidence now. Maybe you should concentrate on rebuilding your life, making a life for yourself now—
Oh!'' He put a hand on her forearm, and she jumped.

On her carpeted floor he'd moved so softly she
hadn't heard him coming. He kept his hand on her
arm for a moment, and then he tugged gently. ''Rachel. Look at me.'' There was a pause. ''Please.''

It was the please that caused her to turn. He was
so close. She looked up, straight into his eyes. His
mouth was so grim, so tight. It was a mouth she'd
once kissed, had teased, encouraging him to open his
lips and take her tongue...

His eyes were hot. ''Rachel, you know me better
than anyone else. How can I pretend I've got a clean
slate here? How can I just 'rebuild my life'? I'm a
convicted murderer. No one will ever really give me
a chance again. I can never take the bar exam, be a
real attorney.'' He paused, and then his voice went

even lower. Huskier. "How can I not try to clear my name?"

It terrified her for a moment, this intensity of his. He'd got through a rough childhood by just that determination, had used determination to make it to school after getting up at three o'clock in the morning to milk cows and scrape manure. To get up and go to school after he'd been up half the night rousting his father out of one of the town taverns. Of course he wouldn't rest until he cleared his name.

And disaster lay ahead.

"Jake, promise me you won't go back to that pawnshop." She had no idea how long the police would be watching the place. "Promise me."

That hand of his was still on her arm. Right through the silk of her blouse she felt it. Warm. No. Hot.

"I can't promise you," he said finally. "I'd be lying to you, and I don't want to do that." He swallowed visibly. "Not to you."

"I have to do my job. Also, Charlie will be back in a few weeks, and he'll take over your case. He's a stickler for protocol. I use my judgment, make the best call I can under the circumstances, but Charlie isn't like that. He's the original bureaucrat."

There was a long pause. "You'll do what you have to do. So will Charlie."

"Jake." She tried not to plead. "You're going to end up back in prison."

She felt the quick, almost spasmodic pressure of his hand on her arm. "No. I'm not going back to prison. Never again."

She shivered and pulled her arm away. He let go immediately and said, "I don't want to get you in trouble over this. That's one of the reasons I didn't tell you about going to that pawnshop before I left town. But I have to do this, and if you find out I've violated my parole when I was trying to clear my name…you'll have to make your decision then."

There was no use in argument. She heard the finality in his voice. She swallowed and found the firmness in her own tone. "Don't push me. I don't want to, but if you go back to that pawnshop, I'll have to have you arrested."

"I don't plan to go back to that pawnshop. That is, unless Danny finds an amber pendant. And you're right, what's the chance of that happening after ten years?"

She felt a spurt of relief. "I'll have to write a memo to Harold." That had been her resolve when she'd decided how to handle Jake. She would document everything that called for judgment on her part. There would be no mistaking her motivations. It was a way to check herself, to be sure she was separating her feelings for Jake the parolee from Jake the man.

"Do what you have to do."

She nodded, glad the discussion was over. "That's it for today. Just…stay out of trouble."

He walked over to the table and picked up the legal pad and law book he'd brought. He was almost at the door when she said, "Wait."

He paused.

"Jake, I… Don't get me wrong. If you go back to that pawnshop, I'll order your arrest. I have to. But I want you to know that I still think you're innocent. I know I wouldn't give you that alibi—"

He made a sound, one syllable. A dismissive

sound, and she wasn't sure if he accepted what she was saying.

Very quickly, she said, "I believed in your innocence then and I believe in it now. Nothing that's happened to either of us has ever changed that."

He had gone completely still. The sunlight from the tall windows at her back cast long, jagged shadows on the carpet. Outside, she could hear the birds. Inside, it was quiet.

Finally, he nodded. "Thank you. Thank you for believing me." Then he was gone.

After he left, she shut her door. It was something she didn't do often, but she was shaky and...raw. Exposed. His expression stayed with her. The vulnerable gratitude on his handsome face, and something more...immediate. Hunger.

His touch lingered. She imagined she could still feel his hand on her skin. He'd only been making a point; the gesture had been almost unconscious. Casual when coming from anyone else. Yet...not casual at all. There had never been anything casual about her and Jake.

She sat down and made herself work. She logged onto her word processing program. The sooner she finished this memo, the sooner she could put Jake Monroe and these disturbing emotions out of her mind.

It was somewhere about the middle of the page that she realized something. Jake had said he had no plans to go back to the pawnshop. But he had not promised to stop trying to solve an unsolvable crime. And he hadn't promised to follow all the rules from now on.

Her heart sank. Jake would never give up trying.

And she couldn't take any more chances. She had a job to do and a child to support.

But as Rachel pushed the button to print, she thought, *Please, Charlie. Get well and come back soon.*

Because then maybe Rachel Penning Drewer wouldn't have a hand in putting Jake Monroe in prison...for the second time.

CHAPTER FOUR

ON SATURDAY MORNING, Jake got up early. He hadn't slept well last night, thinking about his meeting with Rachel. Now he was down in the parsonage garden, feeling the fresh air on his face.

Just a few days ago, he'd vowed not to touch her, not even in friendship. But when he'd been trying to explain about his need to solve this crime, he'd wanted her understanding so badly that he had touched her. And somehow, touching her—even on the arm—had brought back every memory he'd been working so hard to suppress.

He'd meant it when he'd said he didn't want to make trouble for her.

Even as a girl, she'd tried to please everyone. She'd gotten along with others in a way he'd never been able to achieve. She was no risk taker. After all, she hadn't even considered lying for him. But she was a grown-up now, with adult responsibilities, he told himself. Of course she couldn't risk her job.

Yet she believed in him. She'd said so, and that meant more to Jake than he would have liked it to.

He pushed his hands into the pockets of his jeans and headed to the vegetable garden. He stood at the edge and looked at the clean rows of brown dirt. The lettuce was heading up. Full spring had arrived in Grange. Calving season at the farms.

Jake felt his mouth tighten. If it hadn't been for Judge Randall, this time of year he'd be up all night with pregnant cows, helping to pull calves in some cold barn. He really could understand Rachel's fear that he'd blow it. The stakes were gut-tightening high. But he wasn't going back to prison. And he sure as hell wasn't going back to an old farm, either.

The garden at the parsonage was huge, and he'd often seen Reverend Carson working among the rosebushes. Jake didn't have much use for gardens. Instead, he'd always liked the wild places. The spot down by the river where the willow roots had heaved and made a little pocket in the ground, as cozy as a cave. He and Rachel had made love there once. Then there were the ditches on either side of the gravel roads, roads so little used that the county didn't spray the roadsides for weeds. He'd picked Rachel some flowers there once when they'd gone walking: oxeye daisies and mud-orange daylilies, chicory, feathery heads of foxtail.

He remembered the day with perfect clarity because he'd felt so foolish…so silly, picking those flowers. But then Rachel had smiled, and he'd known he'd pleased her. Suddenly, he hadn't felt foolish or silly at all. It was the day she'd said she loved him.

Now Jake saw Reverend Carson come out of the garage, wearing a pair of hot-pink gardening gloves, a plastic apronlike thing and baggy khaki pants. One fluorescent-colored hand was carrying a pair of pruning shears.

Jake turned to go, sorry that the reverend was an early riser, too.

"Hey, wait a minute." Carson picked up his pace, hurrying over to Jake.

Jake took his hands out of his pockets and waited. He'd said little to his landlord since moving in; when Carson was out with his gardening paraphernalia, Jake stayed indoors with a book. The guy was a do-gooder. *Give him a chance,* Rachel had said. But Jake didn't want to be the reverend's latest project.

When he reached Jake, Carson stuck out his hand. "Oops, wait," the reverend said, and pulled off the glove with his teeth. About ten years older than Jake, he had a million freckles on his pudgy cheeks, sun creases around his eyes and a bald spot on his head that he apparently made no attempt to hide. There were freckles there, too.

Jake shook hands.

"How are you doing, Jacob?"

"Fine, thank you. And it's just Jake."

"Ah." The reverend nodded as if there was something significant in that.

"Well, you're busy—" Jake turned to go.

"Wait." A hand shot out and stayed him. "Listen, could you help me with something? I've got a big forsythia that needs moving."

"Sure." The guy was his landlord, after all, and those gloves made him look…approachable. Ridiculous, but approachable.

Carson went to get the wheelbarrow and Jake carried the spade. At the farm his father used to make desultory scratching in the dirt each spring and throw in a few seeds. By midsummer, the garden had always been overrun with weeds. He shook off the memory as they headed over to the large, densely planted shrub border. Behind it was a tall yew hedge, as solid as a wall. Jake took the spade and began to dig around the bush the reverend indicated.

Carson fussed with something in one of his apron pockets. "You like gardening, don't you?" he asked abruptly.

Jake looked up and wiped sweat from his upper lip. "Not especially."

"Oh. I just thought…"

Jake bent again to his task. Obviously, he'd been spotted walking here at night. For a second he tensed, irrationally thinking that the reverend was going to forbid his nightly walks. Then he made himself relax. He was out of prison now; he could go anywhere in Grange County, even in the dark.

"Haven't seen you in church," the reverend said.

Jake felt his teeth clench. "I've been out of town for the last ten years," he said shortly.

There was a second's startled pause, and then Carson…chuckled.

Jake straightened abruptly.

"Point taken." Carson was smiling. "I push too hard with people sometimes. My wife always says so, anyway. These are her gloves, by the way. Never seem to be able to find mine.… Anyway, you're entitled to your privacy."

Jake nodded, feeling a little spurt of…camaraderie. "Thanks."

"Let's lift this baby," Carson said, gesturing to the bush. The reverend's face got red and he grunted as he lifted.

Jake bent to help. They wrestled the root ball from the ground.

Something exploded from between the bushes, a tiny, sleek rush of brown.

"Yikes!" The reverend dropped the bush on his foot and gave a howl of pain.

Jake straightened quickly as the live thing brushed against his leg. A rat or a ferret or...

"Peppy! Peppy!" The yews swayed violently and parted. A kid ran between them. "Peppy!"

It was Andy. Rachel's Andy.

And the rat was a tiny dachshund, long and wiggling. As Andy got closer, the puppy teased, running hither and yon in a dizzying zigzag through the garden.

"Peppy, you're gonna get hurt!" The kid's voice held both exasperation and love.

Jake took a couple of long strides and headed the puppy off at the corner of the shrub border. The dog veered and Andy pounced. A second later, he sat up in triumph with Peppy in his hands, a quivering wiener with shiny black beads for eyes.

Andy looked up at Jake with a big smile on his face. Jake's mind's eye abruptly conjured Rachel. A wide-open smile, nothing held back...

"Hey, thanks," Andy said. "I thought Peppy was gonna run out in the street and get hit by a car." The kid looked down at the dog. "But I got you." He cuddled the puppy to his chest. The dog endured it, but looked up at Jake as if imploring to be rescued.

Jake heard Reverend Carson come up behind him. "Do you know Andy Drewer? He's Rachel's boy."

"We met at the pizza parlor," Jake explained.

"Really?" Andy asked, looking more closely at Jake and wrinkling his nose. It was obvious the kid didn't remember their meeting. Jake would never forget it, though. It was the night he'd met Rachel's child.

Rachel and Chris's child.

Jake bent toward the puppy. These thoughts were

getting him nowhere. He reached out a hand to the dog and scratched the base of one silky ear. Peppy went abruptly quiet, clearly luxuriating in the feel of Jake's fingers on such a sensitive spot.

"Do you like dogs?" Reverend Carson asked.

"Yeah, I like dogs." Spook had gone still this way when scratched in exactly this place on his ear. Before Rachel, that white dog had been his best friend. Spook had always gone along on their walks, had sat in the dusty road and waited patiently when Jake would steal a kiss from Rachel…

He shook his head. Trust Rachel to have a dog. When she was a kid, she'd always wanted pets, but her father hadn't liked the mess. Any kittens she brought home were fed a couple of meals of milk and tuna fish and then taken promptly to the shelter. Funny, though, Jake figured she'd have picked up a mongrel dog at the pound. Mothering mutts was more Rachel's style.

Reverend Carson sat down in the grass. Andy released Peppy and, grand adventure over, the puppy flopped down on his tubby belly. One ear twitched, and then his eyes closed.

Andy ran a hand along the dog's backbone. "I was really scared he was going to go in the street."

He looked earnest, and Jake knew without a doubt that the kid loved the puppy and took good care of him. He looked so exactly like Rachel at that moment that Jake felt a wash of some emotion he didn't want to name. A kind of strange…connection. That was ridiculous, he told himself. Andy was a cute kid with a cute dog, and Jake lusted after the boy's mother, that was all.

Reverend Carson took off his dirt-stained gloves

and laid them in the grass. "You have a fenced yard, and you need to keep the gate closed."

"How far away do you live, Andy?" Jake asked. He cursed himself for wanting to know, for letting Reverend Carson see him wanting to know. He made sure his voice was casual. "I just wondered how far this little guy traveled."

"I live over there." Andy gestured vaguely behind him.

"In the block behind us, about six houses down," Carson explained. Jake was startled; he'd had no idea Rachel lived so close. Carson shot Jake a shrewd look, and Jake knew in that instant what he'd started to suspect a few minutes ago: regardless of the dotty garden garb, this guy was sharp.

Jake needed to get going. He needed to leave this garden, to turn away from this kid of Rachel's. Especially to turn away from the reverend's penetrating gaze.

Pride was a funny thing. You had to hang on to it hard because it seemed as if everyone wanted to take it from you. But something kept him rooted here, sitting on the damp grass.

"I was going to go over to the park and see if there were any other kids there," Andy explained. "But I forgot my mitt, and when I went to the garage to get it, Peppy escaped." He turned serious eyes to the minister.

"You left the gate open," Reverend Carson said, but the words were kind.

"I guess. I'm sorry, though."

"Well, no harm done." Carson reached out a hand and mussed the boy's hair. Jake suddenly had the urge to do the same.

There was a pause. Then Andy said, "Hey, the baseball games are gonna start soon, aren't they?"

"Andy plays on the church league," the reverend explained to Jake.

"Are you going to keep coaching us?" Andy asked Carson, and there was an edge of anxiety to his voice.

Carson grinned at Jake. "No, not if I don't have to. I'm—shall we say—athletically challenged. My idea of activity is puttering in the garden or exercising my jaws at church picnics." He looked at Jake. "You look athletic."

Jake shrugged.

"Ever play baseball?"

"Do you play baseball?" Andy echoed, looking up with real interest.

"A bit." He'd learned the game late, but athletics came naturally to him. As a kid, he'd desperately wanted to be on a team, any team playing any sport.

"Did you play on a league?" Andy asked eagerly.

"Sort of."

"Maybe you'd like to help coach," Reverend Carson said.

"No thanks." *No way.*

Andy leaned forward. "But the games are gonna start, and this time not one of the fathers could help and we're sure not gonna win with Rev—" Andy stopped and got bright red.

"It's okay," Carson said. "Jake, what this little guy is trying to say is that I am 'it' as a coach for these boys. That's the way it goes sometimes. Usually we have plenty of parents to coach, but occasionally we don't. I already told you what my game's like. If you've got playing experience, we could really use you. Think about it.''

Jake got to his feet. Maybe this would qualify as the community service that was part of his parole requirements. Rachel had given him time to set something up, but he needed to decide soon. It sounded sort of…fun. Fresh air, the crack of a bat hitting a ball under the clear sky… The hopeful way Andy was looking at him made him say, ''I'll think about it,'' though he knew better than to get involved.

''Good.'' Reverend Carson got to his own feet a lot slower than Jake had. ''Andy, why don't you let Peppy nap right here, and you go into the house. Mrs. Carson will get you a glass of soda and you can call your mom and tell her where you are.''

''Okay.'' Andy was up and off like a shot. The puppy, alerted by the movement, hopped up too and followed Andy across the grass on fast-moving, stubby legs.

Jake stood looking after them, feeling himself smile at the kid's antics, but feeling sad, too. Andy was a sweet kid. It must be hard on him to have lost his father.

Carson stood quietly next to him.

''How's Andy doing?'' Jake asked. ''I know that Chris hasn't been gone long.''

''He misses him, of course,'' Carson said. ''But Rachel's doing a good job of making sure he feels loved. This baseball thing is unfortunate. Andy's nuts about the game, and Rachel offered to coach. But she's more pathetic at the finer points—like batting, throwing and catching—than I am.'' There was a pause. ''You'd help this kid out a lot if you'd coach.

You've got experience. One thing with kids this age. They like the game, but they like to win most of all. Their enthusiasm goes way down if they can't win a few.''

The idea began to appeal to Jake. He wanted to stand under a warm sun under the open sky and throw the ball to this kid who had such a warm smile. Jake felt a longing that was bone deep. If only he could join something as simple as a baseball team. If only he could just…belong to something. Just once.

''I can't,'' he said, careful to keep the emotion from his voice.

''Rachel says Chris used to throw the ball around for Andy after supper. She says she offers to do it instead, but Andy doesn't like the way she throws. When she told me that, she had tears in her eyes. Rachel hasn't had it all that easy this last year, either.''

Oh, hell. ''I can't,'' Jake repeated. But he felt he owed some explanation. So he took a breath and put aside his pride. ''I didn't play on a league. We did have teams, and the games were pretty intense.'' He took another breath. ''The place I played ball was the penitentiary.''

''Some good athletes there,'' the reverend said mildly.

Jake shoved his hands in his pockets. ''I didn't know if you understood.''

''I'm not an idiot, despite the gloves. I know where you've been.''

''So you should know why I can't do this.''

The reverend nodded. ''It could be tough. But this is a church league. The congregation has had a few sermons on judgment and forgiveness. Andy needs someone like you.''

Jake knew what he ought to do. Say no thanks and go up the stairs at the back of the garage to his furnished apartment. He almost did. But that longing just wouldn't go away; it held sway in his gut, pinched him there.

The puppy was sitting expectantly at the stoop, waiting for Andy. He looked about as big as a brown gumdrop, and Jake again felt that funny, unwelcome sensation of...wanting to connect.

But maybe for now he needed to concentrate on the one thing he thought he had a chance of accomplishing—clearing his name. Maybe he could coach after he'd proved to the town he was innocent of Joann Floutz's murder.

Again Reverend Carson spoke. ''You don't have the guts to face them? Those people who might not like you using your skills to coach their children? How can anyone really object? It's outside in a public place, and I'm there all the time.''

''You don't know what it can be like,'' Jake said quietly. It was a reluctant admission; from his school years on, he'd cultivated the attitude that he didn't give a damn what others thought of him. It was an attitude that had got him in trouble a few times when he was young, and it was an attitude that caused people to say things like, ''The apple doesn't fall far from the tree.''

''You're right, I don't know what that's like. But it must be lonely. Well. Only you can decide when you're ready to trust the human race.''

Jake looked into kind blue eyes. This guy had leased his apartment—the one above the garage of the house where he and his wife lived—to a known felon. He'd asked no questions, had treated Jake as simply a neighbor. "Okay," Jake said. "I'll do it."

"Good."

"I don't go to church," Jake warned. "I never have."

"All right."

"All *right?* What kind of reverend are you?"

The reverend held up the pair of hot-pink gloves. "A strange one, I guess. Let's just take one thing at a time. Starting with friendship." He held out his hand.

Jake took it.

By the door, the puppy had grown impatient, and he put up his nose and yowled, a thin, high, mournful, demanding yowl that went on and on.

The reverend laughed. Jake smiled, and that smile threatened to become a grin.

AT BASEBALL PRACTICE on Thursday evening, Rachel hardly had a chance to put the car in park before Andy leaped out. Leaving the door open, he ran to the edge of the field, smacking his fist into his gloved palm. "Oh, Jake, so you're gonna coach after all!" he shouted. He took off at a dead run, without so much as a goodbye to Rachel.

Rachel's hands froze in place on the steering wheel. Jake was here? She craned her neck. Yes, there he was, tight jeans and lean thighs and all, at the edge of the field. He wore a red baseball cap on his head, crouching as he apparently explained some nuance of the game to another ten-year-old. He wore a red T-shirt like Andy's. When he stood and turned, she could see a word in big white letters, stretching across those broad shoulders of his: Coach.

He was coaching her son. And apparently her son had known this was a possibility. In fact, Andy seemed on downright friendly terms with Jake.

When had this happened? *How* had this happened?

Through the windshield, she watched in a kind of horrified fascination. Andy ran right up to Jake as though they were the best of friends. Rather awkwardly, Jake gave her son's shoulder a light punch, and talked to him for a second. Andy's head bobbed with an enthusiastic nod, and he took his place behind the line of kids waiting for the catching drill.

Rachel usually ran a couple of errands and then picked up Andy after practice was over. This time, well, this time, how could she leave?

During their check-in sessions this past week, Jake hadn't asked any more questions about Andy. She'd decided that Jake had accepted what little information she'd offered about the boy, and had allowed herself to relax a little.

But here Jake was, on a ball field, and she had no idea how he'd come to coach her son.

His son. Their son.

Her stomach gave a quick lurch. Opening the car door, she got out and started to walk over to the field.

When she got close, Jake shot her a quick look before focusing again on the drill.

She waved to Reverend Carson—a wave she hoped looked happy and confident. Then she sat down on the grass near the baseline, close enough to home plate to hear most of what was said. She would stay right here. She would protect Andy from…

What? His baseball coach?

His father?

An old guilt washed over her, but she shook it off. If Jake had been interested in her life, he'd have answered her letters. He'd lost any claim to fatherhood over a decade ago.

She bent her knees and hugged them to her chest.

It was a fine evening, and the kids were in an expectant mood over their new uniforms and the first game on Sunday. There was a lot of chatter and a bit of a ruckus in the back of the line of boys.

"Okay, let's try some batting practice." Jake appointed one of the boys catcher and had the other kids line up to bat. Reverend Carson took his place near the pitcher on the mound.

When it was Andy's turn to bat, Jake stood behind him, his own hands on the bat to show Andy how to choke up a little. Then he stepped away and Andy took a couple of practice swings. "That's it," Jake said. "You've got it now."

Andy swung vehemently at the next pitch, which was high and outside. "Wait for your pitch," Jake instructed. Andy nodded.

The pitcher threw the ball straight across the plate.

Andy swung, and with a hard *thwack* the softball arced high in the air, right over the heads of the kids who'd been stationed in the outfield. Farther and farther it went, until it hit the fence at the edge of the field.

"A home run! A homer! A homer!" Andy threw down his bat and pranced around home plate. "If it'd been a game, it woulda been a homer!"

Rachel smiled, and when she caught Andy's eye, gave him two thumbs-up. Jake yanked on the brim of Andy's cap and gave him a thump on the shoulder.

Then Jake looked over at Rachel. He was smiling, but as he looked at her, he sobered.

Rachel felt her own smile drying up. There was her son, kicking up his heels in utter glee, and the guy who'd made him so happy was Jake.

Jake. Who looked so good in a tight pair of jeans, who looked so good in the brand-new baseball cap. Who'd never had the chance to wear a baseball cap as a boy but was wearing one now.

Jake. The man she'd once loved. She swallowed hard, but she didn't look away. All the background—the sounds of the kids congratulating her son, the sting of the occasional mosquito, faded until there was just her and Jake.

He was tall and strong and dark. Once when he'd looked at her, there had been hunger in his eyes. The depth of that hunger had scared her a little because it was so intense, so much stronger than anything in her eighteen-year-old experience. Once he'd been her whole world, and he'd had a pull on her that…

That she understood all too well. That she felt even to this day. That scared her to death.

"Hey, are we gonna play ball or what?" one of the kids yelled, and Jake turned abruptly away.

Rachel shivered, suddenly cold. The sun was low in the sky, and this time of year it got cool as soon as dark started to fall.

She rubbed her arms. She had a sweater in the car, but she stayed where she was. The kids continued to play, put through catching and batting drills by Jake and the reverend. Jake was everywhere, encouraging, demonstrating, pointing out different plays. Finally, just as the shadows were getting long on the field, Jake called the team into a huddle. She could see him leaning in, explaining something about the game. The last of the sun highlighted his features. He was smiling a little.

Her mind abruptly conjured scenes from long ago. Other teams, church leagues, school leagues, the Jaycees' ball games. Other kids, never Jake. He should have been in that crowd of kids. She might be scared to have him so close to her son, but how could she deny him the obvious pleasure he got in coaching?

A tiny shiver of fear went through her as she realized how important it was to her that Jake smile.

The kids, apparently in response to something Jake had said, hollered, "We're gonna win!" and they gave a banshee yell before breaking up.

They ran off the field, toward the parking area where their parents had come to pick them up. "Hey, Harry, don't forget your mitt," Reverend Carson called to one blond boy, and then he headed slowly out to the parking lot himself.

Rachel got to her feet. Andy came running over to her. Jake followed more slowly.

When they got to Rachel, Andy said, "Did you see my home run?"

"Could hardly miss it, you hit that ball so hard," she said. "I thought for a second it was going to go clear across the street and right through the window of the Dairy Queen. That hit was like magic." She smiled and gave him a hug. Feeling her son's slender body against hers, she suddenly felt a fierce stab of motherly love. Protectiveness. She hugged harder.

"All right already!" Andy squirmed, and Rachel let go.

Feeling herself blush a little, she looked at Jake. He was watching her carefully.

"Do you mind?" he asked quietly.

She didn't pretend not to know what he was talking about. "Of course not," she said. "You're good with the kids, you know."

"It was fun." He flashed a smile, rare and wistful and warm.

Andy said, "I wish my dad could've seen me hit that ball."

There was a second's pause as a cacophony of emotions resonated through Rachel. Regret and sorrow and pain and wishing and...

Jake was still watching her, and now another emotion pushed to the forefront. That motherly protectiveness.

Andy must never know that his father *had* seen him hit that ball.

But...

Jake said, "This must be very hard for you. For you both."

She whispered, "Yes."

Andy used the toe of his cleats to dig at the ground. "My dad would've cheered and cheered." He looked up at Rachel. "Wouldn't he?"

Chris had played baseball for years, had loved the game, had spent long Sunday afternoons holed up in the basement rec room, sitting in his recliner and watching the Cleveland Indians. Once in a while, she'd heard him shout from all the way upstairs, chewing out the umpire for a bad call. It was the only time in their entire marriage he'd raised his voice to anyone.

That safe, quiet life had been hers for a decade, and it was never supposed to change. "Yes," she whispered, conscious of Andy's earnest face and

Jake on the fringes of her peripheral vision. Jake was very still. "Your dad would have been so proud."

Tears pricked her eyes. Oh, she had to do better than this. She cleared her throat. "I think your dad does see when you hit the ball," she said more strongly.

"From heaven?" The toe of Andy's cleat dug harder. "Do you really think he's in heaven and can see?"

She squeezed his shoulder. "Yes, I do, because he was a good man and he loved you so much."

Andy looked up at her. "That's what I figured," he said in a matter-of-fact tone.

"Andy, come here!" Another kid was calling him, and without a backward glance, Andy took off.

For a moment, neither she nor Jake spoke. Most of the parents had arrived now, and they were turning their headlights on against the encroaching dark. A line of cars was forming near the entrance.

"I've got to go," she said finally, stooping to pick up her tote bag and the mitt Andy had tossed on the ground.

"Rachel, I..." Jake hesitated and shook his head a little. "Andy seems to be handling Chris's death pretty well."

"Sometimes I think he handles it better than I do." She dropped Andy's mitt into the tote bag. "Kids are resilient. He misses Chris, but he's okay about it."

"He's a nice kid. Smart, and good at the game."

"Chris taught him," she explained. "That's why... This is good for him. He's going to get better coaching than Reverend Carson's capable of, and he'll have some good games. I'm pleased about that.''

Jake nodded. ''I'm glad. I'd wondered what you'd think of my coaching.''

She clutched her tote bag. ''It's fine.'' He was always looking at her so intensely. ''Why wouldn't it be fine?''

He gave her a look that said she ought to know why.

Suddenly nervous, she said, ''Well, I'd best be going.''

She headed back to the car, certain she'd made a mistake, letting Andy be on a team that Jake was coaching. But what could she do?

She'd just handle it, that's all. The way she'd handled everything for the last ten years.

CHAPTER FIVE

SHE'D HANDLE this attraction too. She would not succumb to the pull of that intense stare. By game time on Sunday afternoon, Rachel had herself firmly under control.

Leora had accompanied them to the game. Andy ran ahead to the field where several of the kids were warming up. The ball caps of the team were dots of bright red against the green of the grass. The diamond had been freshly limed, and the pristine lines of white stood out. Soon, summer would wither the grass, and the dust kicked up as a result of the inevitable summer droughts would make even being a spectator a gritty experience. But today was perfect. Jake was out by the backstop, as was Reverend Carson.

Carrying a couple of folding chairs and some of Andy's gear, Rachel went up to a knot of parents who were watching from the sidelines. A few babies slept on blankets, a few toddlers played in the grass. She kept her eyes on the little crowd, not on the field.

She was *not* going to watch Jake squat in those tight jeans, feeling her mouth go dry at the sight. She was *not* going to watch him exchange a few words with Andy, frightened that he'd guess her secret.

''The kids look terrific this year, don't they?'' she said brightly to no one in particular.

Alva Turner, one of the mothers, turned troubled eyes to Rachel. "The kids look fine. But I don't know about this business of Jake Monroe coaching."

Rachel's stomach had been tight all morning. Now she felt it tighten more.

There were a couple of murmurs of agreement.

Alva's forehead creased. "I've been worrying about it all week. And then I talked to Janna Smith and Patsy Jarenski and they agreed with me. Such a bad influence…"

"Reverend Carson is here," Rachel said pointedly. "Jake isn't alone with the children, though I for one don't think any of you should be nervous even if he *is* alone with them."

Barbara Thomas shifted. "Do you think the reverend being here makes it okay, Rachel?" Barb was always quiet and thoughtful—if naive—and her question was sincere. Barb and her husband were relative newcomers to town, restoring a run-down farmhouse in the countryside. "Convicts use foul language."

Rachel said, "Many do, but Jake wouldn't around the children. In my supervision of him, he's been polite and respectful." She paused and waited until she'd caught the eye of every parent present. "Jake has paid his debt to society. Now he wants to coach a league for a church, for heaven's sake. You all know I wouldn't let Andy play if I felt there was danger to him."

A couple of the parents gave each other sheepish looks. Most had known Rachel for years. After a moment, the talk resumed, but this time the subjects were this morning's sermon and the fact that rain was predicted by midnight.

Rachel breathed a sigh of relief. Belatedly, it occurred to her that if Jake had left the team, it would make life easier for her. But not easier for Andy.

And it wasn't fair for Jake to have to keep paying and paying for a crime he didn't commit.

With short, vehement motions, she set up the folding chairs and she and Leora sat down. Leora put on her sunglasses and watched the kids for a moment. Finally, she asked, "Are you sure this is a good idea, Rachel?"

Rachel tossed her tote bag on the ground. "I've stood up for Jake in front of the parents. Now do I have to do the same with you?" She was a little sorry for her sharpness to Leora, but not for her words. So she didn't apologize.

Leora waited, presumably for the apology. Finally she adjusted her glasses and said briskly, "Well, all this fuss over a Little League game. As if there isn't enough bad in the world to fuss about." She stared straight ahead and Rachel knew the subject of Jake was closed.

The umpire, an older teenager, gathered the kids with a blow on his whistle, and the game began. Rachel started to relax and get into the spirit of cheering the boys on. She'd just cupped a hand to her mouth to yell, "Go Red!" when she heard a voice behind her.

A loud voice. "So it's true." Rachel turned to see Travis Bremmer standing with a hand on his son David's shoulder. David was dressed for the game, but he had an unhappy frown on his face.

"Reverend Carson!" Travis called.

The reverend apparently didn't hear him. So he

spoke to his son, "Go get Reverend Carson. Tell him I want to talk to him."

David shifted uncomfortably. "Dad, the game's already started—"

"Now!" Travis gave David a little push on the shoulder. Feet dragging, David headed in Reverend Carson's direction.

Slowly, Rachel got up. She went over to Travis. He'd gone to school with her and Jake, but he was a few years older than they were.

She'd never liked him, even when they were kids. The son of the town's only real-estate agent, Travis had taken over his father's office a decade ago. There was some competition in the local real-estate business nowadays, but you'd never know it to look at Travis. Even though he was at a baseball game, he was still dressed in the expensive suit he'd worn to church that morning. On his wrist, his gold Rolex gleamed.

Grange, Ohio, had never been a Rolex kind of town.

"Maybe you should just let David warm up so he doesn't miss too much of the game. After all, he did miss practice this week." Rachel's voice was clear and calm.

Travis gave her a pointed glance. "Where, I understand, the practice drills were headed up by a murderer."

Rachel had the most powerful urge to stuff the guy's Rolex down his throat. Instead, she aimed for reasonableness. "I've already explained to the other parents that Jake has given me no cause for concern about the children."

Rachel realized all the parents were now listening

to the conversation. Travis made it clear with a one-syllable sound how he felt.

Barb Thomas said, "Rachel said Mr. Monroe doesn't use foul language around the children."

Travis swore.

Barb covered her mouth. One of the fathers said, "Oh, come on, Bremmer, no cause for that."

"Is there a problem?" Reverend Carson joined them. Beside him, David looked at his feet.

Travis thrust out his chest. "The problem is that you're apparently recruiting murderers to coach little children, Reverend."

There were a couple of gasps from the parents.

Reverend Carson said mildly, "Yes, I have. A murderer who lives above my garage and never does so much as play the television set too loud. A murderer who likes to walk in my garden and scratch the ears of puppies."

"I've never believed he committed any crime," Rachel added.

"Rachel, for God's sake—" Travis cut himself off and addressed the reverend. "If you're getting your information from Rachel Drewer, just remember what a tender heart she has. Remember all those cats she has living in her garage."

Before Rachel could reply, Leora cut in. "I hope you didn't intend that as an insult to my daughter-in-law," she said, coming to stand by Rachel's side. "After all, she was a Penning. She's a Drewer. Both of those names have been respected in this town since long before the name Bremmer has been around."

Several of the parents exchanged uneasy glances. Rachel could hear the sounds of the game going on, but by now nobody was watching. All the parents had gathered, even those from the other team.

Reverend Carson cleared his throat. ''I've been your pastor for four years. Do I have to remind you all what Christian behavior is about?''

There were some shouts from the kids. The sound caused Rachel to look up, and she saw that Jake had come to join them. He looked dark and grim.

At the sight of him, something in Rachel snapped. ''This isn't fair!'' She felt Leora's hand squeeze hers but she went right on. ''Jake didn't kill anybody ten years ago!''

Travis said, ''The jury said—''

''The jury was wrong!'' She started to tremble.

''Maybe I should just give up coaching,'' Jake said quietly.

She whirled to face him. ''Why should you do that? Why, Jake? You obviously like it, and the kids like you. Why should you make it easy for people like—like Mr. Rolex here!''

He gazed at her for a long moment. Time seemed suspended as he searched her face. Rachel almost forgot to breathe. Then he turned to Travis Bremmer. ''As the lady says, why should I give up coaching?''

''Because you're a murderer!''

There was a collective gasp from the parents. Some looked distressed, others fascinated.

Jake asked Reverend Carson, ''Reverend, do you want me on the team?''

''Yes.''

''Then I guess I'm staying.'' He turned back to Travis. ''The reverend asked me to coach because none of the parents volunteered. Where were you when he was looking for coaches?''

Travis's eyes flickered, but he didn't say a word.

"Too busy when the reverend asked, I guess," Jake said quietly. "Yes, I really think I'm staying on."

Rachel felt a stab of pure pride in Jake. Once, he would have pretended he didn't really want to coach, and would have withdrawn with a sarcastic comment. This time, he'd publicly stood up to a bully. Rachel knew how hard that was when, for all Jake knew, he didn't have even one parent supporting him. Jake's shoulders were square, his stance tall and uncompromising. He kept his gaze steady on Travis.

"If you're coaching, we're going." Travis motioned to David. The boy hesitated, and Travis gestured forcefully for him to comply. Not looking Jake's way, the boy went over to his father. When David reached his side, Travis put an arm around his son's shoulders. "I'm looking out for my boy here. Are any of you going to look out for yours?"

For a moment, nobody moved.

Then Alva Turner left the circle of parents. In complete silence, she went onto the field to get her son. Out there, all play had stopped as the kids held their positions.

Rachel knew this day was going to be very hard to explain to Andy.

The rest of the parents watched as Travis Bremmer and the Turners took their children out of the game. A minute later they heard the slam of car doors in the parking lot.

A couple of people squirmed. Jake stood very, very still. Rachel's own spine felt so stiff it was beginning to hurt.

"Well!" Leora said finally. "If that isn't the— Of

course, Travis Bremmer's father was a horse's behind sometimes. It's not surprising his son turned out
that way.''

One of the parents smiled in agreement.

A surge of love went through Rachel. Leora might
be stiff and formal, but she stood up for what she
believed was right. When a couple of parents turned
to go back to the sidelines, Rachel finally felt herself
beginning to calm down.

''Well, that's that, I guess,'' Reverend Carson
said. He ringed his hands around his mouth and
shouted, ''Hey, Ump! Don't you want to play ball?''

Looking relieved, the teenager nodded vigorously
and blew hard on his whistle.

As Jake started to go back out on the field, Rachel
put out a hand and stopped him. The muscle and
bone under her palm felt strong. She said quietly,
''You did the right thing, Jake. But I'm surprised you
didn't quit.''

''Then he would have won.'' There was a tight set
to his mouth, but his eyes were brilliant as they
looked down into hers. ''This time, I wasn't going
to let him win.''

Rachel's heart squeezed. She knew him well
enough not to say what was in her heart—that she
was proud of him. ''Travis Bremmer really had it in
for you,'' she said to cover her reaction.

Jake shrugged and used a hand to shade his eyes
as he watched the game. ''He's had it in for me since
I was in the fifth grade.''

''Really? Why?''

Jake said very evenly, ''I caught him teasing an
injured bird with a stick.''

He didn't say any more, but Rachel remembered

the wiry, athletic boy who liked animals, and, though Travis had been a few years older, she knew exactly what had happened. ''Good,'' she said quietly.

Jake smiled at her. The old way, a good, fine grin.

Rachel felt herself blushing, and that warmth spread all through her middle.

From behind her, she heard Leora cough. They were not alone, and Rachel knew she had to be careful. Her true feelings were dangerous enough when kept to herself. There was no way she could risk providing fodder for gossip today.

Jake seemed to realize it, too, because without another word he broke into a sprint and headed to the field.

The game resumed, and Rachel went back to her lawn chair to watch. Leora was quiet next to her, and Rachel shot her mother-in-law a sidelong glance. She'd expected the support, and in typical Leora fashion—with emphasis on family and breeding—Leora had given it to her. But she was a little surprised now not to be getting a lecture on her defense of Jake…or that smile she and Jake had exchanged.

Unsettled, she made a great show of rummaging in her tote bag for her sunglasses. She could still feel a lingering warmth on her cheeks from Jake's grin.

She tried to focus on the game. Andy was playing first base, joining his teammates in the razzing of the batter as the pitcher sent the ball flying. ''Hey batta batta, hey batta batta, swing!'' they shouted in unison.

She did not look over at the bench, where she knew Jake was watching the game. She had to think about Andy, stick by the decision made ten years ago. If she was having feelings for Jake again, if she

went needy and warm under that brilliant gaze...
most of all, if those feelings were starting to go beyond the physical...

She had to be careful. Very careful.

*SHE'D BEEN IN LOVE with Chris. With another man.
And now he was going to have to trust her again,
because he had no other choice.*

It was Wednesday and Jake was reporting in. He
sat in the chair next to Rachel in her office, pretending to read some new parole regulations from the
state, a long, tedious document. As he pretended to
read, he called himself twelve kinds of fool for planning to trust her.

She'd defended him at the game on Sunday, a passionate defense.

But she'd also said that she'd revoke his parole if
he didn't toe the line, even though she claimed to
believe in his innocence.

So...did he dare trust her? Jake shifted, and made
his decision "I've got to go back to that pawnshop."

She'd been writing something on her yellow tablet.
He'd grown to hate her chronicling his life, but he
was trying to move beyond that.

Her pencil dropped onto the table. "Oh, Jake, you
can't." Her eyes were wide.

"I have to."

She leaned forward. "We're not going to go back
to that discussion, are we? Talking about my reporting you?"

He put his palms on the table. "I hope we're not
going to talk about that. What I want to talk about
is a call I got last night. I didn't plan to return to that
pawnshop, but last night I got a call from the Duke."

She started to say something, but he cut her off. "I asked the Duke to help me out. So he's been looking around, gathering up every amber pendant that's been fenced in the area over the past ten years. He's found about six. One, in particular, fits the description of Joann's. He wants me to come look at it."

She sucked in her breath. There was a little silence as he waited for her to say something. Finally, she said, "How could it be Joann's pendant, after all these years?"

"A friend of the Duke's remembers getting a small, ah, shipment of jewelry nine or ten years ago that had an amber necklace in it. The Duke wasn't too sure of the dates, but he's been asking around." He, too, leaned forward. "I remember Joann's pendant perfectly. I need to look at everything he's got, especially this pendant. It might be the one."

She got out of her chair and paced. "Jake, there are hundreds of amber pendants in the world." Back and forth she paced her small office. "Look. I don't know how to emphasize this enough. Of course you want to solve that crime. I know that, I understand it. But it probably can't be solved, and you're going to risk everything you've earned here. Your job. Your place in the community. Don't underestimate what happened last Sunday. You have a chance for a life—"

"But it's *my* life," he said firmly.

She gestured with her hands. "You're going to risk going back to that shop, having contact with a known felon. No. If you're asking me for permission to go there, the answer is no." Her voice softened. "Listen to me, Jake. I'm a parole officer, and I know better than you how these things look to other people. Forget clearing your name. It isn't necessary. I can help you adjust to the way things are.''

He'd resolved not to let her affect him, not to show emotion. But against his will, he was becoming angry. "I'm not one of your cats, Rachel. You may be my parole officer, but you don't have to watch over me like one of your helpless strays.'' They'd had that argument before, as kids. *I'm one of your strays,* he'd said bitterly, and she'd cried and denied it. He'd been unable to bear her tears, so he'd kissed them away and said he didn't mean it, that he didn't feel that way. But he had.

Now she looked straight at him, and he read in the depths of her eyes that she too remembered that long-ago conversation.

He said without inflection, "The Duke says there's a piece of butterfly wing in that pendant.''

Abruptly, Rachel sat down on the window seat. "Oh my God.''

"Yes.''

"But you can't go back there.''

"Why not?''

"You can't meet with the Duke anywhere.'' She chewed her lip and thought. "I'll go look at it. I'll talk to the Duke.''

"Rachel, I'm not naive anymore. I know how the cops work, how things go. I figured out how you knew so quickly I'd been to the pawnshop. Somebody was staking it out that day. The police, or the tobacco and firearms people. From the way you're trying to talk me out of going back there, I figure they must still be watching that shop, probably with a hidden video camera.'' He paused. "If you, a parole officer, go to a place like that looking for an amber pendant, you could get in a lot of trouble.''

She didn't reply. Jake could see that she was considering the risks to her career. Finally, she said, ''Somebody has to go, and I have less to lose than you. For one thing, Harold's likely to believe me when I tell him the truth. And I think it will look better if I go to the shop, rather than arrange to meet with the Duke somewhere else.''

A rush of something good ran through him, knowing she was prepared to do this for him. He longed to touch her, to take her in his arms and smell her hair and skin, press her to him and feel her warmth, and say, *I won't let you do it, but you have no idea what it means that you've offered.*

He fisted his hands and stayed where he was. ''You don't know what Joann's pendant was like. You hardly even knew her. Besides, the Duke isn't going to talk to you.''

She sighed and thought again. ''We'll go together.''

His heart lurched. Together.

She added, ''I can vouch for you that way. And I can make sure we have this conversation in a, well, in a certain place.''

Smack in front of the hidden video camera, Jake figured. He knew he shouldn't involve her. There was her kid to think of. But she was right: there wasn't a choice.

''I'll stand wherever you say,'' he said, and he meant it.

If he could just clear his name. If this pendant turned out to be Joann's, and they could begin to piece together who might have fenced it, maybe they could discover the thief. Whoever had committed that robbery had murdered Joann Floutz.

Over the rising tide of hope, Jake had another thought. It was half formed, niggling somewhere. As he stood and gathered his law books and research material in preparation for retiring to work, he realized what that thought was.

Was clearing his name enough? Once he achieved that, wouldn't he want more?

He pushed in his chair hard. There was no "more" to be had. If "more" was a relationship with Rachel... Well, Rachel had made her choice ten years ago.

Knowing he was going to clear his name someday had helped keep him sane in prison. The planning had helped. Most of all, the dreaming had helped.

Clearing his name was everything. He'd *make* it everything.

CHAPTER SIX

JAKE GLANCED at his watch and frowned. "We're a bit early. The Duke doesn't get up until noon. I told him we'd meet him around two."

Rachel slowed the car a fraction and glanced up from the wheel at the expressway signs overhead. "Anything else you want to do?"

"Yes," he said, thinking of how much he wanted to do. Other than one quick bus trip to a pawnshop in the seediest part of Columbus a few weeks ago, he hadn't been in a big city since a year before he went to prison. He'd always liked Columbus. The city was busy, and the buildings were modern. Everything seemed brighter than in Grange, somehow. Columbus was a place where nobody knew he was the son of Jake Monroe. "Could you take the next exit, please?" he asked.

"Got something in mind?"

"Yeah," he said. "I've got something in mind."

When they were kids, they'd come into Columbus on the odd occasions when Rachel could borrow her father's car without too many questions from her old man. They didn't want to be seen in downtown Grange, where somebody would undoubtedly tell her father she'd been with Jake Monroe. Walks in the countryside were more their style, anyway.

But sometimes they came to Columbus. Usually

they went window-shopping, sometimes they went to the park, and once they'd gone to the Franklin Park Zoo.

She got off the expressway, and they were in one of the satellite towns, an upscale community with a center that looked like a postcard. He spied a cute, yuppie-style café and directed Rachel to a parking space. She'd fit right in here, he thought, eyeing her expensive jacket and tailored silk blouse.

She got out of the car and looked the place over. "Hungry?" he asked.

"Well, sort of, but not really."

He pushed down a flare of irritation. He knew this game of Rachel's. In the old days, Rachel would pretend she'd just eaten so that he wouldn't feel compelled to pay for a restaurant meal. He shook off the memory. Today was a heady taste of real freedom, even if his parole officer had done the driving.

And, after all, his parole officer was Rachel....

"Well, *I'm* hungry," he said, opening the door of the café for her.

Inside, the place was all blue and peach tile, old wood, bright brass and hanging greenery. He'd been right; Rachel's classy blond looks did fit right in. She settled down in a booth across from him and caught him looking at her.

"What?" she asked.

"Nothing," he said, and she blushed. That blush turned him on. He'd always liked Rachel's blushes. That kind of innocence and freshness she had about her hadn't changed over ten years. She was still so pretty. The slight plumpness of her cheeks and chin only made that freshness and prettiness more interesting.

"I suppose you're going to insist on paying," Rachel said in a kind of mildly sarcastic resignation as she opened her menu.

"Right."

"The county gives me an expense account."

"I'm paying," he said firmly. This was important to him, and he willed her not to spoil the occasion with any more references to her status.

"Women pay for their own lunches nowadays."

"Well, I wouldn't know too much about social mores now." He said the words matter-of-factly; he couldn't shake the good feeling of being out of Grange, with Rachel, and the case so close to being solved he could taste it. He refused to think of what he'd do if one of the amber necklaces wasn't Joann's.

He looked up and caught her eye. They stared at each other for a long moment.

And suddenly, he knew. She still had some feelings for him. The attraction wasn't all one-sided. He thought of those times in her office, other times when their eyes had met, and he knew. For a second, his chest expanded, filling with the knowledge. *There's still something between us.* For a second, the world seemed almost...limitless.

But he had a lot to do before he could even think of a relationship with Rachel. So he said with mock sarcasm, "You going to eat or are we going to argue about it all day?"

"Eat," she said, smiling suddenly, and when the waitress came she ordered some kind of salad with ingredients in it he'd never heard of.

He ordered the blackened red snapper with curry vinaigrette.

"You're going to hate it," she warned, a twinkle in her eyes.

"Maybe so. But I'm branching out." Dinner menus at the farm had been heavy on canned spaghetti, and prison hadn't expanded the choices a whole lot. Somehow, today felt like the first day he'd really come out of prison, and he was going to make the most of it.

He leaned back in the booth. "Do you remember the day I fried us those fish I'd caught in the creek?"

"Do I ever. They were the dinkiest little panfish I ever saw, and watching you skin and gut them was truly gross, and I was worried it was against the law to build a fire. You laughed at me."

"Couldn't help it," he said. "You were such a Goody Two-shoes." The memory should have hurt because he was still having his problems with the law and she was still a Goody Two-shoes. But somehow it didn't.

She put her elbows on the table and her chin in her hands. Her eyes, thick-lashed and lovely, seemed to see something far away. "That fish tasted so good. You invented 'blackened' before it became the yuppie food of choice." She chuckled, a sound that had always seemed so feminine.

He took up the story, the memories coming back as he talked. "About one bite into your fish, you decided we might get mercury poisoning from eating it."

"It was a valid concern. This is central Ohio, not the wilderness."

"So you wouldn't let me eat it." She'd snatched the piece of fish out of his hand, very serious about the possibilities of his being poisoned, though he'd been snitching meals by the creek since he'd been old enough to build a fire that would hold. Jake had pretended to try to take the fish back, but he'd stolen a kiss instead.

She chuckled again. "And I wouldn't let you eat another bite."

"You wouldn't let Spook eat it, either." The dog had begged to no avail. Rachel had tossed the cooked fish back into the middle of the creek.

"Dogs can get mercury poisoning, too," she said. "I didn't want Spook to get sick."

She'd said that back then, too. She'd given the dog a pat and said, "I wouldn't let you eat this unhealthy food, Spook." Jake knew that day he'd fallen in love with Rachel. He hadn't told her then. In fact, it had taken months to work up the courage to tell her.

Now he looked across the table toward her. With a jolt, he realized she was staring at him, and he swore he saw the same kind of longing that kept him up nights, the sheets twisted beneath him.

The server brought their iced herbal tea, and Rachel jerked her gaze away and almost visibly withdrew.

He didn't want to make her uncomfortable. So when the food came and he tasted it, he said lightly, "You're wrong again. I do like this fish."

She flashed him a relieved smile at the change of subject. "For the price you're paying, I'm real glad about that."

He talked about easier things, things more neutral. What he was researching. Television shows, a book she was reading that he'd finished a few months ago.

He enjoyed talking with her, and in this space that somehow seemed carved out of real life, in this golden hour that didn't seem to "count," he made the most of his time. He felt a warmth, a kind of homecoming, that he hadn't felt in ten years.

But as the reproduction railroad clock on the wall ticked irrevocably toward two o'clock, he found it harder and harder to simply enjoy the moment. He began to anticipate. If any of those pendants were Joann's... If he could clear his name...

Well, he would walk down Main Street of Grange, Ohio, with his head held high. For a moment, he let himself fantasize that Rachel would be by his side.

But he'd never in a million years let her endure what he had—the stares, the talk behind his back, the way people drew away from him as though he had some contagious disease. He didn't want her to have to defend him the rest of his life.

There was her kid to think of. He was getting to know Andy from baseball games and practices, and he felt protective of Rachel's child.

Rachel looked at her watch, the fourth time she'd looked at it in the last ten minutes.

"Ready to go?" he asked, picking up the check from the middle of the table.

"Yes. Oh, Jake. What if that necklace isn't—"

"No," he interrupted firmly. "Don't say it. That necklace has to be Joann's. It has to."

IT WASN'T. Jake willed his hands not to shake as he stared down at the necklace in his palm. "It's not Joann's," he said, and he heard an odd, thick note in his voice.

"Are you sure?" Rachel asked.

"I know what her pendant looked like. This isn't it." He waved his hand over the array of necklaces spread out on top of the display case. "None of them are Joann's."

He saw Rachel shoot a quick look at the corner wall, where musical instruments hung, and figured that's where the video camera had been set up.

"I'm sorry," she said quietly.

The Duke shrugged. "Well, you knew it was a long shot." He took the pendant out of Jake's hand. "When you told me there was a piece of bug stuck in it, I remembered this one necklace some guy bought for his girlfriend, and I asked him to bring it in."

Danny "the Duke" Duncan looked nothing like a pawnshop manager or a gangster. He was impeccably and expensively dressed. But he still occasionally spoke in the rough grammar of the streets where he'd been raised. "Just thought I'd try you out on this, you know?" He held up the necklace to the light. "Always thought this amber junk looked like plastic anyway. Now, a nice diamond—well, plenty of chicks been offed for a diamond, you know?" He grinned.

For a moment, Jake had been lost in a crushing, numb fog. But at the Duke's words, Jake forced himself to take charge. Rachel was looking nervously at that camera again. For all that she was a parole officer, such casual talk about murder obviously bothered her. If she kept looking at that damn camera, she was going to blow the police's undercover operation, and the ire of the cops would be nothing compared to what the Duke might dole out.

"Let's get out of here," he said to Rachel.

"Yes." Her shoulders sagging, she started to go out the door.

"Hey, I'll keep looking," the Duke called out. "But, Jake, don't sweat it, man. You're out of the joint, and being out's all that matters."

Rachel turned. "That might be all that matters. But for the record, Jake's innocent."

Jake motioned to the door, urging her to go through it. The Duke cracked a smile. "Listen, honey, I'm telling you it don't matter. Innocent, guilty, it don't matter. Once you've been to the joint, you've been to the joint, you know?"

"Go on," Jake said quietly, gesturing to Rachel.

They headed out the door. As soon as they were on the sidewalk, Rachel stopped. "Jake, I meant it in there. I'm so sorry. I knew there wasn't much chance of any of those necklaces being Joann's but I hoped. I really did."

"I know." His throat felt so tight. His gut felt so tight, his back so straight—always so straight, always so tight, too. "I pinned too much on one of them being Joann's," he admitted. "You warned me."

She reached out a hand to him, and it wavered in the air. With a quick glance at the pawnshop, she dropped her arm.

Jake shook his head, weary to his bones. "Let's get out of here."

When they were in the car, Rachel said, "We won't leave it like this. Some other clue will surface."

"I thought you've been telling me to forget it," Jake said, staring out the window.

Her hands gripped the steering wheel. "I have. That's what I should say, that's what your P.O. would say, but..." She couldn't stand how this day had turned out. She'd been hoping as much as Jake had. At lunch, she'd felt a reckless anticipation, pleasure in his company, and she'd thought, *Maybe it could always be this way. Maybe Jake will really clear his name and then he can go into any restaurant he wants with his head held high.*

In that restaurant, she'd learned something about herself. If she'd been falsely accused of murder, if she'd spent ten years in prison for a crime she didn't commit, if she had to deal with narrow-minded people like Travis Bremmer every day, she'd be trying to clear her name too. At whatever cost.

"I would do the same thing. I'd try to track down the killer," she admitted out loud.

There was a long silence. Then Jake said, "It doesn't matter how either of us feels. There was one clue, and it didn't pan out. End of story."

For several minutes they drove in silence. Then she saw signs for a construction zone. She slowed the car, then stopped altogether as the one-lane zone caused the heavy traffic to back up. Rachel craned her neck. She could see a long line of cars and trucks ahead of her, all the way up the overpass. She sighed, knowing they were in for a wait of several minutes.

"Will all this traffic make you late getting home?" Jake asked. "Andy isn't home alone, is he?"

The concern in his voice warmed her. "He went to Leora's after school. Since tomorrow's Saturday, she's going to keep him overnight." She kept her foot on the brake but relaxed her hands on the wheel.

"Good. I'd hate to have Andy home alone after dark."

Jake's words made her suddenly nervous. His concern for Andy was what a father would feel. No, she told herself, he was just being kind. Being a nice guy.

She said, "Fortunately, Leora's always willing to have him. She seems all stiff and formal. She's never encouraged me to call her Mom, for example, but she loves being a grandma."

There was a moment's silence. Then he said, "I hope you don't get in trouble for today."

"I won't. I was careful."

"You were careful, all right. Every word you said could have carried into the next block. You stared at that wall where the video camera must be for so long I think the Duke thought you were a nutcase. A pretty nutcase, but a real kook, just the same."

She felt her cheeks heat. "I'm not very good at faking things. I'm not a good liar." At the admission, she felt her cheeks grow even hotter. Would he remember that she'd said the same thing ten years ago over a far, far more important subject—his alibi?

Next to her, he cleared his throat.

She was so conscious of him. The car seemed so small, and Jake so large.

"Rachel."

She'd been avoiding looking at him, but now she did.

"Rachel, I just want you to know something. I'll never ask you to lie for me again."

Tears pricked her eyes, and she blinked them away. "I... It occurs to me that I could have saved you a world of grief if I'd just said you were with me when the police came to my house that night."

"That was a long time ago." There was another pause. Jake stared straight ahead. The lights of the roadway and the oncoming traffic threw his regular profile into high relief. "Rachel, now I feel—"

He cut himself off. Rachel's hands on the steering

wheel went suddenly damp. What had he been about to say? That he still had feelings for her despite her refusal to give him his alibi? Despite the passage of ten years? Despite her position as his parole officer?

A shiver went up her spine. *You want him to say those things. You want him to have feelings for you.* At that realization, her shiver turned to trembling. The situation was impossible, for too many reasons to count. And for one overwhelming reason: Andy.

She shot another glance at his profile. She couldn't just up and say, *I had your baby.* Not now. He might have chosen not to know about Andy all those years ago. But since he'd come home, how would she ever justify not telling him that the boy he coached and thumped on the back was his son?

She didn't have a choice. She couldn't hurt her son. He'd just lost the man he'd always thought was his father. And Jake might be innocent, but not in the eyes of the townsfolk. She couldn't ask Andy to deal with something even adults found difficult. That wouldn't be fair. For her son to be hurt now, after she'd spent the last ten years protecting him from just this scenario…

"Rachel."

She jumped.

"You should be moving a little," he said.

"Oh." A space had opened up and she crept up several feet to fill it.

Then traffic was really moving again, and full dark had fallen. Neither she nor Jake said much as she took the exit to Grange fifteen minutes later.

She turned down the two-laner that was the last stretch until home.

Jake, who'd been staring out the window, finally

stirred and said, "I hate like hell to be coming home a failure again."

Rachel couldn't stand the weariness in his voice. "You're not a failure. And you'll find a way to clear your name."

"How? There aren't any clues but that damn necklace. Where is it? It was never fenced anywhere around here. I'd know it in a minute, the way Joann used to dangle it right in front of my nose."

Rachel took a curve. "What do you mean, dangle it right in front of your nose?"

Jake gave a bitter, one-syllable chuckle. "Joann was happily married, but I think she liked the idea of flirting with the hired boy. When I was doing her yard work, she used to call me over, supposedly to ask me a question, and she'd get real, real close. To avoid looking at her…chest, I'd fix my eyes on that necklace at her throat. Look at that trapped butterfly."

At his words, something, some long-ago piece of information clicked in Rachel's mind. She slowed the car, thinking. Then she said, "Do you think she would have done anything more than flirt? If she thought you were interested?"

"I wasn't interested. I used to be afraid you'd find out she was flirting, and think maybe I encouraged her, and you'd be hurt." He paused. "Why, Rachel? Are you thinking something here?" His voice had picked up speed, and she knew he was looking at her.

"Maybe." Her hands gripped the steering wheel harder. "How do you know Joann was happily married?"

"Her husband, Ralph. She was pregnant when she

died. Ralph testified at the sentencing. Talked about how much he loved her. He cried. There was something about the way he acted that seemed sincere, and there'd never been any talk around town that she'd had an affair. You know how Grange is with that kind of thing.''

Jake raked a hand through his hair. ''Her husband did take out a big insurance policy on her about six months before she died. You remember my first lawyer? He thought that was significant, was digging around, before my retainer ran out and I ended up with the public defender. But it didn't matter in the end. There was no evidence that Ralph and Joann were having problems.''

Her heart was pounding. ''Jake,'' she said. ''I don't know if this is significant, but—''

His head whipped around. ''What?''

She pulled over to the side of the road and put the car in Park. ''Chris said once that Joann had flirted with him. A lot. That when he was alone, working in the store, she'd come in and try on tight clothes, get real close, ask him what he thought of her body.'' Chris had told her that one night, his face beet red with embarrassment. She'd never forgotten it, but she'd never thought there was any significance to it. She hadn't known that Joann was flirting with Jake, too.

She took a deep breath. ''Maybe she didn't have affairs. Maybe it was just flirtation with young boys.'' She knew she was reaching, but she couldn't help her rising excitement. ''Maybe her husband knew about it and—''

Jake gripped her arm. ''Ralph had an alibi. He was working at the Treehouse Lounge that night. My first lawyer talked to a waitress there, and she confirmed it.''

The air left her chest like a deflating balloon. ''Oh.'' She ached, she realized, as if she'd been working in the yard all day, a dull ache everywhere. She realized it was in response to this roller coaster of a day—those sweet, long-ago memories they'd shared at lunch, the anticipation of seeing the necklace, the overwhelming letdown.

He still had his hand on her arm. ''I realize what you're trying to do, and I appreciate it. Hell, I more than appreciate it. I'm...overwhelmed by it.'' His voice dropped to a whisper. ''I can't believe, all these years, you've been defending my innocence, and I just...''

She should shake off his arm, she knew. It felt too good, his hand on her light jacket. It felt too right, too...connected.

She looked at him. It was so dark she couldn't read his expression.

His hand slid along her arm, up to her shoulder. She sat perfectly still. Waiting...

His fingers slid up her neck, gently grasped her chin. ''Rachel,'' he said, so softly. She could feel his hand quiver a little. At that tangible evidence of his desire, heat flooded her.

''I've tried to forget,'' he said in a low, harsh whisper. ''I've told myself you have a life now, and not to complicate it. But I just want...just once...to see if you taste the same.'' He tugged on her chin, turning it toward him.

She turned as far as the seat belt would let her, straining, helplessly licking her lips. Because she wanted to know, too. After ten years, she wanted to know if it was the same....

He brought his face to hers. No stroking, no embrace, only his hand still gently holding her chin, their mouths so close and coming closer. He was so close she could feel his warm breath chilling her wet lips. "I can't," she said, and she jerked away at the very last second.

He let out a harsh breath and brought his clenched fist down hard on his thigh.

Rachel sat back in her seat and closed her eyes. She was mortified, and she could feel her own fists clenching. Because she'd wanted, really wanted Jake's kiss. She'd encouraged him, she knew. "I can't," she whispered again.

"I know." There was more disappointment now in Jake's voice than when he'd found out the necklace wasn't Joann's. He sounded more weary. Almost desolate. Her heart squeezed, a physical pain. He'd been hurt so much, and she'd hurt him more.

"I'm sorry," he said after a moment.

She knew she couldn't allow him to take all the responsibility. "I didn't want to pull away," she admitted quietly. "But I'm still your parole officer, at least until Charlie comes back. Jake, if I compromise that position, well, I won't be able to live with myself."

"I know," he said again. "I was selfish and I'm sorry."

In that moment she knew that Jake had gone to prison a boy, but come back a man. And if she'd wanted the boy then, she now wanted the man more. She had cared about him then; she admired him now.

She wanted to touch him. To run her hands down

the crisp poplin of his jacket, to sense the hard chest beneath. To feel his breath on her skin again. To feel...

She couldn't. She couldn't let that happen.

Now what? She thought. She couldn't take the easy way out. She couldn't just palm Jake off onto Harold. No. Until Charlie came back, she had to handle this situation and somehow keep her professional integrity.

But how?

One thing at a time, she told herself. Her insides felt shaky and needy. She forced herself to concentrate on the situation at hand. The first thing she had to do was to drop off Jake and rid herself of temptation. She knew too well what could happen to them in a dark car pulled off the road. She'd learned all about that a decade ago.

And after she dropped Jake off, she would go back to being his P.O. *Only* his P.O. The thought made her lonely, almost bereft. But she'd have to get over it. She'd strive for a professional relationship, and then after she trusted herself again, maybe a distant, kind friendship.

But after Charlie came back and she was off the hook as his P.O., then...

Then nothing. Then she wouldn't see him again, except from a distance, across a ball field. Finally, summer would be over and there'd be no reason to see him at all.

She pulled out onto the highway, careful—very careful—not to look again at Jake.

But she didn't need to look at him to remember every carved line of his handsome face. Every angle and plane, all those angles and planes that had once been hers to touch. She didn't need her thumping heart to tell her what she already knew: she longed desperately to touch her mouth to Jake's.

CHAPTER SEVEN

SPRING TURNED abruptly into summer. A June heat spell took the blue-green lushness from the grass on the ball field and brought all the roses into full bloom in the parsonage garden.

The Raiders were getting to be a good team and might even have a chance at the championship. Jake was getting to know Andy, and they had developed a ritual of shadowboxing and clapping each other on the back that had come to mean more to Jake than he'd ever let on. Andy told him things, too. When Andy was on the bench, he always sat next to Jake, and they talked about baseball, about dogs, about Rachel and Andy's home life.

Jake had tried to forget his trip to Columbus. He'd tried to forget the letdown of not finding the necklace. He'd tried to forget the feel of Rachel's skin on his fingers, the sensation of her breath on his face as he'd leaned toward her. It wasn't easy.

He was going to clear his name, and now he only had one slim lead: the knowledge that Joann had flirted with at least two very young men.

Now, on a warm and humid Thursday night two weeks after coming home from Columbus, Jake sat at a small table in the Treehouse Lounge. He ordered his second ginger ale on ice and smiled at the waitress.

Jake remembered her. Megan. She was about fifty. At the time of his trial, she'd been divorcing her husband, and she'd had a teenager at home. That much he remembered his first lawyer telling him. He also remembered one more thing: she'd been Ralph Floutz's alibi ten years ago, claiming the manager had been working that night. Judging from the way her smile died, he figured she knew who he was, too.

He'd planned this trip carefully. He'd waited for a night Megan was working, but Ralph was off; he doubted he'd get information with Joann's husband behind the bar. The last thing he needed was an argument, because he was violating his parole again. *You are not permitted to frequent taverns or establishments where liquor is sold.* He remembered Rachel's voice reading the words.

Once he'd asked her why. He had no desire to drink, and alcohol had been Big Jake's problem, not his. He was getting damn tired of the sins-of-the-fathers treatment. With some embarrassment, Rachel had explained it was one of Harold's rules for every parolee in the county. Then it had been Jake's turn to be embarrassed. His bitterness had shown there for a minute.

He'd had his first ginger ale at the bar, until he'd figured out which tables belonged to which waitress. Then he'd taken one of Megan's.

The Treehouse was a quiet place, a bar that also did a big trade in hamburgers and onion rings, French fries and Rueben sandwiches. There were a couple of old-fashioned pinball machines in the corner and an equally antique jukebox. The tabletops were plastic wood grain, the chairs old and comfy. Only a couple of dusty artificial vines and a little wooden platform suspended from the ceiling hinted at the name on the door.

Early in the evening, people brought their kids in here, and the serious drinking only began a couple of hours before closing. Big Jake had never frequented the Treehouse—he'd preferred the raucous atmosphere of a tavern a couple of miles out of town.

"Megan." Jake gestured to the waitress as she passed him with a tray loaded with Coney dogs for the group of college-age kids at the next table. She nodded, and when she'd delivered the food, she came back to his table.

"What can I get you?" Her hands on the edge of the tray were damp and a little swollen in the knuckles, and she'd bitten her fingernails to the quick. He noticed she still wore no wedding ring, only a cheap watch. She seemed poised on the balls of her feet, as if ready for flight.

"I'm sorry I make you nervous," he said quietly.

She flinched. "That's okay. Do you want something to eat?"

"No. Just some information."

"What kind of information?"

Yes, he thought, she was definitely wary. "Ten years ago, you told my lawyer that Ralph was working the night Joann was killed."

Abruptly, her eyes filled with tears. "Please don't do this."

He didn't pretend to misunderstand. "I have to."

"If you don't want anything to eat, I've got customers—"

"Then I'll meet you in the parking lot when you come to work tomorrow. I'll come out to your house, or you can come to the parsonage. I live above the garage. If you're afraid, Reverend Carson can be there, too. Or I'll meet you anywhere you want, but please understand.'' By sheer force of will, he managed to keep his voice down. "Understand that I'm going to find out what happened ten years ago.'' He sought her eyes, and when he captured her gaze, he said, "I didn't kill Joann Floutz.''

She brought a hand to her lips.

"I didn't kill her,'' he repeated.

"Well, neither did Ralph, if that's what you've come fishing to find out.'' Her voice had risen, and a few people turned to stare. "I've got to work.''

"Meet me somewhere so we can talk,'' he urged.

"No, I…can't.''

He adopted a hard voice he hadn't used since he'd come out of prison. "I won't let this rest.'' He knew he was bullying her and he hated that. But he had no choice.

"I don't know anything.''

"Just a couple of questions. Please.'' His plea was heartfelt, honest, and he saw her waver. "Please.'' He almost whispered the word.

She fled, and he cursed to himself. One of the patrons at the next table was looking at him with narrowed eyes. Jake tried to place the guy. He was middle-aged, casually but expensively dressed, with logos on every piece of clothing.

As Jake watched, the guy got up and came over to his table. Jake felt his hands tense, but he curled one hand around his glass of ginger ale.

The guy adopted the slightly wide-legged stance that Jake remembered well. Big Jake had used it too when he'd had a few drinks and had to pay attention to things like staying upright.

"Giving the lady trouble?" the guy asked in a too-loud voice.

More people were looking now. Jake cocked his head. "No trouble."

"He's not making any trouble, Mr. Herman," Megan said quickly. "Just sit back down with your friends and I'll get all of you another round." She hustled Herman away with a backward glance at Jake.

Jake watched them go. He remembered now that Gary Herman had owned the drugstore. It was closed now because the supermarket had a big discount-drug department.

He ought to be grateful to Megan for averting what might have been an ugly scene. An ugly scene he definitely didn't need.

Megan had no cake job; those hands worked hard, and Jake didn't want to make grief for her. Only…only, damn it, it was time for him to get a break here.

Rachel's clue—that maybe Joann hadn't been a model wife—pointed to a crime of passion instead of a simple robbery. And in Jake's experience as a jailhouse lawyer, he'd learned full well that in a crime of passion the spouse was the prime suspect.

But if Megan wouldn't talk to him…

Well, why would she? Although Ralph didn't own the Treehouse, he was probably the woman's boss. For all Jake knew, Ralph really *did* have an airtight alibi, which meant Jake was heading down another wrong road.

But he had to do something.

Abruptly, his mind conjured Rachel. After that trip to Columbus, the stakes had risen. Now they were very, very high, because now he didn't just want to clear his name and go to law school.

Now he wanted a life.

THE TELEPHONE in the living room jangled, and Jake stumbled out of bed. He made a grab for his jeans, and carried them out to the living room. The clock over the television set said 3:00 a.m.

The phone rang again. Jake grabbed it. "Hello?"

"He loved her," the woman on the other end said breathlessly.

Jake tried to place the voice. The telephone was an old, rotary-dial style, and the voice had a tinny, altered quality. Finally, it dawned on him who was on the other line. "Megan?"

"Yeah, it's Megan. Before I tell you what happened, I want you to know something. Ralph was my friend. He's still my friend. And friends talk to each other."

Wide-awake now, Jake's heart was pounding in his chest. "What do you know? Tell me. Please."

He heard her take in a deep breath. "I feel like a rat," she said finally. "But I can't sleep. I did wrong ten years ago, and I've lost a lot of sleep over it. The thing is, I can't have you coming to my work anymore. I don't want to come out and meet you anywhere. My daughter…she has a baby and they live with me. I need my job."

"I'm not trying to make trouble for you," he assured her.

"You've got a right, and I know that. I just…" There was a pause so long that for a second Jake thought maybe she'd hung up.

"Are you still there?" he asked.

"Ralph loved her. He said so all the time. If he and Joann had an argument or anything, he'd be all torn up inside."

Jake waited, letting her tell her story, although every pore in his body said *get to it.*

"He loved her," Megan repeated. "I mean, she was going to have their baby."

Jake had known from the autopsy report that Joann was nearly three months pregnant when she died. The prosecution had brought up that fact in sentencing, asking for Jake to get the maximum penalty. "But he didn't have an alibi?" he finally asked, trying to bring Megan back to the issue.

"That night, the night she was...died, well, Ralph was working the bar. That's exactly what I told the police. They didn't ask me too many questions. I didn't have to out-and-out lie. And your public defender didn't question me too closely."

"So you gave him his alibi."

"Yes, he was my friend and he needed me to say that. But he did take off for a bit that night, Jake. That's what I've been keeping secret all this time."

Jake's hand gripped the receiver so hard his knuckles ached. "When? For how long?"

"Early in the evening. For about forty-five minutes."

Joann had been killed between seven and eight o'clock, according to the coroner's report.

"It doesn't mean anything," Megan said hurriedly. "He loved her. He wouldn't kill her."

"If he didn't kill her, he has nothing to worry about," Jake said, and he had a bitter urge to chuckle at the irony.

"I tell myself that, but..."

"You've got to go to the police." His breathing picked up. If she refused, he would be dead in the water, because it would be Megan's word against that of an ex-con.

"I know Ralph didn't do it. For all I know, you really are guilty." She sighed. "At least, I've told myself that for ten years. It helped me sleep at night."

"You have to go to the police," he repeated.

"I will," she said, and Jake sat down hard, his knees suddenly giving out. "I'll do it tomorrow morning. Okay? And then I don't want to see you. I don't want you coming to the lounge. Like I never want you coming there. It would kill Ralph to even look at you."

"I swear I won't come back." There was a pause. "I know this was hard for you, but I want you to know I—"

"It was real hard," she interrupted. "But I guess I had to do it."

"Thank you," he said simply, knowing the words were not enough.

She hung up without a goodbye.

A moment later, Jake got up and strode to the window.

People hadn't been willing to help him ten years ago. The judge. Megan. Even his own lawyer hadn't asked the right questions. But as he stared down at the rectory garden, he thought about how they were trying to make it right.

His lip curled. They were trying to make it right a decade too late.

Rachel's voice popped into his mind. *You might find you can trust people, if you give them a chance.*

At the time, it had been hard not to respond with a mocking, cynical comment. After all, he'd been sitting across from his parole officer, supposed to be grateful that now he could be controlled outside the penitentiary the way his whole life had been regulated inside it.

The garden looked different from when he'd first come home. The pale roses shone in the dark. *Trust people.* The judge had given him a job. Carson was a friend.

Rachel believed in him.

And finally, after ten years, someone was going to tell the truth.

He felt his fists clench, and then he realized just how much he wanted to trust people, just how comfortable and, well, pleasant it would be to be able to look at someone and not tense, not prepare for the inevitable moment when they heard what he'd supposedly done.

"HE WAS DRINKING?" Rachel sat at her desk and held the phone to her ear in disbelief. Gary Herman had just told her that he'd seen Jake, drinking and belligerent, in the Treehouse Lounge the night before. Jake had never taken a drink in her presence, and as a teenager he'd hated the stuff. He'd seen enough of the effects of alcohol with Big Jake for a father. "Were the police called?" she asked. *Please God, don't let the police have been called.* If someone had called the police, she'd have virtually no discretion.

"No. I would have called them, but this waitress got me to hold off. She didn't want trouble. But I should have."

LINDA MARKOWIAK 139

"Did you actually see him drink?"

"Yes."

"What and how much?" Her stomach was sour now.

"Whiskey. At least three."

For a second, Rachel was speechless. Gary Herman and Travis Bremmer were friends. They ran the Grange Downtown Boosters with a zeal that reminded Rachel of her father and Leora taking turns as president of the chamber of commerce. Like Travis, Gary was a member of every organization in town, but the Boosters was the biggest. It sponsored family outings and charitable events. Gary's pharmacy had closed three years ago and now he was making an attempt to sell cellular telephones. She'd heard rumors he wasn't the most successful at the job. She'd also heard rumors that he hit the booze himself pretty regularly these days. And in his younger years, he'd been well-known for having a very hot temper.

"Rachel, you've got to do something about Jake Monroe," Gary said.

"What do you want me to do?" she asked quietly.

"Let's face it. Monroe needs to go back to prison."

"I'll look into his drinking," she promised.

Gary paused. "Look, I've never had anything against you." His voice went higher, as if he was having trouble containing his temper. "But a lot of people are saying you aren't doing your job."

"Who thinks I'm not doing my job?" she asked, not bothering to keep an edge of sarcasm from her voice. "You? Your buddy Travis Bremmer?"

He was silent. Rachel bit her lip. Bremmer and

Herman were known around town as blowhards, but that really wouldn't matter once the rumor mill got going. She knew from experience that fact had little to do with an issue once the townsfolk got to gossiping. Harold was weak and easily swayed, and she could see trouble ahead. "I'll look into it," she repeated. "That's all I'm promising. It'll have to be enough."

To her relief, Gary Herman reluctantly agreed that it was enough.

When she hung up the phone, she tried calling the Treehouse Lounge. Glancing at her watch, she saw that it was too early for the bar to be open. Grabbing her sweater and her purse, she called to the secretaries that she was going to be gone for a few minutes. Best to get to the bottom of this issue; she wouldn't wait for Jake's check-in. Thanks to his regularity with his meetings, Rachel, in consultation with her boss, was now only seeing him once a week anyway. Wednesdays. Today was Friday.

Even Harold had had to agree that by any objective criteria, Jake was functioning in society. His one violation, until now, had been to go to the fence, and he'd had a reason she'd ended up supporting. He had a job, his baseball coaching constituted community charity work and he'd never missed a check-in with his parole officer.

If her cheeks felt too warm at the memory of his hand on her that night they'd gone to see the Duke, if she remembered every second of that moment, remembered how his hand had slid up her arm, how he'd gently touched his fingertips to her chin and she'd wanted him to put his lips on hers, those were her problems—not Jake's.

Forget it, she told herself, picking up her pace. Her office was in an annex of the courthouse that had been built in the 1920s. Now she went outside and crossed the brick sidewalk to the courthouse proper, where Jake worked.

She headed for the judge's chambers, calling out greetings to those she knew. As a few of the courthouse personnel pointed out, it'd been a long time since Rachel had been to "their" part of the courthouse. That fact, of course, had nothing to do with Jake Monroe. Everybody knew that she'd been too busy for casual office visits ever since Charlie went on sick leave.

Jake's office was a small cubbyhole off the judge's chambers. She paused at the doorway, looking in.

The room was a shambles, teetering stacks of papers, briefs piled in the corners, law books pulled from the shelves and opened, stacked one atop the other. Jake's computer screen glowed.

And in the center of it all was Jake, the top couple of buttons opened on his shirt, his tie half pulled off, hanging askew on his chest. His dark head was bent over a thick book.

Black hair and crisp white shirt. A hard mouth that used to soften in gentleness when he smiled at her. Callused hands that had held her chin so gently only a few days ago.

He looked up and saw her. "Hi." There was no real smile of greeting, just a still kind of awareness as he studied her.

Her own awareness of him shivered up her spine. "Hi." She swallowed nervously. "Can I come in?"

"Sure." He got up and grabbed a stack of briefs

that was on the only other chair. "I wanted to talk to you, anyway."

She came into his office. It was so small in here, and with him standing next to her... "I didn't think it would be so small. Your office, I mean. I suppose because it's so crowded..." Realizing she was babbling, she shut up.

"I'm a messy worker. But I'm used to not having a lot of space."

There didn't seem to be anything to say to that, so she said, "Oh."

When she didn't continue, he said, "I'm glad you're here. Let me show you around." His hand swept the bookcase. "The penitentiary didn't have all the supplements to the Criminal Code, but we have them here. And I've got Westlaw on my computer, so I can find the Supreme Court decisions almost the day they're rendered." He gestured again in obvious pleasure.

She felt a spurt of pleasure too, because this meant so much to him, and he'd earned it. She hated to spoil things, but she had a job to do. So hurriedly, she said, "I have a couple of things to go over with you."

"I have a couple of things to go over with *you*. Why don't you have a seat?" He gestured expansively at the chair in front of his desk.

She sat down, folding her hands in her lap, sorry now she hadn't come armed with her paper and pencil. Something to do with her hands. She was suddenly much more uncomfortable than she ought to be. She took a breath. "I found out some things today. For one, Harold told me that Charlie Malchek comes back a week from Monday."

"Oh."

"Yes, so then I won't be your P.O. anymore."

"Oh," he said again.

She couldn't tell what he was thinking. Surely, he must be glad. "Charlie's big on protocol and appearances."

"So you've always said." He picked up a pen, set it down again. "Well, I guess you'll be pleased to get back to working with the kids."

"Yes." She *would* be pleased. She hadn't liked Jake having to check in any more than he had. She'd be glad to be rid of this duty. If she'd learned anything at all these last weeks, it was that it was best if she stayed as far away as possible from Jake.

"The second thing I want to discuss..." She trailed off, then, "I'm here to talk over an alleged parole violation."

Jake abruptly pushed back his chair. "Ah, hell, again?"

"I got a call that you went to the Treehouse Lounge last night."

He regarded her steadily, his mouth hard. "What did your spies report?"

"That you were drinking."

He just looked at her.

"Is that true?"

He made a sound of disgust. "Which? That I went to the Treehouse? Or that I was drinking?"

Her temper suddenly snapped. "Don't mess with me. Don't act like a—a parolee, a common criminal! Answer my questions."

He stood, and he looked so tall standing behind the big old golden oak desk, towering over her. He took a couple of steps over to the bookcase. He said,

"Yes, I went to the Treehouse. I was checking out Ralph Floutz's alibi."

She'd figured that much. "I can understand that part. It's the allegation of drinking. I've got to check that out because your parole rules clearly state—" She fell silent. He knew what the rules stated.

He was still looking out the window. "Rachel, if you have to ask if I took a drink last night, then I wonder—" He shoved his hands in his pockets. "I wonder if you ever knew me at all."

There was a kind of ache in his voice, and suddenly she conjured an image of Jake as a boy. One with an attitude, a don't-even-bother-talking-to-me hardness in his eyes. But it was an act, so much an act that she wondered why she'd apparently been the only one to recognize it as such. The tough kids in the school slipped brown bag–covered bottles of alcohol into the football games and dances, hung out together in a rowdy, boozy crowd, smoked dope in their cars when they cut classes. Jake had never been part of that crowd. Never.

She was suddenly ashamed.

He turned to her, finally. "I had a couple of ginger ales."

"I believe you."

He gave her another faint, half-formed smile. "Well, that's something, anyway."

She got to her feet. "I've told you I won't report you for trying to clear your name. You say you didn't drink—I assume someone at the Treehouse can confirm that. So I guess I'll just write up our discussion for the file."

"You do that." He turned from her and pulled a book from the shelf.

Rachel felt her cheeks flushing at the dismissal. She might have made a mistake, but she'd been trying to do her job, for heaven's sake. "Well, I'll just be going then," she said lamely.

He didn't answer. Then she remembered he'd had something he wanted to talk over. "Was there something you wanted to talk to me about? You said there was when I first came in."

He turned slowly to look at her. "There was." He looked her over. "I was going to tell you what I found out after I left the Treehouse."

"You found out something? Why didn't you tell me right away?"

"Because you were using your P.O. voice. Do you know even your voice changes when you're doing your job with me? You were hell-bent on scolding me for supposedly taking a drink."

Her cheeks felt hot again.

"But I'll tell you, because just now you didn't sound like my parole officer. Just now you sounded like my friend." He took a few steps toward her. "And I've got to tell somebody. I just…" He cleared his throat. "Ralph Floutz has no alibi."

"What?" She was stunned at the news. "But—"

"Megan, that waitress at the Treehouse, was his alibi. But she didn't tell the whole story."

He told her what Megan had said over the phone. At the end, he said, "Even now, Megan may be talking to the police."

"Oh, Jake, that's wonderful. Maybe it was a crime of passion, after all. Now all we have to do is prove Ralph did it." Because of her excitement, she only realized after she spoke that she'd used "we," not "you."

He smiled, warm and wonderful. "We're a long way from proving Ralph did it."

Ralph Floutz had taken out a big insurance policy on his wife six months before she died. Joann Floutz liked to flirt with young boys. *Ralph Floutz had no alibi.* And maybe Jake Monroe would prove his innocence at last. "But we will."

His smile grew a little wider. "Yes."

It was beautiful, that smile. It touched the chiseled angles of his face, contrasted with the hardness, and looked all the more gentle and genuine for the contrast. Quite suddenly, she had a strong urge to trace those firm lips with her fingertip, replace her fingertip with her mouth. Heck, quite suddenly, she had the urge to go into his arms, to feel herself hugged tightly and twirled around.

Jake was looking at her, his eyes dark and intent. He was so close.

A buzzer on his phone rang, startling them both.

Jake was the first to turn away. "That's Judge Randall. He's got some attorneys meeting in chambers, and he must need some research from me."

"Oh. Of course." Rachel turned to go, feeling disappointed somehow. She'd have liked to stay a while, help map out a strategy for proving that Joann's husband was the culprit. She'd like to, well, she wouldn't even think it.

She turned to go. A moment later, she pushed open the outside door. It had started to rain, a few warm, fat drops. She hurried, anxious to get to the annex before it started to storm in earnest.

She ducked into her building just before the clouds opened and the downpour began. She stopped to catch her breath.

Her mind immediately went to Jake.

She'd had no trouble believing him, not once she'd seen him in person. But she had to be objective.

For ten more days, she had to be objective.

But in ten days, she wouldn't be his parole officer anymore. Her official impediment to romantic involvement with Jake would end.

The wind gusted, and rain hit the windowpanes hard.

But there was another reason—a big one—why anything romantic between them was impossible.

"RALPH? Ralph Floutz?" Jake stepped out into the light of a streetlamp in the deserted parking lot of the Treehouse Lounge.

Ralph stopped jingling his keys; in fact, his body went taut. When he spoke, his voice was hard. "Jake Monroe. Why don't you take a hike so's I don't have to call the police."

"I just want to talk to you."

"You did plenty of talking to the police today."

Ah, Jake thought. He hadn't talked to the police, so Megan must have kept her word and gone to them. And apparently, the police had questioned Ralph. He'd wondered if they'd take Megan's story seriously. It appeared they had. "I wonder what you told the police about where you were on the night your wife was killed?"

Ralph took one more look at him, then spat on the parking lot, right at Jake's feet. Turning, he began walking toward his minivan.

Jake followed. "Where were you that night?" He didn't really expect an answer. He'd thought about what to do, and figured to lean on Ralph, maybe make him uncomfortable enough to make a mistake.

Before Ralph could put his key in his lock, Jake caught up with him and put a hand on the car door. There was no way Ralph would be able to get the door open without shoving Jake aside. He tensed, waiting to see if Ralph would make the attempt.

"Get out of my way." Ralph growled the words, but he made no attempt to move Jake.

"I need some answers."

"Why?" The word was tight, angry but almost sorrowful. "What do *you* need answers for? You killed her. All she did was try to help you, give you some work. She felt sorry for you, she said. And you killed her for a lousy necklace, a TV set and a VCR."

Jake was a little surprised at the depth of sadness in Ralph's voice. He'd gotten used to thinking of him as a prime suspect. A killer. But in crimes of passion, the culprit usually loved the victim, he knew. It was the depth of the emotion that provoked the violence in a crime of passion.

Jake had expected the guy to have a hot temper. After all, in his and Rachel's scenario, Ralph had been angry enough to push his pregnant wife off a balcony after arguing with her about her flirtations with teenage boys. But now Ralph made no move against Jake's deliberately provocative gesture. "I didn't kill her," Jake said quietly.

Ralph made a noise, one syllable of disbelief. "Look. It's late and I'm tired. I'm going home and I'll be alone, the way I have been for the last ten years, thanks to you. So if you don't move away from my car door, I'm going to go back inside and call the police.''

Jake shifted tactics. ''You loved her.''

''Yeah. A lot. And you killed her.''

Jake added, ''You loved her enough to take out a three-hundred-thousand-dollar insurance policy on her six months before she died.''

Ralph's head snapped up and he looked at Jake more directly.

Jake felt excitement rising in him. Okay, so maybe it wasn't a crime of passion. Maybe it was as simple as Ralph wanting the money. It happened all the time. If so, Ralph had been pretty obvious about the murder, but another thing Jake had learned in prison was that most crimes were not sophisticated. Even murder. *Especially* murder.

Ralph was looking away now. He swallowed, his Adam's apple bobbing. Then he swallowed again.

Ralph Floutz was suddenly nervous.

Jake slowly took his hand off the door. He'd planted a seed here and now it was time to leave.

Ralph put his key in the door. ''Like I told the cops, I loved her.''

''You took out a big insurance policy on her because you loved her.'' Jake didn't bother to hide his sarcasm.

''No, I took out the insurance policy because a friend of mine from school was trying to get started in the business. Which is what I told the police. I also told them I bought a policy on myself. Not that I owe you any explanation. I loved my wife. Why should I defend myself to her killer?''

Again there was that weariness in his voice, a bone-deep weariness that suggested he'd had ten years to feel his anger and now it was pretty much gone. Jake felt a totally unexpected pang of sympathy.

He shook his head. Ralph had had two motives to push his wife off a balcony, he reminded himself. The guy's weariness could very well be because of the burden of having lived with his guilt for ten long years.

"After all, she was carrying your baby when she died," he mused aloud.

Ralph Floutz didn't say another word. He simply opened his car door and got in, shutting it in Jake's face.

CHAPTER EIGHT

JAKE SAT on his bed and pulled a T-shirt over his head. It was the Sunday after his talk with Ralph, and Jake was thinking about Rachel. He wanted to share his impressions of his chief suspect, get her views.

Come on, admit it. He just wanted to see her. To be with her, to watch the evening sun pick up the pale highlights in her hair. To have her smile at him.

He no longer had any excuse to see her other than the ball games. As of tomorrow morning, Jake's case was being turned over to Charlie Malchek. He was glad. He'd be done answering to her, but thanks to his role as Andy's coach, he could still see her on a regular basis.

He'd been looking forward to the baseball game all day. The league games were in full swing, and the park was busy. The Raiders had drawn the last game of the day.

He got his cap off the nail in the bedroom wall. Grabbing his wallet from the dresser top, he jammed it into the back pocket of his jeans, deciding to head out to the field a little early. If some of the kids showed up, they could get in a good, long warm-up before the game.

He headed down the stairs and passed the garden. The little slips of flowers the reverend had planted were now a row of chubby petunias underneath the bushes. Jake hardly spared them a glance. He liked the garden at night better. You didn't get a sense of its boundaries then. And after being locked up all night for ten years, Jake couldn't quite get enough of being free at night.

At the ball field, one of the players, Frank Meyer, was waiting. His mom was there too, sitting in a lawn chair with a magazine on her lap. She gave Jake a cautious wave, but Frank gave a whoop. "Jake! Can you toss me a couple?"

"Sure," Jake said and he headed out to the field.

He played ball with Frank, and he enjoyed it. He'd never admit to anybody but Rachel how much he treasured this time with the kids. What he'd never admit—even to Rachel—was how he sometimes imagined he was a father, coaching his son's team.

As he tossed the ball back and forth with Frank, he kept watching for Rachel and Andy. They came when about half the team was already there, and Jake had organized a couple of drills.

Rachel and her mother-in-law. Jake was getting used to seeing Mrs. Drewer, though in the beginning it had struck him as strange that the older woman came to all of Andy's baseball games. Little League baseball on a dusty field didn't seem her style. At first, Jake had figured the older woman came because she was undoubtedly on every committee of the church. But in game two, when Andy had hit his first triple, Mrs. Drewer had jumped up from her seat and cheered. Go figure.

Rachel and Leora set up their lawn chairs near the sidelines. Rachel's hair was blowing in the wind. He liked her best that way. A little windblown, fresh like the outdoors, all those little freckles multiplying from the effects of the sun. He imagined if he put his nose to her skin, she'd smell like good, green and open places.

"Jake!" Andy came flying over to Jake.

"Hey, Andy," Jake acknowledged, giving the boy a high five before yanking the brim of his cap down over his forehead. Andy used a knuckle to push it back up.

"Hey, not fair! I can't reach your cap!" Andy grinned and shadowed Jake in their familiar ritual, dancing away when Jake tried again to pull the brim of his hat over his eyes.

Andy always let Jake do it once. And Jake always let Andy dance away, every time pretending he wasn't fast enough to catch the boy and yank that cap again.

Andy grinned and taunted him; Jake kept up the game for a few seconds longer.

He liked all the kids, but he liked Andy most of all. Of course, he was Rachel's kid, and whenever Jake looked at Andy, he could see a younger Rachel. Except for his dark hair, Andy looked almost exactly like his mom, right down to the classy little nose, all dusted with freckles. The way the kid grinned—well, Jake saw Rachel every time.

"All right, let's get you out on the field for warm-ups," he said to Andy. As Andy came toward him, Jake put a hand on his shoulder and turned him toward the catching drill in progress. "Okay, go and take Scott's place, and send him over to batting practice."

Reverend Carson came up to Jake, puffing a little from walking across the field. Most of the players were here now. "The team's looking good," Carson said quietly by his side. "You're a good coach."

"Thanks," Jake said, suddenly feeling an emotion he'd seldom felt in his whole life. It was contentment, he discovered with surprise. He liked being here, in the open space and light, warm breeze, with a bunch of kids in red uniforms that said the Raiders.

One of the players missed a ball that was pitched right over the plate. Before Jake could offer encouragement, Andy called out, "That's okay, Kev. That ball was coming real fast. I couldn't have hit it, either."

Just like that, Jake felt a rush of emotion, the kind that thickened his throat. Andy was often like that. Apparently, thanks to all that practice in the backyard before Chris's death, and his love for the game, Andy was one of the best players on the team. But he was always the first to offer encouragement, to commiserate with another kid who wasn't so good. Last week, one of the players had been hit on the shoulder by the ball. Andy had rushed over as fast as Jake. It was that rare thing in Jake's experience: a kind child. And that made Andy special.

The teenager who was umpiring the game got there a little late, but made up for it by a loud, long blast on his whistle. "Play ball," he yelled.

Jake consulted his roster and lined up the players to bat. Andy was second in the lineup and hit a single on the first pitch. The game was off to a good start.

The game was in its third inning when the catcher on Jake's team, Brian Thomas, decided he had a stomachache. "Musta been somethin' I ate," he said solemnly.

Jake looked over the bench. The Raiders didn't

have too many decent catchers. "I hate to spare you from right field," he said to Andy. "But we're two runs up, so maybe this is a good time. Want to try catching?" It wasn't a drill Andy had practiced much.

"Sure." Andy jumped up, caught the catcher's mitt and mask that Brian tossed him and headed to the plate. Jake turned to see that Rachel was shading her eyes, watching her son. Well, Andy would have a story to tell at home tonight, he thought as he took his seat on the bench.

Andy squatted behind the plate, his mitt face out, ready to catch. The pitcher sent the ball right over home plate but too high. The kid at the plate started to swing. Andy straightened, trying to catch the high ball...

"No!" Jake leaped to his feet.

The swinging bat caught Andy on the side of the head. Hard. He went down. And was still.

RACHEL GOT THERE almost as fast as Jake, and Leora wasn't far behind. Jake knelt on the ground beside Andy. "Andy, are you all right?"

She also knelt in the dust of home plate, her heart pounding against her ribs. Around her, the parents were coming up to stand in a ring around her son and Jake. His catcher's mask lay in the dust beside him.

Andy's eyes were open, but a little unfocused. She started to scoop him up in her arms. Jake put out a hand to stop her. "Don't. Let's wait a minute and make sure he's not hurt too badly to move."

A head injury. Dear God.

Her eyes met Jake's for a panicked second.

Andy coughed, and both looked down immediately. The boy struggled to sit. The skin around a cut on his temple was already starting to discolor. The cut was oozing blood. A lot of blood. There was blood in his ear, too, and more of it was beginning to soak his hair.

Jake put his arms behind Andy's shoulders. "Don't try to sit," he said.

Through her own fright, Rachel noticed how thin Jake's voice sounded.

Andy sat up anyway. Droplets of blood ran down his cheek, and Rachel felt another spurt of panic. Jake kept an arm firmly around his shoulders and used his other hand to take a handkerchief out of his pocket. He pressed it against Andy's temple. He said quietly to Rachel, "Cuts on the face bleed a lot, and it usually looks worse than it is. That blood coming out of his ear might just be from a scratch. I saw a lot of those kind of cuts in prison. They were never serious, Rachel." Nevertheless, his voice sounded strained. "They were never serious," he repeated, almost to himself.

"I couldn't breathe," Andy said, sounding more perplexed than hurt. "I got hit with the bat, didn't I?"

Rachel almost sagged with relief. Her little guy, talking at least. He couldn't be hurt that bad if he was talking to her, could he?

"Are we gonna lose the game?" Andy's voice was gaining strength.

"No," Jake said quietly.

"But you don't have a catcher," Andy said, starting to get up, only to fall back with a moan of pain.

Jake picked him up in his arms and stood. "Can

you finish up here, Reverend?'' he asked Carson, who was standing with the knot of worried parents. Without waiting for an answer, Jake carried Andy off the field. The spectators gave a smattering of encouraging applause.

"Do you hurt a lot?" Jake asked Andy.

Andy started to lift his head to look at Jake and let it fall back. "Yeah," he said. "It hurts."

"You're going to be okay, sweetheart," Rachel said, trying not to show how frightened she was. She reached out to touch him lightly on the top of the head.

"S'okay, Mom," Andy whispered. "I'm not gonna die or anything."

Her throat nearly squeezed shut. "Of course you're not going to die." She'd intended her voice to sound firm, brisk. Instead, she sounded fierce. Scared.

They got to Rachel's car. Jake whispered to her, "We could call the paramedics, but I think we'd get there faster without scaring Andy if you drove. Can you?"

At the chance to actually do something, Rachel rallied. "Of course." But after Jake had laid her son gently in the seat next to her and strapped him in, she realized her hands were shaking. Jake opened the back door for Leora, and without asking, got in the back seat on the other side himself.

It was only a short drive to the hospital, but it seemed long. Andy was so quiet. Rachel felt her heart thump in double time as they passed under the blue sign that said Emergency. Chris had been pronounced dead at the scene of the car accident that had killed him. He'd already been dead by the time she was called. She had no experience with this, with injury and waiting to find out if a loved one was all right.

An orderly took Andy into a cubicle, and Rachel watched as the doctor used a lighted instrument to check Andy's pupils and asked him all sorts of questions. To Rachel, his voice seemed thin and reedy, and his answers a beat long in coming. *He's just scared, being in a hospital,* she thought, and she tried again to reassure him. Andy didn't acknowledge her voice, and that frightened Rachel, too. The doctor finally said quietly to Rachel that he wanted to run a few more tests. "What for?" she asked.

The young emergency-room doctor was kind. "Probably for nothing." He hesitated. "He's had a trauma to the head. We're looking for concussion. Hematoma."

Blood on his brain, she thought, sick. "Okay," she said and watched them take her son away.

When she got to the waiting room, Leora was standing by a window, looking out. Jake was pacing.

"Is he all right?" they both asked at the same time.

"Yes, I think so." Rachel took a deep breath. "But he's kind of quiet, and they're running some…tests…" Despite her best efforts, she started to cry.

Jake was at her side in a second. "Sit down, Rachel." With infinite gentleness, he steered her to one of the vinyl chairs in the waiting room and sat beside her. Leora sat on her other side, silent, her back held stiffly, her hands clenched over the clasp of the purse in her lap.

Jake took Rachel's hand. His palm was rough.

Warm. She sighed and almost leaned into him before she remembered she couldn't.

"Hey," Jake finally said softly. "It's going to be okay. I've seen a lot of guys get hit and they were always okay. The skull is so hard."

"He's just a little boy," she whispered.

"I know," Jake said gruffly. He used his fingertip to wipe away a tear from her cheek. "He's a special kid. Don't you think I know that?"

His voice had thickened. She raised her eyes to his and saw the feelings there. Feelings for a child he didn't know was his.

He didn't know, but he obviously cared. Rachel gripped his hand harder.

Then they just sat. The three of them—Leora and Jake on either side of her. Once, Jake asked her if she'd like something to drink; she said no thanks. The minutes ticked by.

"Mrs. Drewer?" It was the doctor again. All three of them jumped up.

"He's fine," the doctor said, and Rachel's shoulders sagged in relief. "He's got a slight concussion. We're going to watch him for a little while here, and then release him to you." He paused. "Would you like to come and see him? We gave him a little something because he's hurting, so he's a little groggy."

Without a word, Rachel reached for her purse and followed the doctor down the hallway. Leora trailed after her.

Jake had to physically restrain himself from following. Instead, he sat back down on the vinyl couch and rubbed his eyes. His throat felt thick, the muscles of his neck and shoulders tight. When he'd seen Andy lying on the ground, so still...

When he'd seen all that blood... His words hadn't been meant only to reassure Rachel, but to reassure himself. In the moment when he'd knelt in the dirt beside Andy, he'd realized something.

He cared about Rachel's son.

He didn't just like the boy, appreciate how special he was, see bits of Rachel in his expressions. He really cared. He felt protective, possessive almost of Andy. It had been hard not to follow Rachel and Leora down the hall just now, because on some level he felt he ought to be there.

It was a ridiculous notion. He had no right. He was a caring friend to Andy, and his mother's client.

He waited for about fifteen minutes. The waiting room was quiet. The only other patient on a Sunday night, an older woman with a sprained ankle, had gone home. He tried to read, but the weeks-old newsmagazine just wouldn't hold his interest.

Leora came back down the hall. Jake got up. "How is he?"

She gave him a half-formed smile. "Pretty lively, all things considered."

Jake took a deep breath. Okay. That sounded all right.

Leora continued, "He has a concussion, but it's minor, and all Rachel will have to do is wake him up a time or two tonight to make sure he's focused and alert..." Her voice trailed off. "Anyway, Rachel's signing papers and they're gathering Andy's things. They'll be going home soon." She studied him, an odd expression on her face.

She finally seemed to make up her mind about something. "Can I call you a cab?"

"I'm going home with Rachel."

Leora flushed. Ah, hell, Jake thought, realizing how intimate his words had sounded. Falsely intimate, he knew. "She might need help with Andy," he explained.

"Oh. I see."

Her cheeks still held high color. That embarrassment was kind of odd, too, now that he thought about it. Rachel had taken pains to keep their relationship at the level of friendship. Leora couldn't have known about their past. So why would she assume his going home with Rachel had any significance?

Regardless, he felt uncomfortable under her scrutiny. She had a way of looking at a person with her lips pursed that conveyed disapproval and a refined arrogance.

He didn't deserve that from Leora Drewer. He hadn't deserved it since age eight when he had delivered a humiliating apology for the theft of a pair of shoes.

He tossed his magazine on the pile on the table. "Have you got a problem with my going home with Rachel and seeing to her hurt son?" he asked levelly. He tried to keep the mocking note, the big-A Attitude out of his voice. But he suspected he hadn't quite succeeded, because her lips pursed tighter than ever.

"Rachel's an adult," she said finally.

"Right," Jake said, and he turned from her. Fishing a couple of quarters out of his jeans, he went to the soda machine and punched buttons for a cola. When the can banged its way down the slide, it sounded loud in the quiet room. He couldn't see Leora behind him, but he could sense her watching him. He took the can to the window and stood looking out. His thoughts were in turmoil. Leora Drewer was the living, breathing embodiment of everything he'd always resented about Grange. Yet somehow, even now, like an eight-year-old boy, he wanted to please her, and he hated that about himself.

"Jake." She'd come right up by his side.

He just looked out the window.

She stood next to him, looking out too. "The hospital has a fine garden this year. The garden club is doing all the planting and weeding, you know."

"No, I wouldn't know."

"No, I guess you wouldn't," she said quietly. Then she added, "You never had the chance to experience some of the nicer things in life, did you? Gardens, for example."

New shoes, Jake mentally added. He was sure Leora was remembering that long-ago incident. It was there like a wall between them. He'd stolen something maybe six times in his life, and he remembered every time. When he was little, the packages of Twinkies and the Kit Kat bars from the convenience store. Then later, a book from the bookstore. Parts to fix the old truck. He remembered the sick feeling of guilt as if it were yesterday. He never could take pleasure in the things he stole, even when he'd gotten more clever and hadn't been caught. Anyway, after he'd been caught with those shoes, he'd never stolen anything again from Drewers.

Beside him, he could hear Leora take a deep breath. "I know you think I don't like you." There was the smallest plaintive note in her voice, so small that he wondered if he was imagining it.

"You're right. I think you don't like me because you don't."

"Well," she said. He turned to look at her and saw that her cheeks had that high, defined spot of color in them and her eyes were hot with embarrassment.

He was suddenly embarrassed himself. She was all buttoned up, and even her sporty blouse was real silk, he was sure. Her clothes looked expensive, her hair so perfectly coiffed, her lips so perfectly painted in old rose that he figured she must have taken a detour into the bathroom to groom herself before coming out to talk to him. But she looked older than he remembered. Her skin had a few age spots. A web of lines crisscrossed the skin around her eyes. Her glasses showed a faint line where the bifocals were. He'd always thought of Leora Drewer as somehow ageless, the reigning queen of the Emporium. Now his mind's eye flashed to the meager stock there and realized that things weren't quite what they seemed.

"I think I misjudged you," she said abruptly.

He went absolutely still.

She bit her lower lip, and for a moment he thought she wouldn't meet his eyes. But he'd underestimated her, because in the next second she looked directly at him. "I've got a bit of a thing for good blood, you see. Class. Rachel's been on me about it for years." She paused, then hurried on. "Rachel's made me see over the years that blood isn't everything. That it's possible for a person to be of good character no matter who they come from."

He still felt that curious stillness, as if his body was too heavy. "My father was an alcoholic. That's an illness, they say. But if so, I don't have it."

She nodded. "I've seen no sign of it in you."

He said, "I also didn't kill Joann Floutz."

There was a long silence. "Rachel has never thought so."

"But you do."

"I did. But now...I don't know. You really don't seem like a murderer to me."

She put out her hand, a most formal gesture of reconciliation. He took it, feeling the big diamond ring on her wedding finger, the fragility of the bones of her hand.

Before he could speak, he heard "Here we are!" He turned to see Rachel coming down the hall next to an orderly. The orderly was pushing Andy in a wheelchair. A big white bandage dressed one side of his head.

Leora forgotten, Jake headed over to Andy. They stopped in the doorway. Jake knelt by the boy's side, and felt that thick, hard-to-swallow feeling in his throat again when he saw how pale he was, how every freckle stood out on his cheeks.

"Hey," he said softly, using his palm to brush Andy's hair off his forehead.

"Hey, yourself," Andy said groggily. Then a second later, he said in a far more vibrant way, "I got injured in a *game*. Just like a real player."

"Yeah. Injured for your team." Jake's voice was husky.

"So, did we win?"

Jake said, "I don't know. I've been here instead of at the game."

"Really?" Andy looked at him askance, the bandage making him look even younger. "You mean, you came here when you could've been coaching ball?"

Jake smiled. "Yeah, kid, I came here when I could have been coaching ball."

"Well, that's kind of cool. Kind of dumb but kind of cool."

Jake gave him a soft punch in the arm, and Andy gave him a wobbly grin.

When he straightened, he became suddenly conscious of the women. Rachel and Leora. Rachel had the strangest expression on her face. A sort of tenderness or something soft, though she wouldn't meet his eyes. But Leora's lips were pursed in that high-chinned aristocratic disapproval. As if she hadn't offered her hand to him not five minutes ago.

Rachel was fiddling with her shoulder bag now, in one of those nervous gestures she'd never had as a girl.

The only person he understood here was Andy. The kid was still grinning at Jake—and that grin felt so incredibly good it hurt.

CHAPTER NINE

"IT'S THE SECOND DOOR to the right," Rachel whispered, leading the way down the hall toward Andy's room. Her son was asleep, utterly slack in Jake's arms. She was glad Jake had offered to help, because she would have hated to have to wake Andy to send him upstairs to bed.

She walked ahead of Jake into the room and pulled back the bedspread and sheets. There wasn't much moon, and the night-light in the bathroom next door barely illuminated the space. But it was light enough to see Andy's baseball posters on the walls and, on the dresser his precious autographed ball from one of the Cleveland Indians' players. The ball shared space with Andy's most elaborate Lego creations.

Jake laid Andy carefully on the bed, and his gentleness brought a sudden prick of tears to Rachel's eyes. She blinked them away, reminding herself that she'd had a huge fright today and all of her emotions were on the edge. Andy was going to be all right, and that was all that mattered. There was no reason to get emotional now.

"Shoes?" Jake whispered, turning toward her a little. "They're cleats, and they'll tear up the sheets."

Shoes? "Oh," she whispered belatedly. She stepped forward and untied Andy's cleats and pulled

them off. He was still in his uniform, and she'd seen
at the hospital that evening that it was dusty and had
a grass stain on one knee.

She decided Andy was better off comfortably
asleep than clean. She pulled the sheet up to his
shoulders. She couldn't help smoothing a hand over
his cheek. He didn't wake up. Chris used to say a
freight train crossing in the middle of his room
wouldn't awaken Andy. Not even Peppy's barking
when they'd come home had caused her son to do
much more than stir in Jake's arms. And the big
clock in the hallway had struck midnight just as they
passed. That hadn't woken him, either. She smiled,
glad her son could sleep so comfortably. She bent to
kiss him on the cheek.

When she straightened, she became aware of Jake
watching her. He was standing by the dresser, his
body very still. She found herself swallowing hard,
maybe at memories, mostly at the sight of him where
she'd never pictured him to be. In her son's bedroom.

She headed out of the room, and Jake followed,
closing Andy's door softly. In the linen closet, Rachel picked out an old, mechanical alarm clock that
she kept in case of power outages. They went downstairs.

In the kitchen, she gave Peppy a little rawhide
chew, which he took gratefully to his box in the laun-
dry room. Over on one of the kitchen chairs, Waldo
raised his head, yawned, then went back to sleep. The
bookends and Carmen Sandiago were nowhere in
sight. Rachel fiddled with the alarm clock. "I'll have
to set this for three hours, because I need to wake
Andy and see if he's focusing on me properly. The
doctor told me to do it."

She turned the little keys, trying to concentrate on a task that didn't need much concentration. She was trying to blot out the picture in her mind of Jake carrying Andy upstairs, laying him down on the sheets so gently. She tried even harder to push away the feeling of guilt she had about her secret. And she tried hardest of all to forget the image of Jake in her little boy's room. It was a scene she'd fantasized about long ago, one she should dread today. But somehow it had felt so...right.

She felt sad that Andy would never know Jake was his father. But she needed to keep things as they were, for her son's sake.

"Thank you," she said softly. She had meant her words to come out as politeness for his help, but they had a husky sound.

"You're welcome." He stood next to her, leaning a hip against the kitchen counter. "I like the house. Was it like this when you moved in?"

"Oh no." To distract herself from her thoughts, she was happy to rattle on. "The paint was peeling. The cabinets were metal and painted pea green. I had a choice to do a little at a time or wait. We decided to wait. We needed new wallpaper and flooring, but we lived with what we had for a long time. Finally, we could afford to remodel the whole kitchen."

She waved her hand in the air. "I chose the wallpaper and the chandelier." Done loosely in Victorian style, the kitchen featured lace curtains and a William Morris–type wallpaper of densely patterned beige leaves on a cream background. Golden oak cabinets cast a yellow glow at night. The only color in the room came from brilliant stained-glass flowers on a Tiffany-style chandelier.

"Did Chris help you?" Jake asked.

For some reason, Chris's name was a jolt. She'd said "we" not "I," but still, with Chris gone and Jake in her kitchen...

And Jake laying Andy down on those sheets just now...

"Of course. He liked things nice." That was fudging things a little. Chris had liked her decorating, but he didn't have much interest in picking things out. After working at Drewers all day, nearly every day, he had never liked to shop.

Jake was still looking around, and when he spoke, his voice had a faraway sound. "I always knew you'd live in something old. I could picture it."

Her father had owned a modern, ranch-style house. Jake had envied her that house in their youth, but Rachel had always wanted something more solid.

"We used to talk about it," he said.

She knew what "it" meant. They had talked about being married, where they'd live. Jake had opted for a place somewhere far from Grange, but he liked the country. A big old house was their dream. He'd lie on the grass and stare at the sky as Rachel described this imaginary house. Of course, he never contributed to the conversation, but he'd get this little indulgent smile that just barely turned the corners of his mouth on the days she waxed eloquent about wainscoting and wide front porches. And sooner or later, he'd roll over and press his body to hers and kiss her and then she couldn't think anymore about porches or wainscoting.

"I always knew you'd have something classy," he added. "That's my earliest memory of you. Classy."

She warmed at the compliment. It was undeniably cozy here, with Jake in her kitchen. But it was more than cozy. He was big and dark and male, and he was leaning with a casual grace that had always made her mouth go a little dry. She should offer him coffee, she thought. Andy was safely asleep upstairs, and it seemed the polite thing to do. But if she did so, then he'd be staying for a while. Pleasure and fear mingled again. She needed to use good sense here. They'd crossed a line today. Jake was in her house. Suddenly, he'd really become her friend. Friends learned things about each other. Shared secrets.

"It's late," she blurted.

He nodded, looking at her, and he slowly straightened. "Past midnight," he agreed. "I heard the hall clock strike when I took Andy upstairs."

He was *really* looking at her now. Staring in that intense, can't-look-away way he had. The sense of power in that stare, the sense that she was the only thing that mattered at that moment, the glittering depths of those eyes...

The day was telling on her, she realized as she started to tremble. "Well, you've got to work in the morning, so I'll show you out."

She had to pass him to get around the kitchen counter. His arm shot out, grabbing her hand. He tugged it and she turned toward him. "Jake—"

"It's past midnight," he interrupted. "Past midnight, Rachel. Do you know what that means? You're not my parole officer anymore."

The reality of his words stunned her. Slowly, he pulled her toward him. His eyes darkened to black in unmistakable desire, a desire she knew they'd been avoiding since they'd come down to the kitchen. No. Longer than that. Desire they'd been denying since the day he'd come home.

She was trembling for real now. Helplessly, she let him draw her toward him.

She rallied a little when she was within inches of his chest. "The official changeover might not be until morning, when Charlie actually comes in to the office, so I guess technically—"

Abruptly, he pulled her against his chest. She smelled the dust of a ball field and the sweat of a man. Helplessly, she pushed the tip of her nose into the thin cloth of his shirt, feeling his hard chest behind it.

He tipped her chin up. His lids were half lowered, but still she felt the impact of his eyes on her. "I don't give a damn about the technicalities," he said in a harsh whisper. Then he kissed her.

And, oh, she welcomed that kiss. She opened her mouth for his tongue, and the delighted shock of feeling it enter her mouth mingled with a sense of finally being complete again.

Because as she put her arms around him, as her hands touched the back of his neck, she remembered everything about the feel of him against her. His lips on hers, working at hers, molded to hers, as if he had to have her now. The feel of his arousal, demanding and hot against her belly.

There was his harsh breathing, then a moan, which she dimly realized came from her own throat. His kiss made her feel warm and fiery and alive. As his tongue penetrated and withdrew, she sagged against him, wanting him, needing him.

Still he kissed her. He dragged his mouth from

hers to plant kiss after kiss on her face, on her cheeks and chin and nose and eyelids. He used one hand to sweep her hair aside and hold the back of her head as he licked and nibbled at her neck. She moaned again.

He used his other hand to press her hips to his, and as they made more firm contact, she couldn't help moving her hips a little, trying instinctively to get more of him. Against her neck, he groaned, the sound loud in the still kitchen.

That groan sent another shot of sensation through her. At the same time, it brought her to her senses. What was she doing? She had to stop. She *had* to. She pushed on his shoulders, but it was a puny effort.

In fact, he didn't seem to even feel it. Instead, he turned her, pressed her against the counter, pushed his hips blatantly against hers. His hand came up and cupped her breast. Even through the cotton of her blouse and the lace of her bra, her nipple went instantly hard against his palm.

"Ten years," he mumbled against her neck. She felt his breath on her skin. "I've waited ten years and more, and nobody, nobody could taste like you… I want all of you…"

He was tugging at her blouse, pulling it out of her jeans.

Oh, if she didn't stop him now…

She pushed as hard as she could against his chest. "Jake! Stop."

He went abruptly still, the tails of her blouse in his fists.

"Please. Stop."

He moved so slowly it was as if she were watching stop-action film. That slowness was painful to watch.

His fists uncoiled. The crisp fabric of her shirt was crumpled and they both watched as it wafted back into place over her midsection. For a frozen moment, neither moved. She could still feel his arousal, his thighs against hers. She wanted to feel his skin against hers so much she could have wept.

He said, "You're not my P.O. anymore."

She'd led him to believe her job was the only impediment between them. She remembered bringing it up the first time he'd tried to kiss her, the night they'd sat together in a dark car after seeing the Duke in Columbus.

He said, "I thought you wanted this."

"I don't." Her voice sounded thin, doubtful.

Suddenly, he stepped away. "For someone who doesn't want it, you certainly gave a pretty good imitation there for a while."

Her cheeks went hot. "I know," she admitted.

He looked her in the eye. "So why did you tell me to stop?"

She broke eye contact and focused on his chest. Through the thin cotton of his T-shirt, she could see his chest rising and falling, still heard his breathing, heavy and raspy.

She said quickly, "It's been a long time for you. I mean, since you had—were with a woman, and I think—"

"Don't!" he said harshly. "Don't do that. I admit, when I came out of prison, I wanted a woman. I'd missed so much. Everything. Yes. I wanted to get laid." He put a thumb on her chin, forcing her to look up. "That's the truth. The rest of the truth was that as soon as I saw you again, you were the one I wanted. Only you. And just now, you responded to me.'' The pressure of his thumb didn't let up, a gentle but steely reminder that he wanted an explanation. ''Why, Rachel?'' He searched her eyes. ''Why did you tell me to stop?''

She couldn't tell him why. She couldn't say, *I want you to touch me. I ache for you to make love to me. But I couldn't live with my secrets and my lies tomorrow morning.*

Instead, she said, ''I really do think it's more generic than you do, Jake. You've gone a long time without—without intimacy.'' She tried not to wince at her preachy tone. ''Surely you know that those memories between us make it easier—''

He swore, one low syllable, and abruptly let her go. She almost sagged against the counter, as if the gentle pressure of his thumb on her chin was the only thing that had held her up.

''I'm going, and I'll show myself out.'' He turned from her.

She ought to just let him go, to let him think what he would.

She followed him. ''I'm sorry.''

He stopped at the front door. ''It was memories that made you kiss me, is that what you were saying?''

She nodded. That was the truth, or part of it, anyway. Those memories had been so good, so compelling.

''And you felt sorry for me because I haven't had a woman?'' The anger in his voice seemed to come from somewhere bone-deep.

''No!''

He waited, as if she was going to add more. When she didn't, he said, ''I loved you once. But even then,

I hated the idea that I was one of your stray cats. Something to love, something to feel sorry for.'' He opened the door. The night air, cooler and more humid than the air in the house, rolled into the hallway.

Without a backward glance, he stepped out onto her porch.

She almost called him back, sick to her stomach. To protect her son, she'd let Jake think she felt sorry for him. She'd resurrected his feelings of shame, and that hurt her, a physical pain.

What hurt worse was that she wondered who she was really trying to protect—Andy or herself.

Because if he ever found out she'd married Chris and let Andy believe Chris was his father, he'd hate her. He had so much pride. If he learned that even now, a year after Chris's death, she was keeping this knowledge from her son, he'd hate her for it. She couldn't bear it if he hated her.

She shut the door and stood leaning with her back against it. She'd had a good reason for her decision a decade ago. She had good reason for it now. But despite her reasons, Jake would still hate her, wouldn't he?

She was a coward; she was afraid to find out. Better to let him think she felt sorry for him, that he was one of her stray cats, instead of a grown man, an intelligent man with a hard chest and a hard mouth that went soft against hers, and a way of looking at her that melted her insides.

After all, what was one more lie? For a woman who'd never been a good liar, she was learning fast.

ONE NIGHT almost two weeks later, Jake sat on his bed wearing his briefs, telling himself if he didn't get some sleep he wouldn't be much good in the morning. The judge had asked him to sit in on a trial that was starting tomorrow. Jake wanted to be around for the process of jury selection, which would begin at eight. He'd been trying to watch as many trials as possible, knowing that he needed to get some practical courtroom experience—even if vicariously—to round out his research and writing skills.

But he knew he was probably kidding himself. There wasn't much likelihood of a good night's sleep. Not tonight.

He snapped on the bedside lamp and pulled this morning's newspaper toward him. The article was in the bottom left-hand corner of the first page, right underneath the one about the thirty-fifth annual Downtown Boosters picnic to be held a week from Saturday. The one of such profound interest to Jake wasn't a big article, and the headlines weren't the two-inch kind that announced elections and assassinations. But to Jake the small article seemed so prominent it almost glowed.

Floutz Murder Case Reopened. Husband Questioned and Released. In a calm, almost stark way, the paper stated that Ralph Floutz had been questioned in the ten-year-old case of the murder of his wife. The chief of police emphasized that Ralph Floutz was not a suspect in his wife's death, just that some "alleged new evidence" appeared to "throw some light on the case," leading to the questioning. "We had a conviction in that case," the chief had gone on to say. "As far as we know at this time, that conviction is still good."

It was a fine piece of waffling by the chief, Jake thought now as he scanned the article one more time.

The man was taking pains to treat Ralph Floutz as innocent until proven guilty. An old bitterness ate at him, because Jake had never had the benefit of the doubt, but he pushed it aside. Besides, the chief was new, not the one who'd questioned Jake with such zeal ten years ago, the one who couldn't help a slow smile when he'd casually informed Jake that Rachel Penning wouldn't confirm his alibi.

Besides, Jake could read between the lines. The county had to be careful this time. Sending the wrong man to prison could result in a very expensive lawsuit. Oh yes, this time they'd tread carefully.

He put the paper down and shut off the light again. Lying back on the soft, worn bedspread, he wove his hands together behind his head and stared at the ceiling. The police were not discounting Ralph as a suspect. The chief had gone on to state that the investigation was being reopened. The story's last lines had been a sentence or two describing the stolen property, including a description of Joann's amber pendant, and a final note that, with the exception of a tape deck found at Jake Monroe's dairy, none of the property had ever been recovered.

All day at the courthouse, people had talked about the article. If Jake rounded the corner unexpectedly, he'd interrupt conversations, and glances would skitter away. It was almost like his first day at work, when he'd look up to find everybody supposedly very busy but watching him nonetheless. At midmorning, the county prosecutor passed him near the stairs. Over time, Gerry Pendask had thawed a bit. Today, he'd made a point of pretending he didn't see Jake.

Jake had made no friends at the courthouse. He'd

always been so careful to keep his distance from strangers that it was easy to come to work alone, concentrate on his cases, avoid the coffee area at peak times and pack a sandwich from home, which he ate at his desk.

At three o'clock in the afternoon, Judge Randall had called him into chambers. The judge was as messy a worker as Jake; his spacious office was piled with papers. The dregs of his lunch were on the conference table, a bit of bun and a wadded fast-food bag next to a few equally wadded sheets of yellow legal paper. Jake held a tablet of his own, waiting for instructions. Instead of launching into a legal problem, the judge had rummaged on his crowded desk for the newspaper. He found the section he was looking for and held it out to Jake.

"I assume you saw this?"

"Yeah," Jake said. "I read it this morning when I got to work."

"Looks like you might actually get out from under this after all these years."

Jake knew it was still a long shot. He shrugged.

The judge motioned him to sit. Jake sat on the edge of one of the leather conference chairs. The judge was quiet for a moment, stroking his upper lip as he thought. Finally, he said, "You've done a good job here."

Jake nodded. "Thanks."

"I knew you would."

"Thanks," Jake said again. He started to rise.

"Sit." Judge Randall waved him back into his seat.

Their relationship was professional, cordial but not

warm. The judge had made overtures these last months, but Jake had rebuffed them.

Judge Randall swiveled in his chair. He looked over at Jake, his eyes kind. "I want to help."

Jake pushed down a flash of bitterness, the words *like you helped ten years ago?* unsaid. He'd be a fool not to take any help that was offered.

The judge stroked his upper lip again. "Do you want me to pull those records, look at the trial transcript, see if there's any way for a late appeal?"

"I did that long ago."

"Oh. Okay."

There was a beat of silence. Then Jake added, "Thanks."

"I could go to the chief of police, tell him I think there were errors in the trial."

"But there weren't any errors. There were no technical errors, no legal screwups. I spent the better part of a year looking and researching, trying to find one."

Judge Randall pushed a piece of paper aside, exposing the wood of his desktop, then rapped out a beat on the desk with his fingers. "You're right. It was always more a feeling I had that you were innocent, rather than the evidence, though there was that issue of your only having one piece of the property that was supposedly stolen. Anyway, I've been a judge for fifteen years, and the chief and I go back a ways. I can make sure this investigation they're doing is thorough, that they don't blow off any evidence they get."

Something—Hope? Warmth?—leaped to life in Jake's chest.

The judge cleared his throat. "I can't fix what I did ten years ago, Jake."

Jake shrugged, studying the tassels on his loafers, thinking of the sneakers that had been his only footwear in the penitentiary. It was true. Nobody could give him back ten years of his life.

But what was the point of clearing his name if he was going to nurse these grievances for the rest of his life? Confused suddenly, he didn't say anything.

The judge leaned forward with a squeak of his massive chair. "I can't fix it, but we can go on from here. We can be true colleagues." The judge waited a beat more then said, "We could be friends."

Jake's hands were flat on the conference table. They were rough; since coming from prison, he'd cut his nails more evenly, but the cuticles were ragged, the palms calloused, the knuckles dry and cracked here and there. There was a scar across the top of his wrist, the remnants of a fight in the cafeteria between two prisoners, a day when Jake had been caught in the crossfire. He thought of that long, irregular scar on his thigh. Some things about prison would always be there. On his skin.

But he knew suddenly that he didn't want those things in his soul. So he stood slowly, and even more slowly, he held out his hand.

The judge got up and met Jake's hand with his. At the contact, Judge Randall let out a small breath. Jake was surprised, even as they shook hands. Surprised that his action apparently meant so much.

When he withdrew his hand, he shoved it in his pocket, suddenly a little embarrassed by the emotion in his boss's eyes, and even more embarrassed by the warmth that stole over him.

Randall said, "I won't pretend that this will heal everything between us. But it's a start, Jake. It's a start."

It *was* a start. And now, tonight, Jake kicked the spread aside and rolled over onto his side. The sheet was bunched around his thighs, but the night was warm and he didn't need the covering.

The day had been good. But he still couldn't relax enough to sleep. And he knew his restlessness came from more than thinking about Ralph and the case.

All day he'd been waiting for something, and that waiting had contributed to the edginess that had him flopping over onto his back again.

Tonight before bed, he'd eyed the phone a couple of times, realizing he was willing it to ring. It hadn't. Now, here in the quiet dark, Jake finally acknowledged the truth.

He was not going to hear from Rachel.

All day he'd been waiting for her to appear in his office, a flush on her cheeks, her eyes bright, waving that newspaper and saying he was on his way. He knew she got the paper; he'd seen a couple of days' worth of the Grange *Post Gazette* on her kitchen counter the night he'd carried Andy upstairs. So today when she didn't come, he'd told himself that she was out in the field somewhere, counseling some kid, and she'd call. She hadn't.

He felt like a fool now. Of course she wasn't going to call. She'd made it clear that night in her house when he'd kissed her that they were going to have no relationship whatsoever. Now he knew that kiss had had a high price indeed. It had apparently killed even their friendship.

Of course, it hadn't been friendship he'd been feeling for Rachel that night. He'd been very aroused, had sensed her own arousal. You couldn't miss the way she'd pressed herself to him and moaned, the way she'd met. his tongue with hers, explored his mouth with the same sensual purpose he'd displayed.

He felt himself grow hard just thinking about Rachel's response, remembering the softness of her skin, the feminine width of her hips.

Hell. He sat up and raked a hand through his hair. Then he got out of bed and pulled on his jeans, careful with the zipper. Shoving his bare feet into loafers and grabbing the T-shirt he'd left on the back of the chair, he headed downstairs. He pushed open the door and headed down the main path of the garden.

There he stopped. It was cooler out here, and the coolness prickled his forearms. But he was still hard as a rock. He sat on a bench, trying to relax.

Rachel didn't want anything from him. Not his friendship, and certainly not his touch. When she hadn't come to the game this past Sunday, when he'd seen Leora arrive with Andy, he'd told himself maybe she had to work. Andy had looked good and was his cheerful self. When Jake had asked him how he was doing, Andy had said his mom was making all his favorite foods and hugging him and stuff, adding that Jake ought to come and have some spaghetti after the game.

Jake had smiled and ruffled the kid's hair, wondering briefly what Rachel would do if he just showed up at her house, Andy in tow, saying he'd been invited for spaghetti. She would have been dismayed.

He felt the cool, welcome breeze ruffle his hair and told himself he understood her reluctance. She'd lost her husband only a year ago. She'd had no chance to get used to Jake without the damn fact of her being his parole officer being between them. And he still hadn't proved his innocence yet. Given that, there was Andy to consider. And he'd left angry, the remnants of an old argument between them.

He guessed he'd pushed her too fast.

But it sure wasn't too fast for him. A decade had passed. Now Jake knew he'd spent those ten years waiting for more than a chance to clear his name. Now he knew he'd also been waiting to touch, to kiss, to make love to only one woman.

CHAPTER TEN

CHARLIE MALCHEK rapped a hand on Rachel's door frame.

She took her eyes from the computer screen and motioned him in.

He came rather hesitantly into her office. It had always amazed her that Charlie had had a heart attack. His only risk factor seemed to be his age. In his fifties, he was so slim he didn't have even a slight potbelly, and he was the mildest of men.

He was happily married, with two girls who hadn't caused him a lick of trouble. He drove a years-old station wagon with real wood sides, a relic that never broke down, and Rachel didn't think he had a type-A pore in his entire body. And he'd apparently never had the slightest doubts when it came to his job. While Rachel struggled with her juvenile delinquents, trying to be counselor or strong arm of the state or even substitute mom, Charlie read his regulations and sharpened his pencil and went through the motions.

His chief complaint had always been boredom. Waiting for parolees to show up, listening to their lies, checking the boxes on their forms, then—if it was Tuesday—ordering beef barley soup to be brought in from the diner for lunch. That was Charlie's life.

"Come in," she said with a smile. She didn't have much respect for him, but he'd always treated her and everyone else in the office with kindness. Besides, she reminded herself, he'd just gotten back from a long illness.

"How are you feeling?" she asked as he sank into one of her side chairs.

He smiled. "About the same as yesterday, Rachel. You don't have to ask every day." He sighed. "I'm getting a little tired of popcorn without butter and five-mile walks, but—" He stopped and shrugged with a smile. "At this rate, I'm gonna live forever."

"Good." She fiddled with her pencil, wondering how early in the conversation she could introduce the subject of Jake Monroe.

It had been just as well that she'd missed Andy's game last Sunday. The mother of one of her clients had called; the woman thought she smelled pot in her son's room and wanted Rachel to come over. Rachel had done so, though she hadn't smelled any marijuana when she'd got there. Anyway, she and the boy had ended up at his kitchen table and had had a good talk.

Yes, she'd made some progress with the teenager and avoided Jake. Andy had been delighted to see Jake, of course. When Leora had brought him home that night, it had been Jake this and Jake that, so much enthusiastic talk that neither she nor her mother-in-law could get a word in edgewise. In consequence, Rachel had expected a lecture from Leora about letting a convicted murderer spend so much time with her son. It hadn't come. That had been a little puzzling.

Last Sunday, she'd had no excuse, so she and

Leora had gone to see the Raiders beat the Penguins seven to four. And she'd watched Jake the whole time. Secretly, behind her sunglasses, which must have hidden how avid her stare was, because Leora hadn't noticed. A muscled back and lean hips had caught her eye. When the wind ruffled his hair, she thought how it was getting longer now, and she remembered how thick and vibrant it had felt between her fingers. When he squatted, she'd had her eyes on his rear and thighs. When the game had ended, she'd felt a relief so profound she wondered how she was going to endure the rest of the season. Later at home, Andy had gone to bed saying something about how Jake liked spaghetti and Rachel ought to have him to dinner.

When that newspaper article had appeared ten days ago, it had taken all her willpower not to go to his office and share what must be unfettered joy at the first piece of really good news he'd had in ten years.

But that kiss they'd shared had scared her. The fire in her body had been wonderful and terrifying, and she'd known she had to make a clean break. Anything else would be confusing and unfair to Jake. So she'd stayed away and let him think the worst of her—that she wasn't willing to share in his good news, that she wasn't willing to be his friend.

At night with the lights off, though, she lay awake in her big Victorian bed and felt her limbs ache with a longing to hold him close.

Now Charlie was going on about something and she tuned in belatedly.

He finished, ''Anyway, she's a nuisance but she's cute.''

Huh? "Who?" she asked sheepishly.

"Cleo. My new cat?" He snapped his fingers in a wake up, Rachel, motion, but he was smiling. "The doctor said pets are a great stress reliever." Charlie got up and meandered around her office, stopping finally to look out the window. "Got to relieve the stress in my life, the doc says, but hey, a cat is a lot of work and I'm thinking, come winter, that Cleo will kill the birds at my feeder. How can that be less stress?"

"I don't know, Charlie. My seven cats are hardly stress free." She thought of Waldo, who would wait for hours trying to catch a bird, always without success. "Maybe Cleo won't be into birds."

He turned to look at her as if she'd just sprouted ears and a tail herself. "She's a *cat*. Cats catch birds. It's like this, see." He scratched his nose and thought. "Cats are cats and birds are birds and criminals are criminals."

Rachel gritted her teeth and remembered why, sympathy over his heart attack or no, she'd never really liked Charlie all that much. "I don't agree. Every person is an individual and entitled to be treated as such."

Charlie just shook his head. "Look at Jake Monroe."

She leaned forward abruptly. "Jake? What about Jake?"

"That's what I came in to tell you. I figure, you were his P.O. for so long, you'd want to know. By the way, I'm not sure I thanked you enough for taking over my cases. I mean, Harold told me not to worry about my job, and I said, 'Harold, I'm not a worrier, but you know how something like—'"

"What about Jake?"

"Well." He drew out the word, and Rachel felt her fists wanting to clench. "It illustrates my point about Cleo, see? About cats and cons? There was this robbery last night, and the chief thinks Jake did it."

"Oh my God." Rachel almost forgot to breathe for a second. Then she stood. "Come on, Charlie. What happened?"

"Well, there was this robbery. It happened about three in the morning, too late to make the morning paper, but I got a call from the chief because Jake's a suspect."

"Oh my God," Rachel repeated, softer this time, her thoughts in a whirl. She knew Jake was innocent, but this looked very bad for him. "Why do they think it's Jake?" When Charlie didn't answer right away, she took a step toward him.

Charlie held out his hands as if to ward her off. "Take it easy. Jeez, you're going to have a heart attack yourself if you get so excited about every little thing. Don't worry, I know Harold won't do anything to you for not reporting his parole violations those times. Harold is a good guy about our jobs."

"Charlie." Rachel forced herself to calm down. Charlie had one way of telling a story, and attempting to hurry him was useless.

"Well, the thing is, there was a burglary. Guess what was stolen? Electronics, that's what. Jewelry." Charlie dragged out the last word. "Sound familiar?"

"But there are burglaries every once in a while. This might be Grange, but we do have crime." Her thoughts raced. "Cripes. I could pull the crime stats and show you probably five dozen break-ins when Jake was in prison. Besides, what does any burglar take? Electronics and jewelry.''

"Yeah, but most robberies are done when the people are out. In this case, the lady was home and got a look at the guy."

"She claims it was *Jake?*" Her throat closed and she reached behind her, grabbed the arm of her chair and sank into the seat.

"Looked like him," Charlie said. "I told you, a criminal is a criminal, and I knew Jake was up to no good, going to that fence and going to a bar and maybe getting drunk. The preview before the movie, you know?"

Think. Rachel barely heard him. "Did the lady actually identify Jake?"

"Well, not exactly. But the burglar had dark hair and was tall with big shoulders, she said, and he was like thirty or forty."

"Thirty or forty? That's a ten-year difference, Charlie!"

Charlie shrugged. "Yeah, well, he was dark."

"Do you know how many thirty- or forty-year-olds there are in town with dark hair?"

"It wasn't Mrs. Evesham's fault Jake Monroe was wearing a mask," Charlie said, the tiniest edge coming into his voice. "He was running away with a TV in his arms."

"Is Jake in jail?" she asked, her voice barely above a whisper.

"Nah." Charlie shook his head slightly. "The police didn't have enough to hold him. Got the impression the judge vouched for him or something. But Jake did it, just like he robbed and killed that lady, and they'll get him now like they got him then.''

While Charlie had been grinding out his story, Rachel had been relatively calm. Now in the silence that followed his last statement, she started to shake. She imagined Jake in jail and her heart squeezed. ''Where is he now?''

With maddening deliberation, Charlie pulled a pack of chewing gum from his pocket and started to tear off the cellophane. ''Don't know. It's not his check-in day.''

Without further thought, she grabbed her purse. Jake was either at work or at home. She'd look in both places.

JAKE SAT at his desk but he couldn't concentrate on the cases spread out before him. He had the creepy feeling that the walls of his small office were closing in on him, that they had the faint, constant stink of urine. He knew it was his imagination, but he'd find himself straining to hear the clank of metal doors being shut and locked. A trickle of perspiration trailed, hot and wet, down his side.

He was shaken. Very shaken. His throat felt tight and his chest tighter.

''Jake! I'm glad you're here.'' Rachel rushed into the room.

Just like that, he was back in the present, in a cubbyhole next to the judge's chambers in a courthouse in Grange, Ohio. His sense of relief was overwhelming, easing the muscles in his chest. He stood and she hurled herself into his arms.

In a kind of daze, he folded his arms around her and held her. Her hair smelled exotically perfumed, spicy, a different smell than in her youth, but comforting and real just the same. He let the relief of her presence sink into his very bones.

A while later—a minute? an hour?—it occurred to him that he shouldn't be standing in his office with the door open holding his former parole officer in his arms. Gently putting her from him, he took a few steps to the door and kicked it shut.

"My God, Jake," she was saying. "Were the police rough on you?"

He pushed her gently by the shoulders, urging her to sit. She sat on the edge of his one chair, and he sat on the edge of his desk facing her. "It wasn't so bad," he said quietly. There was a short pause during which she looked up at him with round, shining eyes. It hit him in a flash that she was very close to tears, and that touched him deep inside.

"It was bad," he finally acknowledged, unable to lie or even pretend to be tough. Not when he saw the tears she was blinking away.

"It was bad," he repeated quietly. "No rough stuff this time, though. They didn't threaten me. But they're the police. They have a way of making you feel guilty even if you're not."

She nodded in understanding.

"They finally let me go about six this morning. I went home but I didn't know what to do there, so I came here. To work."

"You could have called me."

"I didn't think you wanted that." He heard the bleakness in his voice and knew he was sharing a bit of what he was feeling. How he'd needed her and she hadn't been there.

She lifted her hands in an almost prayerful supplication. "I'm sorry. I'm sorry I gave you the impression you couldn't come to me."

He had to look away. "It doesn't matter now," he said gruffly. "They let me go."

He couldn't sit still any longer, so he got up and paced the small room. "I thought I was ready to go back to jail if it was necessary. I told myself I'd take chances to solve the crime, and if that resulted in my being returned to prison the price was worth it. But being in that jail last night just..." He took a deep breath. "It's dark in jail, Rachel, and everything in the world is painted gunmetal gray or swamp green. Everything is gouged and filthy. I sat on a cot last night, and everything I touched was slimy. Everything is so closed in. No fresh air anywhere." He took another breath. "I realized I'm not ready to go back to jail. Not for anything."

She leaned forward. "You won't have to. You're innocent, and the chief of police is a fair man—"

"I have no alibi," he cut in.

He saw her close her eyes for a second.

"In fact, when they came for me, I wasn't even in my bed, asleep. Instead, I was fully dressed, and I was outside."

"Oh God."

"Yes."

"Why were you outside? Charlie said the robbery happened at three in the morning."

He made another turn. "I can't sleep sometimes. I lie there and my room begins to close in on me. So I go down to the parsonage garden to walk."

She thought. "Does Reverend Carson know you do this?"

Hope started a faint beat in his chest. "That I do

it almost every night? Maybe. We sat out there once. We've never talked about it, though." He paused. "But if he didn't see me last night, what difference does it make?"

"Well, that you had a reason to be down in the garden in the middle of the night."

He felt his spine start to relax. "I suppose so."

She said, "Could you sit down, Jake? You're making me nervous."

He sat, but he drummed his fingers restlessly on the desktop. "The thing is, do you think this could be a random burglary? I mean, unconnected with my case?"

"It does happen in Grange."

"Do you think that's what it was?"

She bit her lip. "I don't know. This seems more like the kind of burglary done by kids. Surely no thirty- to forty-year-old robber would let himself be seen like that."

Jake put his palms on the desk for a moment, then stood again. "That's what I've been thinking. Why would the guy break into a house where someone's home? Unless he wanted to get caught. Or at least be seen. Doesn't it seem like a coincidence to you that a burglary like the Floutz robbery occurred in town after a story broke that the investigation has been reopened?" He gave a harsh chuckle. "After all, it didn't take the police long to make the connection, did it?"

She jumped to her feet. "It's possible you're being set up, Jake."

He nodded. He'd thought this through for hours, and he'd come to one conclusion. "I think the bastard who murdered Joann Floutz is still in town. And he doesn't want the police to go poking around.''

"Ralph? He's about forty, and he's big and dark.''

"The police officer who let me go this morning said they were checking all angles when I mentioned my suspicions.''

"We need to know if Ralph had an alibi.''

"He was probably at home and in bed. Of course, he could have hired someone to commit the robbery, but he's not very sophisticated. And he doesn't have the criminal contacts he'd need.''

For a second, they looked at each other. The tension was thick. He remembered old times, old alibis, and most of all, he remembered that jail cell this morning. He looked at Rachel, at her luminous eyes, realizing her distress and her determination.

He took a couple of steps her way and pulled her roughly into his arms. "Let me hold you,'' he said, his voice a harsh whisper. "Let me know that you're alive and here and in my corner. Just let me hold you.'' He'd wanted her, he'd lusted after her. Once, he'd loved her. And now Jake realized he loved her again. Under the glaring light of his office, he held her tight, gaining strength from her touch. Strength to face whatever he had to face.

THE JUDGE CALLED Jake into his office at five o'clock and told him he'd just gotten off the phone with the chief of police. The chief had reported that Ralph Floutz had been visiting his brother the night before. Apparently, Ralph often had trouble coming down and relaxing after his shift at the bar, so he tended to go to bed late. His brother worked a three-to-eleven shift at a factory and had the same problem.

At three o'clock in the morning, he and his brother had been drinking a couple of long necks and watching an old movie, *The Day of the Jackal,* on television. In other words, Ralph Floutz's alibi was airtight.

Rachel had long since gone back to her office by the time Jake got back to his. Jake was glad of that. He'd needed her desperately this morning, but it wasn't wise to involve her. She wasn't his P.O. anymore, but hell, she shouldn't have been in his office hanging on to him like that, either. She didn't need this. She didn't need him. Not now.

But he wanted to go to her. He wanted to say, *I'm in despair and I'm scared to death I'll end up back in the joint and I don't have a clue what's going on. Ralph Floutz has an alibi. So he probably isn't setting me up. So who is? Who the hell is?*

And then he wanted to take her in his arms and undress her slowly and push these thoughts away— if only for a time—and take something wonderful and good from this terrible day. She might not need him, but he sure needed her.

He stuffed papers into his briefcase and went home alone and took the phone off the hook so she couldn't call.

CHAPTER ELEVEN

RACHEL HAD BEEN GOING to the Downtown Boosters picnic for many years. Leora loved the picnic because anything involving the Boosters took second place only to the chamber of commerce in Leora's mind.

Rachel had a headache, and she responded only vaguely to Andy's chatter as he walked beside her. The park was crowded with families. Each family had set up their meal at one of the picnic tables, and the bigger, more extended families had spread blankets on the grass. Some of the younger kids had fishing poles to catch the sunfish and crappie that swam in the pond. She shaded her eyes, seeing who was here, as Leora recited names.

Andy said, "This is gonna be fun."

She smiled. Later, she'd compete with her son in the three-legged race, and the one where they'd transfer a Life Saver candy from toothpick to toothpick without dropping it.

"Gosh, I wish Dad was here," Andy said.

Her heart skipped a beat. "Me, too, honey," she said gently.

"Remember when we won the three-legged race, me and Dad? Man, you and me were *putrid* last year."

Rachel sighed. She'd tried. "I'm a klutz, kid."

She ruffled his hair. "That's the way of the world for Rachel Drewer."

"But Dad wasn't."

"Your dad was very athletic," Leora said with a smile.

Rachel's mind conjured Jake. She'd thought of little else this week. Jake's case. Jake the man.

Andy shrugged and shifted the old blanket he held to his other hand. "But you know the best thing with Dad was, you could talk to him."

Rachel stopped dead. She tipped his chin up. "If you want to talk about something, I'm here," she said, and knew her reaction was too strong when Andy averted his eyes and did a kind of shimmy.

"Never mind. You don't know baseball and stuff."

For six months after Chris died, Rachel had read the sports page of the newspaper. But Andy didn't like talking baseball statistics with her any more than he liked her pitching. She was raising a sexist son, that was the long and short of it, she thought, making a mental bid for humor. But she'd always felt she'd failed. She couldn't take the place of Chris. Who knew what Chris and Andy had talked about, joked about in the yard after dinner all those times they threw the ball around? She knew what Andy was getting at, and it had little to do with baseball. He was just a ten-year-old expressing loss.

"Jake's not here?" Andy asked after they'd gotten closer to the picnic area.

"Jake is not in the Boosters," Leora said, but it was without her old prejudice and stiffness. Rachel looked over at her in surprise.

Leora added, "He has to work a lot. He has an

important job working for the judge, and he doesn't have time for the Boosters.''

Rachel's mouth gaped.

"You're going to catch a fly in that mouth of yours, Rachel, if you don't find a way to shut it,'' Leora said briskly, winking at Andy. ''Remember, you're in the country now. No sense attracting bugs.''

Andy chortled. Then he spotted a friend and was off like a shot, his little tackle box and fishing pole in his hand.

Rachel and Leora called greetings to the others, then found a table that was unoccupied. Rachel pulled the lid off the picnic basket, and unpacked a container of cut-up melon. Leora put a hand on her arm. ''Andy loves being around Jake. You can see that, can't you?''

Rachel felt herself flush, and she occupied herself with unpacking the sandwiches. ''Of course I can. They both like that infernal baseball, don't they?''

''I think there's more to it than that. Face it, Andy needs a man.''

Rachel looked up at her mother-in-law. ''I thought you hated Jake.''

Leora colored a little, the made-up spot of pink on her cheek getting a little broader, more natural looking. ''I never said I hated him.''

''But—''

''No buts, Rachel. Now, let's get this food ready.'' She didn't look at Rachel as she busied herself setting up a rather elaborate place setting.

Rachel was quiet, thinking. She assumed Jake's kindness to her family when Andy had been injured was what had caused this softening of Leora's attitude. Leora loved Andy more than anything or any-one in the world. But there was something about the way Leora wouldn't meet her eyes...

She'd had the sensation before, that Leora knew who Andy's father really was. If so, they should discuss it, get it out into the open. How wonderful it would be to talk about Jake with someone she trusted. How wonderful to say she had these feelings...

She choked suddenly and took a quick sip of lemonade from a paper cup. What if Leora didn't know? How could she tell her mother-in-law that her precious grandson was not Chris's flesh and blood? Leora's being fair to Jake, allowing him to coach her grandson, be a role model for Andy was a far cry from wanting him in their family life.

No, she had to go it alone. Her secret had been kept for a decade; it could be kept a good while longer.

She couldn't seem to stop thinking about Jake. She and Jake had talked some about the crime; he'd stopped into her office on Wednesday after his check-in with Charlie. Her door had been open, and he'd stayed a good distance away from her. But they'd talked. Someone was setting him up, trying to make sure the police still believed Jake had killed Joann Floutz, but who? There were simply no suspects.

Now Andy brought his friend Josh over to eat with them, and Rachel relaxed, absorbing their happy chatter. Almost against her will, the pleasant day started to seep into her skin. It was hot in the sun, cool under the pines. The pines in the picnic area had been planted fifty years ago and had lost their lower

needles. It was a green-dark room under them, carpeted with needles, their thick, acid mulch insuring
that no undergrowth snagged at clothing. The shelter
house in the distance sported a beautiful stone chim-
ney, solid and sure; it had been built by the townsfolk
as part of a W.P.A. project in the Great Depression.
The pond had been dredged and deepened then, too.
It was a beautiful, peaceful place.

"Rachel! Come join us." Barb Thomas waved her
over.

Andy and Josh decided they'd rather fish than sit
with the adults, so, carrying a last glass of lemonade
and a plastic bag full of cookies, Rachel and Leora
joined their neighbors.

They talked in a quiet, casual fashion. The kids
were all down by the pond, and the talk was mostly
about the children and the Boosters' plans for a charity peanut sale at the fall parade.

There was a little commotion as Travis Bremmer
arrived. He was an hour late, and his wife trailed him
with David and their daughter. The children went
down to the pond area as Travis called jovial greetings in a very loud, booming voice. The low hum of
voices changed, and the sense of peace was gone.

Gary Herman jumped up and hurried over to
Travis. Doubtless getting ready to conduct very important Booster business, Rachel thought uncharita-
bly. Next to her, Leora made an unladylike snort.

Rachel looked at her in surprise.

Leora fiddled with the strap of her purse and spoke
in a low tone only Rachel could hear. "Well, Rachel,
he is an idiot. Bremmer, I mean. Herman is, too. The
blood's thin in that one. And the way they go on and

on about the Boosters, hogging the presidency... Oh, forget it.''

Rachel fought the urge to smile a little. Once, Leora and her father had cared about the chamber of commerce just as passionately, and they'd ''hogged'' the presidency of *that* organization between them for over twenty years. She'd often noted in her work as a counselor that people criticized in others the faults they themselves had.

Gary and Travis turned toward them, and Barb sucked in her breath.

The sound captured Rachel's attention. ''What is it, Barb?''

She looked embarrassed and troubled. ''A few of the men, especially Travis and Gary, want to have an informal meeting to talk about Jake Monroe.''

Shock dried Rachel's throat. ''Here? Now? Why didn't you say something before?''

''Because I knew how you felt about Jake. When I saw Gary here and not Travis, I figured maybe Travis wasn't coming. You know Gary's just a side-kick, he'd never start something on his own. I thought it would be okay.''

Travis stepped between their table and another. ''We're going to have a short business meeting,'' he announced.

''This is a picnic,'' Rachel said quickly. ''Not a business meeting.''

''We've got to decide what to do about Jake Monroe,'' Travis said. ''I'm calling a special meeting.''

Rachel started to stand. Leora put out her hand, staying her. ''Point of order, Mr. President,'' Leora said. ''The bylaws of the Boosters don't allow the calling of a special meeting without written notification to all the officers and an agenda printed and posted.'' She said the words calmly, as if they were discussing mundane business.

Travis looked nonplussed and shoved his hands in his pockets. Gary Herman turned red.

Leora's mouth was pursed but her gaze was steady.

Rachel's heart surged. From all those years leading the chamber of commerce, her mother-in-law had obviously learned her Robert's Rules of Order.

Travis turned an irritated face to Leora.

''Well, it's an emergency meeting, not a special meeting,'' he said tightly. Rachel noticed he was clenching and unclenching the hand he had in his pocket. He was nervous, and that seemed out of character for the man. From what she knew of Travis, he relished scenes like this one.

''Point of order, Mr. President.'' Leora straightened her spine. ''There is no provision in the bylaws for an emergency meeting.'' She didn't smile, but Rachel suddenly realized from the gleam in her eye that Leora was enjoying herself.

She knew her mother-in-law was tough; she'd been the driving force behind Drewers, even when Chris had been alive. She'd never admit defeat, not even when the chain stores and the mall outside of Grange had ruined most of the hometown merchants. Rachel felt a fierce stab of pride in her.

Gary Herman stood up. ''Leora, we've got to listen to Travis.''

''Not as president of the Downtown Boosters. He doesn't speak for us or for the organization.''

Barb shot a concerned look Rachel's way as the other adults began a low murmuring.

Gary looked for a moment as though he were going to explode. Finally, he said in a tight voice, "Look. It was one thing for him to be in town working for the judge with Rachel watching him." He paused until he had the eye of every adult present. "But now there's been another robbery, and he's a suspect. We've got the kids to think of."

Rachel felt her heart sink as she heard sounds of assent from the other parents.

Travis was nodding vigorously. "We've tried to be fair—"

Rachel jumped up. "The hell you have!"

Travis nodded at her as if he'd been expecting the outburst. "You see how just the mention of his name is causing all this trouble at a small-town picnic. We got along so well before he came back."

Rachel was so outraged she almost sputtered. Grange was a nice place to live and most people were decent. But people were no better or worse in Grange than anywhere else. Rachel looked around, her heart sinking. Perhaps the people in Grange were worse than others in their rush to judgment.

Alva Turner spoke up. "I took my boy off the baseball team a long time ago, and I've never regretted my decision. Jake Monroe is entitled to his job until the judge sees the light or until Monroe gets caught. I for one don't think it'll be a long time before that happens. But our children are what's important here."

Travis nodded. "Let's face it, Jake's been a loser at everything he's ever tried. He got caught once and he was almost caught the other night."

Gary nodded vigorously.

Rachel felt hot tears of rage pricking her eyelids.

But she knew she wouldn't help Jake with an impassioned defense; most of the town probably thought she lacked good judgment when it came to Jake.

"Just a minute," Barb Thomas said thoughtfully. "Has it ever occurred to anyone to wonder why, if Jake Monroe is such a bad guy, the judge keeps him on and Reverend Carson thinks so much of him?"

There was silence for a moment, and Rachel shot Barb a look of thanks.

Travis started to speak, his tone unexpectedly mild. Persuasive, as though he'd read the indecision of the crowd. But those fists in his pockets were still clenching and unclenching. She knew the man needed to feel powerful, and he'd obviously had it in for Jake since they were kids. He said, "Look, it's my opinion he's guilty. I'm just trying to protect this town, our young people, from an evil influence. Who wants to take a chance with their kids?"

Rachel's stomach rolled as she saw the indecision on most faces, and then a few nods.

Ohmygod, do something! she thought. When she spoke, her voice was shakier than she'd planned. "Andy will be on that team if there's only one player."

Gary turned to her. "Rachel, how can you take that chance? What would Chris say if he knew his son was hanging around that guy?"

A couple of people gasped, and Rachel struggled again with her voice. "How dare you," she finally said. Beside her, Leora took her hand, but Rachel hardly noticed the pressure. "Chris was good and decent and he didn't play the self-righteous ass and he didn't judge people."

Barb said, "Rachel, please don't get so upset."

But Rachel heard the plea only dimly. She wanted to scream at the people around her. Gary and Travis had been leaders in town only because most people didn't want the work of running civic organizations. The two hadn't garnered much respect. Until now.

One of the parents said slowly, "If it were just me, I'd give the fellow a chance. But ever since that robbery, well, there's my child to think about."

Rachel's eyes filled with angry tears. Through them, she looked around at faces she'd known since childhood. Many of the parents had been classmates of hers and Jake's. Some looked uneasy; a couple of the mothers looked at their hands. Most looked sad. Many looked determined.

"Mom?" Rachel looked down to see that Andy had joined them, along with a couple of the other kids, all holding fishing poles. A tiny fish flopped around in Andy's bucket.

"The coaching is the thing," one of the other parents said. "Jake shouldn't be around our children."

"Mom?" Andy repeated. "What are they saying about Jake?" His voice was high and tight and worried.

"Come on," Rachel said to Leora and Andy. She wanted to stay and defend Jake, but she needed to get her son away in case this conversation got ugly. He idolized Jake; she didn't want him to hear the worry and fear in the voices of the parents, nor the triumphant venom in Travis's. "We're going. Away from narrow-minded people."

She did her best to keep her spine straight as she and her family went back to their picnic table. A low buzz of conversation went on behind her as she and

Leora silently packed up their things. Andy asked at one point what was going on, but Rachel asked him to wait. She'd burst into tears if she told him here, and she didn't want to do that in front of Gary Herman or Travis Bremmer.

Finally, they were done packing and they headed for the cars. When they were almost there, Andy said, "Well, I waited. So will you tell me why we have to go home?"

Rachel and Leora glanced at each other. Leora said, "Why don't I go on ahead to the car? Come when you're done here, Rachel."

Rachel nodded. She and Andy sat down on a concrete bench that had been crafted to look like a log. "They were talking about Jake," she said gently.

"They don't like him. I could tell." There was pain in her son's voice. "Why don't they like him? He's a cool coach, he never gets mad and stuff the way Ray's dad always did if we goofed up. He knows everything about baseball but he doesn't care if you choke up on the bat or miss the double plays. He says it's only a game and we're just learning and we should have fun. Jake is…" He stopped, obviously thinking hard. "Well, he's cool."

Rachel put her arm around him. If things had gone as planned, Andy would never have had to hear this story about Jake. She'd managed to sidestep the issue when Travis Bremmer and Alva Turner had pulled their children from the team early in the season.

But Jake had become a part of her son's life. And Rachel had always held to the belief that kids were ready to hear things when they asked the questions. So she told him about knowing Jake when they were younger, and how a lot of people blamed Jake for the bad things his father, Big Jake, did.

Andy's forehead creased in concentration. "That's not fair."

"No," she said as gently as she could. "It's not fair, but sometimes life isn't fair."

"So Jake didn't have any friends?"

"Not too many," Rachel said, her voice almost a whisper. "Until me. I was his friend."

Andy said, "There was this kid, Joey Norris, who didn't have too many friends in first grade because he used to have accidents and pee in the classroom. And Zach Broward has some friends but they call him blubber buns." He paused. "Zach is okay, though. He likes science. We talked about the stars once, and he told me how they make pictures in the sky. He's a friend of mine."

Rachel smiled at him a little. Andy was a terrific boy. She knew he was kind to others, and she was more proud of that than all his good grades and athletic prowess. "It's just like I always told you. Kids are mean to any other kid they think is different. And Jake had a father who didn't take care of the animals on his farm, and stole things from the shops in town. Jake didn't have nice clothes or lunch money, and all those things made him different. So maybe you can imagine how Jake felt."

"Sure." Andy nodded his head vigorously. "So those parents don't like him because he was like Zach. They don't like him because he didn't have friends when he was a little kid. Weird." Andy's forehead wrinkled again.

Rachel took a deep breath, because now came the hard part. "That's not really why they don't like

Jake." She explained to Andy that Jake had worked for Joann Floutz. "Someone pushed Mrs. Floutz off a balcony and a lot of people thought Jake did it because he was there that day. Mrs. Floutz—"

"Died," Andy finished for her.

"Yes. How did you know?"

"The kids talked about it a long time ago. They said how Jake pushed that lady and she died." There was a small silence. "But I don't think he'd do something mean like that."

"He didn't push her," Rachel said firmly. "But people thought he did."

Andy grew more serious, and he drew up a knee and studied it. Rachel waited. Finally, her son said, "Danny Turner told us all about it after his mom took him off the team. He said his mom said Jake is a murdering person and so Danny couldn't be on the team. I said Jake was cool and Danny said Jake wasn't cool because he was that murdering person." His voice had slowed.

Rachel gave his shoulders a squeeze. "Why didn't you tell me about this?"

He turned dark eyes on her. "I was afraid if you found out that they said Jake was a murdering person, you wouldn't let me play baseball. I *have* to play baseball."

The squeeze turned into a hug as Rachel swallowed sudden tears. "We could have talked about it. I've always told you we can talk about anything that's bothering you."

There was a long silence. Then Andy said, "I didn't want you to take me away from Jake."

The tears threatened to spill over, but she swallowed them down. She had to be strong for her son. She had to think about Andy.

Andy said, "Some of the other parents were taking their kids off the team, and I know how you always are about safety, like walking my bike when I cross the streets, so—" He cut himself off and shrugged. "But it's weird. I knew I was safe on the team. Like I just kind of *know* Jake didn't push that lady off that balcony. So why doesn't anybody else know?"

Rachel knew that Andy couldn't possibly grasp the complex emotions of this ten-year-old crime. But he'd grasped one essential fact right away. Jake was innocent. "Some people prefer to believe the worst about people."

"Why?"

She sighed. "Oh, for a lot of reasons, I guess. Because they know they've done some wrong things, too, and maybe they feel their wrong isn't so bad if they can compare themselves to someone else they think is worse." She thought of Travis. "Or maybe they just like to feel important, and making someone else feel bad makes them feel important."

"That's pretty dumb," Andy said very solemnly.

Rachel gave him another squeeze. "Yeah, it is, isn't it?" She hesitated, not really wanting to tell him about the robbery and the new suspicions of the townspeople. But here, alone under the trees, seemed as good a time as any. So she told him about the robbery, and the man loosely fitting Jake's description seen running away from the house. "But we always lock our house, so we're safe. The police will get the real robber," she finished.

Andy thought about that for a few moments. Then

he said, "If anyone says something bad about Jake, I'll punch them in the nose."

Aside from a couple of shoving matches when he was much younger, Andy hadn't ever been in a fist-fight. Heck, Andy never even *talked* about being in a fistfight. "That's not going to solve anything," she said gently.

"Somebody's gotta stand up for Jake!"

"I do. I try, anyway. But people believe bad things sometimes, and you have to show them by example you're right."

Andy was thoughtful for a few moments. Then he said in a hopeful voice, "So I get to stay on the team?"

"Of course, as long as there's a team, you'll be on it." She hugged him, then, a good, fierce hug.

A few minutes later, she and Andy headed toward the car. Andy was quiet and pensive, and Rachel decided to let him work some of this out on his own. But it was obvious that her son had learned some painful things about how people could behave.

Damn Travis for teaching the lesson.

Rachel couldn't help worrying. She didn't want Andy to get in a fight, have his nose bloodied defending Jake. She didn't want him to lose his friends. She'd tried so hard to protect him.

It was so...unfair. The word seemed inadequate, but it was the only one that fit. Unfair. Unfair!

She could feel time running out. The robber, who-ever he was, had upped the stakes. Because, if there were more robberies, sooner or later, Jake would be back in prison by popular demand. All his P.O. would need was some little bit of evidence that pointed his way, just a small excuse...

Would Jake have the time to clear his name?

And if he didn't, if he was returned to prison...
Well, just how old would her son have to be to handle the news that his father would be in prison for the next fifteen years?

THAT NIGHT, Jake sat on the bench in the garden of the rectory and told himself not to lose heart.

Earlier that evening, after receiving a contingent of "concerned parents" consisting of Alva Turner, Gary Herman and Travis Bremmer, Jake had known what had to be done, though he hadn't given the group the satisfaction of hearing him say so.

He'd been standing there listening, absorbing their words like a kick in the gut, when Reverend Carson had come up the stairs. Carson had listened, too, and then suggested the group go home. They'd finally left.

Carson, of course, had wanted to come in and talk. Jake had been rude. He didn't want to talk.

Tomorrow he'd give Carson his letter of resignation as coach of the baseball team. It was a little thing, he told himself, small in comparison with the other issues in his life. His need to clear his name. His job and his desire to go to law school. His longing for Rachel, the ache in his bones when he thought about loving her.

So coaching ought to be a small thing. But it hurt like hell. Not to see Andy again, to help him with his swing, to pull down his cap over his eyes, to shadowbox and clap the kid on the shoulder...

For Andy's sake he had to quit.

He leaned forward and clasped his hands between his knees, thinking. The backyard looked gray, almost silvery. It was high summer, and those big white flowers that only bloomed at night were scenting the air with their distinctive perfume. For the moment at least, he was free, free to roam in a garden at night.

The back door opened, and Reverend Carson came out, dressed in a pair of sagging jeans and a T-shirt. Jake tensed. The guy would want to talk again, and Jake wasn't in the mood. But he was good and trapped as Carson made his way down the path toward him.

"I couldn't sleep," Carson said as he got close to Jake. "You, too?"

Jake shrugged. Carson had told the police Jake was out here in the garden nearly every night, giving him an alibi of sorts as to why the police had found him out here the night of the robbery.

"Mind if I join you?"

Jake considered refusing, then said, "The garden belongs to you."

Carson sat next to him on the bench.

Jake said suddenly, "What's the name of that big white flower, the vine that only blooms at night?"

"Ah. The one with that scent. It's moonflower, related to morning glory. But it only blooms at night because it's pollinated by moths. Actually, it doesn't always bloom in this climate. But I babied those plants and gave them a head start on life under lights indoors." There was a pause. "I've always felt that if you give things the right conditions, with a little blessing, most do all right."

Ah, hell, Jake thought. He'd planned to forestall a lecture, and Carson had managed to sneak one up on him anyway. He debated how long it would be before he could escape upstairs to his apartment.

"Those moonflowers are like people," Carson said now.

"I got the point," Jake said dryly.

Carson chuckled. "A bit too obvious, huh?" He stretched out his legs. "But you've got to admit, Jake, you've done well here. You have a job and an apartment and friends."

That was true, Jake thought in some surprise. Once, his only ally had been Rachel, now he could count the judge and the reverend as friends. But that group of parents tonight... He leaned back on the bench and closed his eyes. He'd been protecting himself against that kind of hurt all his life. Would it ever end?

As if he could read Jake's thoughts, Carson said, "When people are unfair to you, you just have to keep doing what's right."

"That's never worked. All my life, I've tried—" He cut himself off. He wasn't going to sit in this garden and bare his soul.

"You haven't been blessed, have you?"

Jake gave a bitter chuckle.

"All the more reason for you to stay on the team."

"I told the parents I wasn't quitting. You heard me tonight."

"Ah, but I know you. You're planning to quit, aren't you?"

"Yes."

"You can't do that," Carson said firmly. "You can't give in to this kind of pressure."

Jake hesitated, wondering if he should confide in the reverend. *Take a chance.* He heard Rachel as if she'd spoken. "It's because of the kids," he said finally. "Andy. I don't want them—him to suffer because of a bunch of town bigots."

Reverend Carson thought for a moment. "I wonder, when it's all said and done, how many families will actually take their children off the team. Once they've had a chance to think about it."

"It doesn't matter now."

"It does. That's why I'm not accepting your resignation."

"What? It's a *baseball team.* I can resign if I want to."

Carson smiled. "Not really. I'm in charge, and you signed papers."

Jake could have laughed. He knew full well that the paperwork he'd signed for insurance purposes didn't mean he couldn't resign. "I don't even go to church."

"I'm working on that," Carson said, still smiling.

That stopped Jake short. "You are? You haven't said a word to me about coming to church."

"I'm working on it," Carson repeated.

Jake decided not to ask how. He'd sure missed in his initial judgment of Carson as a flighty do-gooder. The guy might be a do-gooder, but he was anything but flighty. For a second, Jake felt something, some kind of finger down his spine that was downright otherworldly. He shook his head. He was going nuts in this town. He'd managed to stay sane in the joint only to go nuts back in Grange.

But he realized he felt better. Carson next to him was a warm presence. He could now view the contingent of parents as merely a small-minded group of people. "I'll think about what's best for the team," he said to Carson.

"Okay. And if you really decide quitting's best for the team, then I'll tear up those papers." The reverend paused. "But if you're thinking about Andy Drewer and what's best for him, you'll stay on. The kid's been doing pretty well since his dad died. Rachel has seen to that. But he needs a man around. All kids do better with a father figure, and I've watched you. You're it, Jake, whether you like it or not."

At Carson's words, the funniest surge went through Jake, a kind of tight-gut fondness for Andy, a sense of real responsibility for another person. That responsibility shook him.

"Do you think it would be good for Andy to see that you quit whenever it's the easiest way for you?"

"I don't do that!"

"No. You don't." The reverend's words were measured. "And that's an admirable trait. One I think you ought to show Andy."

Jake paused, and then repeated, "I'll think about it."

"Good."

For a few minutes they were silent. Jake looked at the sky, where a few stars shone through wispy clouds. He looked at the moonflower vine, the dish-shaped flowers glowing in the night. He looked at the outlines of the rosebushes. He always felt loose out here. He'd always liked the wild places, but he was coming to see that a garden made by a person could be a very peaceful place.

Carson was quiet beside him, but Jake felt little tension now. The ugly scene in his doorway was fad-

ing. He finally said, "I can feel time running out.
That's what—" He stopped and then just let it out.
"That's what scares me. With this robbery, I can feel
that I don't have too much time to clear my name.
Somebody's setting me up. I'd thought the killer was
Ralph Floutz, but it probably isn't."

"Why not?" Carson's voice was still measured,
as if they had all night to talk.

Jake thought with wonder that perhaps they did.
That if he wanted to stay up all night and share his
plans, his fears, Carson would stay with him and listen. "Well, I figure whoever pulled that robbery was
trying to put the blame on me. So he has to be the
killer. Ralph Floutz had an alibi."

"Oh."

"I wanted to believe Ralph did it, but I met with
the guy one time, and something didn't ring true. He
loved Joann. I felt it."

"A lot of people have been killed by those who
love them."

Jake stretched out, getting more comfortable on
the hard bench. "I know. But things were looking
good for them. After all, they'd been married twelve
years and she was pregnant with their first child
when she died."

He sensed Carson's sudden stillness, heard his
sharp intake of breath. He stiffened slightly himself,
though he didn't know what he'd said. Of course, the
fact that Joann was pregnant added to the heinous-
ness of the crime, but he'd never felt judged by
Carson before. "She was pregnant when she died,"
Jake said again, waiting for a reaction.

Carson gripped his arm hard, the suddenness of

the movement sending Jake instinctively to his feet. He realized his mistake and sank back on the bench.

"Are you sure she was pregnant?" Carson asked. The pressure on Jake's arm increased.

"The coroner testified to it at my trial. Three months pregnant."

"That can't be, Jake."

What? *What?* "What can't be? Tell me." Jake could feel his blood pounding in his veins.

"I had no idea," the reverend said, his voice intent in a way Jake had never heard it. "Listen to me. You know I've only been here four years. Last year I was cleaning out my old files, the ones left by Reverend Ogden, and even the ones left by Reverend Sandleton. You might recall Reverend Sandleton died about two weeks before your trial."

Jake hadn't known that. While he was preparing for his trial, the death of one of the town's ministers would have been totally irrelevant.

Carson shook his arm. "Sandleton was counseling Joann Floutz. She was upset, had trouble in her marriage. I saw the paperwork."

Excitement gripped him. "Ralph and Joann were having marital trouble? She was a flirt, but that's all we know. At the trial, Ralph just kept saying how much he loved her."

"But Joann Floutz was murdered, and remember, Sandleton was dead. It took the congregation months to recruit a new minister. Nobody was going through old files at the time of your murder trial to see who was coming in for counseling and why."

Jake told himself not to get excited, though the blood was zipping through his veins. He'd been shot down so many times before. So he forced himself to say, "It doesn't prove anything—"

"Oh yes it does." The reverend took a deep breath. "Joann Floutz was having marital difficulties because her husband was impotent. According to the file, he'd been impotent for years."

The world tilted on its axis. For a moment, Jake's brain refused to function. Then it raced, ideas and theories tumbling so fast through his mind that he couldn't articulate them in words, only feel them. "Then..."

The reverend brought a fist down on one thigh. "Here I was, sitting on evidence in a murder trial, and I never knew it. Joann Floutz was pregnant, but it wasn't her husband's baby. Do you know what that means?" There was a quick pause. "Of course you do. Someone else was the father of Joann Floutz's baby. It means that Joann Floutz had a lover."

CHAPTER TWELVE

RACHEL PULLED ON her robe and dashed down the stairs to answer the doorbell. It was after midnight, and her heart raced at the late summons. She looked through the peephole and her heartbeat picked up some more as she recognized Jake. She yanked open the door.

"Jake. Has something happened?"

"Joann had a lover."

"What?"

"She had a lover. Reverend Carson found out."

"Reverend Carson?" She realized suddenly that her mouth was gaping, and she made herself shut it. "Come in." But trying to calm herself was futile. How could she calm down when Jake was at her door, a coiled tension in his body, a shiny darkness in his eyes?

She led him into the living room, but he didn't sit. Instead, he paced. She stood still, watching him, her hands folded across her breasts. But she felt an almost unbearable excitement. "Okay, tell me everything."

He told her about Reverend Carson looking over an old file, but not knowing its significance. "Oh, Jake," she kept saying. The words sounded lame, but heck, what else could she say?

"I wanted you to be the first to know," he said.

He finally stopped pacing and took a few steps toward her. He studied her face. "A few people have believed in me since I've come home. They've given me a chance. But you were the first, and you were the one who never stopped believing in me."

Those eyes of his. His gaze hit her with such intensity that she suddenly shivered and held her robe more tightly around her. "Yes," she said softly. "I always believed in you."

There was a long pause. Finally, Jake shook his head slightly and said, "Well, I wanted you to know."

"Yes." She didn't know what to say. "Well, why don't you sit down and I'll make us some coffee. We've got a lot to talk about."

"Yeah, we do. Rachel, I need your help. I want to talk about what this could mean."

"Sure. It could mean—" She stopped. It could mean a number of things, she realized. He was looking at her again, and she was suddenly conscious of how she was dressed. Her robe was a modest cotton knit, but it clung in a few places. They were places he'd once seen and touched, but...

But he could never see and touch them again. "I'll just go get dressed and put on some coffee." She gave a shaky laugh. "It'll give me a chance to think."

"Right." His gaze, with the remnants of his excitement in his eyes, flicked over her robe.

She resisted the urge to flee the room, to overreact. Instead, she left with dignity. She hurried when she was upstairs, though, pulling on a pair of shorts and a baggy top. In the bathroom she combed her hair and splashed water on her face. She looked in the mirror. Her color was high and bright, and her eyes sparkled.

Jake could do that to her. He always could.

She gave herself a mental shake as she went back down the hall. He was excited about his case, and she was, too. That was what had brought him over here. If she'd decided it would be better if they weren't even friends, much less...anything else, it seemed that events had overtaken them. She would always be willing to brainstorm with Jake, she would always be willing to help him. So friends they would be.

Once she had coffee made, she felt more in control.

In the living room she persuaded him to sit down on the couch. But he made no move to pick up his cup of coffee. Rachel sat in the armchair. Jake leaned forward, his knees apart, his hands squeezed tightly between them.

She said, "So, tell me what you're thinking."

"One of the things I'm thinking is that maybe Ralph found out she had a lover and got angry and killed her."

"We've discussed that. We thought if he knew about her flirtations with teenagers, he maybe got angry and pushed her."

"But that motivation never worked for me after I met him. The guy didn't have that bad a temper, not from what I observed and was able to find out from Megan. Even if he knew Joann was a flirt, it would take real rage to kill her." His hands tightened. "But this, her having another man's baby, a baby he couldn't give her. This is the kind of thing that could send him into a murdering rage."

He paused. "So I shouldn't discount Ralph. But I'm going in another direction here. Ralph Floutz's alibi was airtight the night that burglary took place a couple of weeks ago. So I'm thinking Joann's lover was both the murderer back then and the burglar a few nights ago."

She nodded, and her skin prickled with goose bumps.

Jake was looking off into space, obviously concentrating. "Here I once thought this was a premeditated crime, that Ralph had killed his wife for the insurance money. Now, look at the emotion here. Ralph can't make love to his wife, but somebody else did. And her lover, well, who knows what made him decide to kill."

A shiver went up Rachel's spine as she thought of Joann Floutz. Joann's betrayal of her husband. How frightened she must have been, carrying a baby that her husband would know wasn't his.

After all, Rachel knew all about being frightened and trying to protect a vulnerable baby. Had Joann feared her husband's reaction? Her lover's? Perhaps she'd told her lover she was pregnant, and in a fit of rage he'd pushed her off that balcony. Had she died clutching her belly, trying to protect the life inside her?

Sudden tears sprang to Rachel's eyes. But she had no idea what kind of woman Joann Floutz had been. If Rachel let herself identify too closely with the dead woman's plight, it wouldn't help Jake reason this out.

"What was she like?" she asked abruptly.

"What was who like?"

"Joann. Was she—well, was she the kind who

would want this baby, no matter what, do you think?''

He seemed to relax finally, and sat back a little as he thought. ''She was quite pretty. Young-looking, and she dressed just provocatively enough to send a kind of message to a guy. You know, she'd wear a pair of slacks and a blouse, and the blouse would just have one too many buttons undone. She was a flirt, but she was careful about it. If she had an affair, my first lawyer wasn't able to turn up anything about it.'' He paused. ''I mean, of course she *did* have an affair, but she'd covered her tracks really well.''

''Did she flirt with older guys?''

''I think if she did, we'd have heard something about her behavior. If it was only kids, they probably wouldn't talk much about it. I mean, the woman used to scare me a little, the way she'd come on to me, but at the same time, I'd tell myself she wasn't really coming on to me, you know. To a nineteen-year-old, it seemed pretty weird to have a thirty-year-old married woman interested in me. But, hell, I don't know.''

''Her lover murdered her.''

He stood up and took a couple of paces. ''What teenager would have the guts to push her from that balcony? But it makes sense. It makes *sense*. After all, whoever did that robbery in town a couple of weeks ago was my age or up to ten years older.'' He turned to look at her. ''Okay, here's what we know. If we discount Ralph, Joann's lover is the only suspect in the murder, and we know his age within ten years, and that he's got dark hair.''

She got to her feet, too, unable to sit. It seemed

they were making progress at last. "So we just need to figure out who her lover was."

"But how are we going to do that?"

She shook her head. "I don't know. Grange isn't that big, but there are a lot of men living here who would be your age or a few years older, assuming we're right and her killer was a young man. Really, what would be the motivation? I work with teenagers. If they get a girl pregnant, there are a lot of options besides murder. They marry the girl. Or she puts the child up for adoption, or raises it herself."

She felt her cheeks color at the parallels to her own story, so she hurried to add, "But in the case of Joann, she was already married, and it would seem as if the guy was off the hook. Nobody would expect a teenage boy to do anything about the baby of a thirty-year-old married woman."

Jake went to the window. The curtains were drawn, but he seemed absently focused on the crack between the drapes, where Rachel could see a sliver of the window. She went up to him and stood next to him, seeing a reflected fragment of his face in the glass.

He said, "There are dozens, probably hundreds of men who were around then and who fit the description. We just need to know more." He shoved his hands in his pockets. "We've always needed to know more."

"We just have to think."

There was a long pause. Finally, he said, "I've thought and thought."

"We'll find a way."

There was another pause. He put a finger up and

slowly traced the edge of her drapes. "You keep saying 'we.'"

Had she? She hadn't realized that. Or perhaps only her heart had realized it. She took a deep breath. "Yes, I guess I have been. I guess I am saying 'we.'"

He looked down at her; she met his eyes. She licked her lips. He watched the motion, and the intentness of his gaze sent desire running through her.

She swallowed. It was getting harder and harder to ignore the pull of this man. She felt a real urge to set things right between them. There were some things she couldn't tell him, but some things she could. She said slowly, "Jake, I want to tell you something. I—well, I wish I'd told you this when you first came back. I owe you an apology. I'm so sorry I didn't give you that alibi you needed ten years ago."

"It's okay." His voice was rough.

The hallway clock ticked. But otherwise there was silence in the living room. The one lamp she'd lit made a pool of light, as if she and Jake were all alone on a vast stage.

"It's not all right. If I'd supported your alibi, you might not have gone to prison." If he hadn't gone to prison, she wouldn't have had to make that bargain with Chris, the bargain that had changed everything.

"We weren't together that night. It would have been a lie for you to tell the police we'd been together. Just as you once said."

Pain squeezed her heart for every lie she'd ever told, and every one she hadn't. "You were right all along. If I'd believed in you, I should have done whatever was necessary. Lied to save an innocent man.''

He shook his head, his mouth hard but his eyes tender. ''I know a lot more nowadays about how the cops work. They would have questioned you in detail about our supposed night together. You would have got some detail different from the story I told. In the end, that alibi wouldn't have stood up. I would have gone to prison anyway, and the whole town would have known that you slept with Jake Monroe.'' He paused. ''I'm glad it happened the way it did.''

She reached out and touched his arm. ''I should have tried. Please forgive me.''

He put his other hand over hers. ''Believe me, I forgave you about two weeks after I went to prison.''

''Two weeks after...'' It was hard to think with his hard, warm palm on hers. It was hard to think with him next to her, with his powerful presence so close. With all her emotions so near the surface. ''But you didn't answer my letters. All along, I thought you were angry with me when you wouldn't answer my letters.'' Memory washed over her.

''Jake, I sent you four letters. I took out a post office box. I'd tell myself to wait a few days, to give the postal service time to deliver those letters, then some time for you to write back. But I could never wait. Each time, I'd go to the post office the very next day after I mailed those letters and go to my box. The box had a little door with a window, and I could look into it and see whether there was anything in there, before I even put the key in. But there was never a letter. Each time I...hoped so hard. I wanted a letter from you so much.''

She didn't even realize she was crying until he put

out his hand and touched her cheek and caught one of her tears on his finger. He lifted his finger and stared at the wetness there.

He whispered, "Please don't cry."

She gulped, trying to stem the flow of tears. "I'm sorry. I just...needed you so much."

He reached out suddenly and grabbed her shoulders. "You didn't need me. Don't you see? I didn't want you to need me."

"I did need you. But you were angry. I knew you had a right to be angry, but it still hurt...that you didn't care about me."

His eyes went bleak. "I was the worst thing that ever happened to you. I was bad for you even before the police came looking for me that night. We couldn't tell your father we were seeing each other, and I knew you hated the secrecy. Then I was sent to prison for manslaughter. You were only eighteen."

His hands gripped her shoulders harder. "I had no life. But *you* had a life. A chance for a good life, and I wanted you to have that chance. So I didn't answer your letters. I wanted you to think I was still angry about the alibi. I wanted you to think I didn't care."

She was shaking her head. "The worst thing in the world for me was thinking you didn't care. I loved you. I needed you to love me, from Grange or prison or anywhere."

"I knew I was doing the right thing. It damn near killed me inside. But I wanted you to have what we'd talked about, what I knew you wanted more than anything else. Not a sterile place like your father had, but a real home. A family."

Rachel's heart lurched. He'd wanted those things,

too. Desperately. A home and a family. But he was right; in that time and place he couldn't have them. So in an act of incredible generosity, he'd given them to her.

And now he didn't even know the boy whose hair he ruffled, the kid who he clapped on the back in encouragement, was his son. "Jake—"

He put a hand on her lips, shushing her gently. "Let me tell you this. I don't want you to think I was angry. When one of your letters came, I would hold it, imagine you writing it, think about what it might say. That you loved me and you'd wait for me. At first, I'd leave your letter around for a few days, just so I knew somebody cared about me. Then that got too hard. I knew if I left your letters in my cell, someday I'd open one. And if I opened one, then I'd answer. I know you, Rachel. If I'd answered those letters, you would have put your life on hold for me for a decade. I couldn't allow that."

He shoved his hand in his pocket and looked away. "So as soon as I got a letter from you, I'd give it to one of the other guys. I'd have him put it in the next batch of mail to be returned to you unopened." He turned to her again, and his gaze seared her. "But never, never think I didn't care."

Her whole body shook at his words. He'd loved her that much! If she'd only known, she could have held the knowledge to her, cherished it...

"You know what?" His eyes searched hers. "I'm glad you didn't lie to the police. It wouldn't have worked, and it would have just...dirtied what we had. I want to remember you as the girl who couldn't lie."

Shame washed over her, thick and hot. She'd kept

so many secrets. She'd had no choice ten years ago. But she'd had one when Jake had first come home. Should she have told him about Andy then? It was too late. How would she explain to Jake now?

And there was still the question that had haunted her since Jake's return. How would she explain to Andy?

Jake, too, had wanted a family. He deserved one. He deserved to know.

She feared that no matter how good her reasons for not telling him had been, he'd hate her if he knew. She reached up and touched his cheek. He went very still. "You're a good man," she said through the urge to break down and sob out her ten-year-old loss and right-up-to-the-present fear.

"Not so good. When I came back and realized you'd done what I wanted—found yourself a decent man and married him, it made me angry. It made me real angry to see how quickly you got on with your life."

"Jake—"

"I'm just a man. No better or worse than any."

"Not true," she said, her voice wobbling uncontrollably. "You're the best…man…I know—"

His mouth came down on hers, sealing the sob that had been about to break forth. He held her gently, but with purpose. He kissed her, and there was an ache in that kiss, as if his throat was tight and she was absorbing that tightness, taking it into herself.

Her throat was tight, too. She was overwhelmed by him. By his generosity. He'd been alone and scared in prison. She knew without asking that her letters were the only ones he'd ever received.

She couldn't help responding to the feel of his

mouth on hers. She knew she shouldn't, that she should pull away. Instead, her mouth accepted his tongue, touched it with her own in a greedy taking. And she gave, too. Of their own volition, her arms went around his waist and she pressed her body to his.

His mouth left hers. His breathing had picked up. "Do you want me?" he asked in a harsh, gritty whisper. He tipped her chin up. "This time, I don't want to hear about responsibilities or your feeling sorry for me. I just want to hear it straight. Yes or no. As a woman to a man. Do you want me?"

She couldn't lie to him anymore. She couldn't make her lips say no. So she took a deep breath and said. "Yes. But Jake—"

Again, he cut off her words. But this time his mouth was not gentle. It molded to hers with bold demand. His arms went around her, and he bent her backward, kissing her mouth and her throat.

Every movement of his tongue sent desire racing through her veins. Every press of his lips, every push of his hips, every movement of his hands sent a signal to the very heart of her. It had been so long. It had been too long, ten years too long.

How long it was now, how many minutes they touched and kissed and touched again, their hands hot, their bodies on fire, how many moans of desire mingled in the still room, she never knew. She was utterly lost. Time had once meant so much. It had no meaning now.

Jake finally dragged his mouth from hers. "Upstairs?" he asked in a harsh whisper.

"Andy..."

"We'll lock the door. And I'll go before morn-

ing.'' He had her hand and he was already pulling
her toward the doorway.

She wanted to go. But Andy... The woman who'd
had to make hard decisions surfaced through the fog
of desire. She knew that no matter how much she
wanted to capture this moment in time without past
or future, she knew that he would leave her bed, that
morning *would* come.

Time didn't stand still anymore. ''We can't,'' she
said, her words barely above a whisper.

''Rachel—''

''I can't.''

He stopped and shut his eyes, and a groan of pure
frustration came from his lips.

He gripped her shoulders. ''Why?''

Her body still trembled. She was so hot she could
feel a flush on her skin. She raised her hands to cup
his cheeks. She said, ''I care about you.''

He shut his eyes for the briefest of seconds. When
he opened them, she was astonished to see how much
emotion she could read in them.

''Then why won't you let me make love to you?''
he asked. ''I know I haven't cleared my name. But
I won't complicate your life. I swear, I'll be gone
before morning. No one will ever know I'm here.''

''I'm not ashamed of you!'' she said fiercely. She
tried to govern her voice. ''I can't tell you why. But
I have my reasons. Please don't ask me what they
are.''

He searched her face. ''I'm asking.''

''I can't tell you. Please. If you care about me at
all, accept that—''

''I know you've got Andy to think about. I know
it wouldn't be good for him to have me in his life,

not while this crime is unresolved. It's about Andy, isn't it?''

She nodded. ''Andy and other things.''

''Just one night, Rachel. Just tonight. Nothing has to change.''

Everything would change. He was offering her a night of love, no strings attached. But there were strings, the connection of a child, the connection of the past. ''I can't. If you care about me as you say you do, you won't push me.''

He looked at her for a long moment. Finally, he said, ''I won't push you tonight.''

Profound relief washed over her. She hadn't lied to Jake, and she'd be able to keep her secret. Just for a while longer. Just until she decided Andy was ready. When she finally told Jake, and he hated her for not telling him sooner, at least he would not have a night of lovemaking to think about, lovemaking that would be the same as another lie.

''Thank you,'' she said softly.

He said little as she led him to the door. But the tension was thick, and she knew he didn't consider the issue closed. She opened the door for him.

He went through it. But as he was moving down the walk, she was unable to help herself, to keep from calling his name. He turned. She said, ''You're going to be able to clear your name. I can feel it. You're getting close.''

There was a long, meaningful pause. ''And then I'll be back. Make no mistake about it, Rachel. I'll be back.''

CHAPTER THIRTEEN

JAKE HAD BEEN LOST in thought and hadn't realized he had visitors until he heard the pounding of feet on the stairs and the sharp knock at the door. It was 10:00 p.m. on a Thursday night, and he'd been immersed in a brief. In fact, he'd been barely aware of the rain beating on the panes of his living-room window, beyond a vague thought that if the rain kept up it would make the ball field muddy come Sunday afternoon.

The clouds had made the evening prematurely dark. His desk lamp had been lit since the storm had started a couple of hours ago.

Still holding his ballpoint pen, Jake answered the door. Two uniformed police officers stood there.

Jake's hands tightened around the pen as his heart started to beat in double time. *Damn. What now?*

"Jake Monroe?" one of them asked.

Jake felt his mouth harden. "I think you already know that."

The older of the two said, "I'm Officer Farrell and this is Officer Lyndhurst."

Jake's hands started to shake, so he shoved them in his pockets. Farrell apparently caught the gesture, as his eyes narrowed. Jake forced himself to speak evenly. "I recognize Lyndhurst from that motion hearing last week. How are you, Officer?"

Lyndhurst shifted his weight to his other foot. "Ah, fine. I, ah, understand the judge ruled in favor of the state, given the research you did. I was kind of surprised at the stuff you came up with."

"The judge pays me to give him an objective analysis. In *that* case, the police were right." He allowed plenty of sarcasm to creep into his tone to keep from showing how rattled he was.

Farrell ignored the conversation. "Mr. Monroe, where were you one hour ago?"

Jake glanced at the clock again, and not until he turned back to the uniformed cop and made eye contact did he realize his motion had looked suspicious. "I've been here since six o'clock. Since I got home from work."

The officer looked around, noting the desk piled high with papers, the plate of crumbs from Jake's sandwich, the wads of paper on the floor.

"Messy place," the officer said.

"Yeah, well, nowadays I get to be messy if I want to." Jake had practiced this tone in the joint—just enough cynicism and belligerence to show you wouldn't be pushed around, just enough deference to make sure a guard didn't have an excuse to break a couple of your bones with a nightstick.

Both officers were looking at his piled desk. The mess should make it obvious he'd been busy working for some time, but Jake felt the sweat begin a slow trickle down his armpits. He'd never get used to cops. Never. He suddenly itched to go outside, despite the rain. In fact, he longed to feel the rain on his face, running down his neck, soaking his jeans. Suddenly, his apartment seemed small and airless.

He fought the sensation of being confined. He

knew the officers were being deliberately quiet, letting him sweat. "Why do you want to know where I've been?" He cursed himself for asking.

"Claire Bartholomew was robbed tonight, about an hour ago."

Jake closed his eyes for a second. "What's that got to do with me?"

"Well, now," Farrell said. "Maybe it doesn't have anything to do with you. If you were here in your apartment as you say, it shouldn't be a problem, should it?" He paused for impact. "I don't suppose anyone can vouch for you being here?"

Alibis, Jake thought bitterly. Would he ever be free of the need for an alibi? "I've been alone."

"No Reverend Carson to vouch for you this time?" Farrell's voice had a little edge. "No Carson to say you're in the garden every flaming night? *Were* you in the garden, Mr. Monroe?"

"No." He straightened his spine. "Am I being arrested?"

"Not yet. Mind if we have a look around?"

Jake hesitated. One part of him said to let them look so they could be on their way. After all, Jake didn't have anything to hide. But ten years in prison had made him cautious. He'd given permission to the police to search the farmhouse ten years ago, and they'd made a whole case out of that tape deck.

And he was being set up by somebody.

He'd been working pretty much nonstop since he got home from work, stopping only to make a sandwich. He hadn't checked through his dresser drawers to see if anyone had planted something in his apartment while he was at work.

"I think," he said slowly, "if you want to search,

you'd better get a warrant. This is still the United States of America. Even a convicted felon has a right or two.'' He heard the bitterness in his voice and thought he caught a flash of sympathy in Lyndhurst's gaze.

Then Lyndhurst looked around Jake. ''Ah, Farrell? His jacket's wet.''

Jake's jacket was slung over the arm of a chair. It was a navy blue poplin, and the rain had made it splotchy dark.

Heat and nausea rushed through Jake. He'd taken out the garbage an hour or so ago. He'd forgotten the quick trip through the driving rain. He looked up and caught Farrell watching him speculatively. If he said so now, he'd only make them think he was fabricating his story, which would make him look more guilty. Carson wasn't home, couldn't support his statement.

There was a short pause, then Farrell said, ''I'm taking this jacket in for evidence. I'm sure you know from your work with the judge, I can confiscate anything I can see in plain sight, even without a warrant.''

It was true. Why in hell hadn't he taken the time to hang up his jacket? Jake was nauseated for real now. ''Are you arresting me?'' he repeated.

Farrell looked him over. ''Your shirt doesn't look wet, but you could have changed. If we look in your bedroom or bathroom, are we going to find wet jeans and a shirt?''

''No!'' *Careful, Jake. Cool it, man.*

Officer Farrell said, ''You willing to stand in a lineup, Mr. Monroe?''

''If my lawyer recommends it. Otherwise, not.''

Farrell's eyes narrowed. "Funny thing. About fifteen minutes ago, Ms. Bartholomew looked at some photos. She picked out your mug shot. She saw the burglar running away."

Running away again. Breaking into occupied properties. Wanting to be seen. "I'm sure if Ms. Bartholomew had any trouble recognizing me, you... helped her a little."

Farrell didn't say a word and Jake knew what was going to happen next.

He kept his cool when they handcuffed him, though it was one of the hardest things he'd ever done. He'd gone willingly with the police ten years ago. He'd have gone willingly this time, too; they didn't need to cuff him. But Farrell hadn't given him a chance. Jake tried to resist the urge to pull his wrists apart, to test the tightness of his bonds. To fight being shackled.

"I suppose Ralph Floutz has an alibi?" He cursed himself for speaking, because he heard the trembling in his voice. He couldn't stop it. The cuffs had done it. Now he just concentrated on trying to keep from bawling out his rage. And his fear.

Farrell smiled. "Airtight."

Jake had known it would be. He didn't think it was Ralph who was setting him up anyway, but—

Lyndhurst spoke up. Familiar words. Sickly familiar. "You're being arrested for burglary of an occupied dwelling. You have the right to remain silent. If you give up the right to remain silent, anything you say can and will be used against you in a court of law. You have the right to an attorney. If you can't afford an attorney, one will be appointed for you..."

Jake shut his eyes, trying to block out that voice.

Rachel, he thought. *Please come. I can feel the walls closing in on me for real, and this time, I don't think I can go it alone.*

SHE CAME at ten o'clock the next morning. He felt filthy, greasy and damp from his night in a cell. Sometime during the wee hours of the morning, a drunk in the next holding tank had vomited, and Jake imagined he could smell the stench of it on his own clothing.

She looked wonderful, all buttoned into a butter yellow linen jacket, her cheeks pale with worry. "Why didn't you call me right away? For heaven's sake, why didn't you call last night? I had to hear this from Charlie this morning."

He shrugged. He'd needed her desperately, but something—pride, he guessed—had kept him from calling her last night. The vestige of an old shame, maybe. Being rescued by Rachel like a stray cat was not a scenario he wanted to play out, even now. Even when he was desperate.

But she'd come for him anyway, and he was so glad to see her he pushed aside his pride. "My lawyer was going to get me out of here sometime this morning," he explained as he was signing for his wallet and keys. He'd hired a young but trustworthy local attorney, whose work he'd admired when the lawyer had appeared in front of Judge Randall.

"I didn't want you to see me like this," he admitted when he was free at last. He stood on the steps of the jail and breathed in great gulps of fresh air.

"Oh, Jake."

"I look like hell. I need a shave and a shower." He remembered holding her in his arms, how fresh she'd smelled. How vibrant and pliant her body had been. "I know I smell bad." He paused. "But it's not only that. Mostly, I didn't want you to think I was weak."

"Oh, Jake," she repeated, and she put her arms around him right there on a public street and held him fiercely.

He felt her strength flowing into him, as if she was giving it to him, and he took it greedily. To hell with being strong. This was love, to need another human being, sometimes to take from that love. It only required a couple of seconds for him to realize with a certain astonishment that instead of feeling weak, he felt strong.

Her voice was muffled by his chest. "My God, if I'd spent that night in a cell, knowing they were trying to pin a robbery on me, I think I would have...gone crazy."

A flash of pride went through him. He *hadn't* gone crazy, even though he'd been confined to a small, dark cell. It would be easy to go crazy. Many did in the joint. You could hear them at night, calling, crying, singing, their voices echoing in the hallways.

"I'm keeping it together for now. But I *can't* go back," he said, and he held her in a bone-crushing grip.

After a moment, she pulled away. She took a step up so that she could reach out and cradle his cheeks with both hands. "Listen to me, Jake. We're going to find this guy."

He was at eye level with her. The fierceness of her gaze felt good somewhere in his soul. But he couldn't ignore reality. He was in deep trouble. But he knew she was scared, and he needed to prop her up, meet her needs as she was meeting his. "I know we're going to get him, too," he lied.

"I'm making a list of every man who is thirty to forty years old, dark-haired and living in Grange ten years ago. I'm going to use the phone book, the newspaper, my high-school yearbook. Anything to jog my memory."

"But you don't even know what you're looking for."

"I realize that. But I have to do something, Jake!"

Because time was running out. She knew it the same as he did. "There must be two hundred guys who fit that description."

"Do you have a better idea?"

"No," he admitted. "I'll help you."

"Good."

He looked into her eyes, loving her, not caring if his feelings showed. He must have shown more than gratitude, more than friendship, because her cheeks went bright red.

She turned from him. "We don't have much time."

He knew that. His gut had been tight with the knowledge ever since ten o'clock last night. "I've got time before my trial. Unless Charlie Malchek's got a parole-violation hearing sooner."

"I hate to have to tell you this. Charlie set the wheels in motion this morning. He's added in everything he can, even some of those old incidents when I decided not to report your violations. Your parole hearing is in two weeks. If you don't have some evidence in your favor, you'll be sent back to prison to serve the rest of your sentence."

The rest of his sentence amounted to fifteen more

years. Jake made himself face the possibility. He told himself that he was strong, he could—

He couldn't. He couldn't go back there. Not this time. Not ever again.

"Oh, Jake, I'm so scared."

Me, too, he thought. Me, too.

JAKE PAUSED on the steps of the church. He realized he should have come earlier, before the opening hymn. Now he'd end up making a grand entrance, when he'd have liked to slip in unnoticed and sit at the back of the church.

He knew he was making excuses, looking for a way not to go into the church. He'd never even seen the inside of a church, except on television. Big Jake had never had any use for religion. Except for his belief in the numbing effect of a bottle of booze, Big Jake had never believed in anything.

Jake had never believed in a higher power, that was for sure. If God had been around ten years ago, why would he have sent Jake to prison?

He put a finger inside the collar of his dress shirt, pulling a little. Then he loosened his tie. He could hardly breathe in the thing, which was really strange because he was used to a shirt and tie by now—it was his everyday work wardrobe.

Even as he asked himself what he was doing here, even as he told himself to go on back to the parsonage and walk in the garden if he needed to quell his restlessness, Jake walked up those steps.

He needed to believe in something. He was in trouble, and he needed help. He needed inner strength, he needed inner peace to face what he'd be facing in less than two weeks. Loving Rachel had made him not only physically hungry, but spiritually hungry as well.

He and Rachel had been working for the last two nights, and they had a hundred and twenty names on Rachel's list. They still had no motive, but tonight after Andy was in bed, they'd start the arduous task of checking out alibis and crossing off names.

They didn't have enough time. He knew it. He suspected she knew it, too. Last night, he'd been unable to bear her fear, the almost frantic concentration she brought to bear on their task.

He'd kissed her right before he'd left, but gently. He hadn't wanted to upset her, only offer her comfort. And he'd taken comfort in return.

Now he walked up the steps of the church and opened the door.

The choir was singing an old hymn to the accompaniment of an organ. Jake didn't know the words, but he recognized the tune from somewhere. Probably television again.

The place was crowded. He moved alone down the aisle, his feet feeling heavy and too big for his shoes.

People were turning to look at him.

He kept his eyes roving, looking for an empty seat, not meeting the curious glances of so many faces.

He paused at the end of one of the pews. There was a place in the middle, but he didn't relish climbing over bodies to get to it. Then people shifted, and a place opened up for him right next to the aisle.

He took the seat.

There were a couple of coughs.

Reverend Carson was taking the podium, and Jake stared straight ahead, toward the minister.

Carson smiled at him. Abruptly, Jake remembered a night in the parsonage garden. *I don't even go to church.*

I'm working on that.

You haven't said a word to me about coming to church.

I'm working on it.

Jake smiled back.

As the service continued, Jake opened his hymnal when directed to do so. He listened to a sermon about boundless, unconditional love. But feeling the stares around him, feeling the whispering, he told himself the sermon was a crock, that he'd made a mistake coming here this morning.

And then something started to change. The words started to mean something. He stared at the images of suffering and triumph on the walls, and a curious kind of peace came over him.

It shook him, that feeling, but he reveled in it too. He let that good feeling, that ease, creep over him, let in the voice that said, *It's going to work out. It's going to be all right.*

And in the next moment, he caught Rachel's eye. She was clear across the church. His own gaze drank her in, the classy rosy-pink sheath, the little designer purse. Her sleek cap of American-girl blond hair. Andy waved frantically, trying to get his attention.

Leora looked over at him, too, an odd, intent, questioning frown on her face.

Rachel smiled.

Jake believed, suddenly, in a higher power. In God, he guessed with astonishment. Because God hadn't left him empty-handed all those years.

Surely, only God could give him someone as good

as Rachel to love. Only God could have kept that image so vivid in prison. The memory of her, the one good thing in his life, had been his to hold on to, to cherish.

She'd insisted he trust people. She'd made him think, decide not to be so bitter. She'd made him reach out to others. Her love had made him a better person. Inside, where it counted, where nobody could take it from you.

Their gazes met and meshed, and Jake tried to convey his love for her. She blushed and looked down. She'd never told him what her feelings were. She'd treated him strictly as a friend, had accepted but not shared in his gentle kiss last night.

His head said that was better, that he might not be able to save himself, that she was better off not loving him. His heart told him something different.

As SOON AS RACHEL opened the door that night, she could see that Leora was upset. Startled, Rachel said, "What's wrong? Has something happened?"

Leora's usually perfectly coiffed hair was in disarray. She rather self-consciously tried to pat it into place. Her motions made the teased and sprayed mass look even worse. "Nothing's happened."

But in addition to the hair, her color was too high. Rachel held the door open, nudged two of the cats back with the toe of her sneaker as Leora marched past, obviously a woman on a mission.

Rachel said, "Well, I guess I'll just see if Andy's ready to go home with you—"

"I'm ready," her son called, running into the hallway, Peppy on his heels. Leora bent to hug him, and the dog tried to wiggle between them. When Leora straightened, Rachel was startled to see her mother-in-law's eyes wet with tears.

Her instincts hadn't been wrong; something was the matter. "I've got to talk to your grandma," she said to Andy. "Can you go outside and play with Peppy for a few minutes?"

Andy ignored her. "Did you bring Peppy's treat?" he asked his grandmother.

Leora dug in her purse for the little can of dog treats she'd taken to keeping there. Peppy sat expectantly, his nose in the air, quivering as if he could already smell the tempting aroma of liver. But instead of carefully extracting a treat from the can, Leora held the container out to Andy. "Here. Why don't you go in the backyard and try to teach Peppy a few tricks? You can use these for rewards."

"The whole can? I can have the whole can?" In almost as much puzzlement as Rachel, Andy looked at his grandmother. "I thought you said it wasn't healthy to let Peppy have too many snacks. That if he had the good stuff, he wouldn't eat his dog food."

"Go on now," she said briskly, shooing him away.

"It won't hurt him if I give them all to him?"

"It won't hurt him," Rachel said. "Go, and I'll call you when Grandma is ready to leave."

Andy shrugged a little and, holding out a treat, told Peppy to heel. Instead, the dog danced around him, begging with his eyes. Andy chuckled a little and gave the treat to him anyway. "Peppy, you aren't ever gonna learn any tricks, are you?" he said with affection as he and the dog went back down the hall together.

A moment later the screen door to the outdoors slammed.

"Now," Rachel said, putting a hand on Leora's arm. "What's really wrong?"

"There's nothing wrong, exactly. It's just that I've been doing a bit of thinking, and I want to talk something over with you."

"Oh. Okay." For some reason, when she'd sensed something wrong, Rachel's mind had conjured one word. Jake. Of course, Leora wouldn't have come with bad news about Jake. Was it something about the store? But it was Sunday, and Drewers was closed on Sundays. Leora had been very quiet after church that morning. Rachel hadn't thought much about it at the time, because she herself had been coping with the extraordinary sight of Jake Monroe, come to church.

"Whatever it is, we'll deal with it," she promised quietly.

"Could I maybe have a cup of tea?"

"Sure." Rachel led the way to the kitchen. Once there, Leora got out spoons and sugar while Rachel filled the teakettle. Outside it was hot, but Leora had always liked a cup of tea. They could both hear Andy prompting the dog. But he hardly gave the puppy enough time to try to perform the trick before consoling him with a treat.

Leora smiled and glanced out the window, but her smile was strained. Rachel waited for the water to boil in the kettle.

"Rachel, I've been thinking," Leora said.

Rachel nodded.

Leora asked abruptly, "Were you happy with my son?"

Rachel looked up, her heart doing an odd flip at the unexpected question. "Yes."

"Always? Even from the beginning?"

Rachel hesitated. "He was a good man. An easy man to love."

Leora abruptly snapped a spoon against the table. "I know that. He loved Andy, too."

Rachel looked across the room. Her mother-in-law's glance was steady but haunted. And Rachel suddenly realized without a shadow of a doubt that Leora knew. She *knew*. Maybe not the whole story, but enough to know that Chris wasn't Andy's biological father. Maybe even that Jake was.

The world spun a little. She squeezed her eyes shut for a moment. "How—"

"How did I know?" Leora let out a bitter chuckle. "Well, I suppose there were clues, but I didn't notice them at the time. I mean, you and Chris were friendly enough as teenagers. But I could see he loved you. You, on the other hand, always treated him like a big brother."

Leora's eyes strayed to the backyard for a moment. "Your father and I had always planned— Well, you know what we planned. And when you and Chris announced so suddenly that you were getting married, we both—your father and I—figured you were pregnant, that Chris was doing the right thing and marrying you. If you seemed a little unhappy, a little unsure, I thought, well, of course you were unsure. Here you were, eighteen, with plans for college that had to be put on hold, and a baby on the way." She paused. "But your father and I decided it would all work out."

A little unhappy, Rachel thought. She'd seemed a

little unhappy. Actually, she'd been terrified, then miserable. She couldn't have been that good an actress. But then she met Leora's eye and knew that Leora and her father must have seen what they'd wanted to see. What she and Chris had wanted them to see.

The teakettle whistled. Rachel jumped and pulled it off the heat, but she made no move to pour. Her hands were shaking too much. "But if you figured I was just unhappy about the baby, how did you find out…"

"That the baby wasn't Chris's? That Andy's real father is Jake Monroe?"

There was silence in the kitchen for a long time. Rachel felt a lump in her throat and so many questions in her heart. She leaned back against the counter, wanting its firm support. Leora knew everything. She whispered, "How long…?"

"How long have I known?" Leora completed the question. "Since Andy was about five."

"Oh my God."

"Yes. My sentiments exactly." Leora's voice sounded gritty, old. "When Andy was five, you and Chris got into an argument. You'd wanted to finish school and go on for your master's degree. Chris wanted you to go to work right away."

Rachel remembered the argument, one of the few serious ones they'd ever had. Usually, Chris went along with all her decisions. Their argument had been pointless and hurtful, because they'd fought about what couldn't be changed. Chris didn't earn enough at Drewers to support them anymore. Her father had died that year, and there had been enough money to cover her school loans, but that had been it. In a small town, the appearance of wealth could be very deceiving, and both her father and Leora had done a good job of deception. She was never going to be able to go on with school.

She shivered. In her life, there had been so many lies and half truths. So much of keeping up appearances. She clenched her hands together as Leora continued.

"After you'd argued, Chris left to take a walk and cool off. I was out on Main Street when he came by the convenience store to pick up some beer. I knew right away something was wrong. I insisted he tell me." She smiled faintly, without any warmth. "I can be a little...pushy sometimes. Chris finally told me what a failure he was. That he couldn't support you. That he couldn't make you happy."

Rachel let out a little cry of distress. She'd tried so hard to make sure Chris never felt that way.

Leora sat down abruptly. "Up until that day, I thought you were happy."

"We were," Rachel said, feeling the tears start to clog her throat. She left the kettle and went to her mother-in-law. Leora's hand was resting on the tabletop. Rachel took it in hers.

"Yes. Well. Anyway, that day, we took a walk to the park. We sat on a bench. Chris cried. He told me everything that evening. He said you hadn't wanted him in the first place. Then he talked about Andy."

Rachel sat down next to her mother-in-law. "At first, it was Chris who insisted it be a secret. He thought it would be better for Andy, for everybody, if no one ever knew."

Leora nodded.

"I don't know why he told you," Rachel said.

"We had our secret, and we had our marriage. We made it work. It took some time but in the end, I loved your son."

Leora nodded again. "Thank you," she whispered. Then more strongly, she said, "I was shocked and it took me a while to get over it, but then I decided Chris had done the right thing. That you could have a good life, and Andy would never have to know."

Rachel sighed. "We should have talked about this when Chris died. I've needed someone to talk to, ever since—" She cut herself off, the heat creeping over her skin.

"Ever since Jake came home." Her mother-in-law seemed fixed on their hands, resting together on the tabletop.

Rachel blinked hard.

"I was afraid," Leora whispered. "Andy was everything to me. Chris had grown up, my husband was dead, my hopes for Drewers—well, Andy had always seemed like a fresh start. New life. He was such a sweet child. I didn't want to believe for a long time he wasn't my flesh and blood."

"But you're his grandmother. I mean, you're the only grandmother Andy has ever known. He loves you." A fat tear slipped down Rachel's cheek. "Chris was his father in too many ways to count."

Outside, a friend of Andy's had come over, and now there were two voices shouting in the backyard. Peppy erupted over something or other, giving an excited series of yapping barks.

But in the kitchen, it was quiet. Leora was so still, her spine straight, her mouth pursed, and Rachel had the awful feeling Leora was about to cry. And Leora

Drewer didn't cry; the only time Rachel had seen her cry was at her son's funeral.

Rachel didn't know what else to say. How could she explain to Chris's mother that she'd managed to be married to and love Chris, at the same time she'd never stopped loving another man? She didn't understand it herself, really. To still be in love with Jake after all this time...

She barely stopped herself from a sudden hard squeeze of Leora's hand as realization dawned.

She loved Jake? She'd never stopped loving him?

She did. She loved him for his determination and his intelligence and his fundamental goodness, for what they'd shared long ago and what they'd shared since he'd come home. Heat, then cold, then heat again swept over her, and she had the almost giddy urge to laugh and a more profound urge to cry. Abruptly, she pulled her hand from Leora's. She clenched her hands in her own lap against the tide of emotion.

Andy was supposed to go home with Leora, to stay the night at his grandmother's. She'd have a bit of a breather before Jake came over later to go over their list of possible suspects. Time to calm her racing heart, to think.

"Rachel, look at me," Leora said quietly.

Now she just needed to be alone. Reluctantly, Rachel met Leora's gaze, afraid her feelings for Jake might show on her face. "I'm sorry," Rachel said softly. "I'm sorry I caused you hurt. I'm sorry I couldn't have loved Chris first."

"Rachel—"

"I'm sorry because I didn't tell you, or maybe I'm just sorry you found out."

Leora let out a long, sad sigh. "After Chris told me, I said to keep it a secret forever. Andy's father, a convicted murderer?" She shuddered. "No way should a child have to bear that. Andy loved Chris so much, I wondered what it would do to him to know his father was another man. I was so afraid."

"Me, too." Those damn tears of hers. Rachel swiped at her eyes.

"Every time you defended Jake, I wondered if you still loved him, if you'd do something stupid to ruin Andy's future."

She jumped to her feet. "I wouldn't!"

"Women in love do stupid things." Her mother-in-law straightened her shoulders. "Jake was in prison, and I'm ashamed to admit I was glad he was there. That he couldn't ruin all our lives. Then that day in Drewers, when I looked up to see Jake Monroe, home, in my store buying a tie, I just—my God, it was like my worst nightmare come to life. What if he found out? What would he do?"

"I know," Rachel said miserably, and she started to pace in the small breakfast area. Every time she turned, she could see her son through the window, out on the lawn. He was laughing. "I was afraid, too. But then Andy started to idolize Jake when he coached the Raiders, and I was even more afraid of them getting close, but I wanted that for Andy. At the same time I started to—" She cut herself off just before confessing that she, too, had come to care for Jake.

Leora let out a long breath. "Pretty soon Andy and that dog and his little friend are going to be back in this kitchen, wanting a cold drink or a snack or some mothering. So I need to say what I came here to say. I've been thinking about something for a long time now." She paused. "You need to tell Jake about Andy."

Of all the things she'd expected her mother-in-law to say, that was the last. Rachel turned to look at Leora, her mouth open.

Leora's gaze was steady on hers. "I was a fool years ago not to see that Jake was a person of good character. In a way the whole town—me included—is as responsible for your secret as you were. He shouldn't have been treated the way he was. He shouldn't have gone to prison. I've been thinking that for some time, especially when Andy was hit by that ball and he was so good with him. Then I saw Jake in church and knew that he deserved to be told the truth. He cares about Andy. He deserves to know the truth."

Rachel started to shake all over. "Do you know what you're saying?"

"I do. As I say, I've been thinking about it for some time, but today in church, seeing him there, trying to make something of his life, with everything against him... Well, I knew. We've done him a grave injustice. Chris is gone, but Jake has his whole life ahead of him. You can't fix everything for Jake. But you can put one thing right."

Rachel swallowed. Her mouth and throat were dry. "He'll want some kind of rights. Fathers have rights nowadays."

"I know that. I read the papers," Leora said with a touch of her customary briskness.

"He'd maybe try to take Andy away."

Leora said nothing.

Shame washed over Rachel. "Okay, he wouldn't

try to take Andy away. But he'll want to tell Andy. Do you honestly think that's something Andy should be told only a year after Chris has died? When he's barely adjusted to his loss? When he's at that age when he sees everything as right and wrong, black and white?'' All the books on child behavior she'd read, all her training said that Andy couldn't handle the news. Had she sacrificed for him ten years ago only to fail to protect him now?

Leora's eyes were troubled as she glanced out the window. "I don't know if Andy can handle the news or not. Sometimes kids take things better than we believe they will, and Andy is a smart little boy. But if you don't think the time is right for Andy, you could still tell Jake. You could ask Jake to keep it a secret for a while longer."

Rachel's hands fisted. "You've seen how Jake is. He wants his life back. He wants what's his. Do you think he'd keep it a secret if I asked him to?"

"You know Jake better than I do, but it seems to me that he cares about Andy. If a parent loves a child, he'll do anything to protect that child." Leora paused, obviously thinking. "All along, everybody's thought the worst of Jake. Maybe we should start to give him some credit for a change. Give him the chance to do the right thing, whatever that turns out to be."

"He'll hate me for what I've done!" Rachel turned from the window. She went to the counter for a tissue and blew her nose, trying to calm down. She kept her back to Leora as she felt the scalding shame at how selfish her words sounded.

Leora got out of her chair and came over to stand

behind Rachel. When Rachel felt her mother-in-law's gentle touch on her shoulder, she stiffened.

"Is that what's keeping you from telling him?" Leora asked.

"I am worried about Andy. It's a valid worry. Oh, heck," Rachel said abruptly. "I'm worried about Andy, but I'm worried about what Jake will think of me. If he'll hate me. And I don't want him to hate me."

"He might hate you. He might not." Leora's hand tightened. "But this is about Andy, not you."

That shame again. It burned her in the belly. It made her hands clench.

Her first concern *was* Andy. But she had to believe that the man she loved would do what he thought was best for her son. Trouble was, Rachel wasn't sure what that was anymore. If Jake had to go back to prison, maybe Andy shouldn't be told. But if Jake was able to clear his name, shouldn't he be allowed to build some kind of relationship with his son?

She was a coward. Jake Monroe, the unloved son of the town drunk, was a person of courage. But Rachel Penning Drewer, daughter of one of the town's leading citizens, admired by many, was a coward.

She did not want to be a coward. She didn't want to be the kind of person who took the easy way, who thought first and foremost of herself. And with that realization, she knew what she had to do.

"You're right," she admitted. Her throat was so tight with tears and fear that it was hard to say the words. "I'll tell him. He's coming over tonight to share some of what his attorney's turned up, and to go over our list again. Andy's going to be staying

the night with you.'' She took a deep breath. ''I'll
tell him tonight.''

Leora did something she hadn't done since Chris's
death. She hugged her daughter-in-law. Hard.

CHAPTER FOURTEEN

THE LEAD IN Jake's mechanical pencil broke and a bit of graphite flew past Rachel's head.

"Oh!" she said, starting.

He stared at her from across her kitchen table. It was almost ten o'clock, but not quite dark. The late-summer twilight was warm. Rachel had put on the overhead light so they could work, and the light had attracted insects that hummed and moved against her screen door.

"Oh, sorry," she said with a funny little laugh. She tossed her head.

Rachel was acting very strangely this evening. Downright weird. When he'd first arrived, she'd said rather abruptly she had something to tell him. Then she'd changed her mind, said it could wait.

He'd figured it had something to do with the case, some theory or other that she considered too wild to tell him. They both had come up with some wild ones these past days as they'd gone over Rachel's list.

But as the evening wore on, he'd become convinced that whatever was on Rachel's mind didn't concern his case.

She was too upset. Take her cheeks, for example. They were too bright. When he'd inadvertently touched her hand, he was surprised to find it ice-cold. She'd snatched it away, getting even more nervous.

"Are you all right?" he asked for the second time. "You're not sick, are you?"

"Of course not. Don't be silly. I'm always healthy as a horse. There's stuff going around the office all winter long, and the kids on my caseload get colds and things, but I never do. A single mother can't afford to get sick—" She cut herself off, blushed even more deeply and added quickly, "Anyway, I'm feeling fine."

He cocked his head, studying her. Andy was spending the night at Leora's, she'd said. Jake would have liked to have seen him, but it seemed real...convenient that Andy was away tonight. As soon as she'd told him that the boy was away, Jake's mind had conjured bedrooms, open windows, cool sheets on a warm night. And no need to be quiet.

Looking at her across the table, knowing her son wasn't home, had made it hard for him to concentrate. Instead, he'd kept watching her, noticing again the smoothness of her cap of hair, her clear skin dotted with all those golden freckles. The softness of curves, the fullness of her breasts that proclaimed her a grown woman. He remembered everything about her skin, her warmth.

He'd flirted a little, maybe. He'd watched her lips. He hadn't been able to keep from touching her as she handed him a glass of soda or a piece of paper.

He'd made her nervous. Maybe that's why she was so skittish.

He leaned back in this chair. "Let's put this stuff away for tonight."

She frowned and shook her head. "We've finally

got some leads. Seven of the men on this list have been in some trouble with the law.''

Jake's attorney had checked the criminal dockets. The theory was that the person who'd murdered Joann might have an antisocial personality, and might have committed other crimes. ''We only have three who have committed minor felonies. And a couple of misdemeanors don't make a guy a murderer.''

He paused. ''Besides, we have several names on this list of men who've moved away from Grange. It'll take weeks to get their records back.'' He didn't say what he knew she was thinking. He didn't have weeks.

He stood up. Gently, he grabbed her wrist. ''Come on. Let's go outside.''

She let him pull her to her feet, but she looked uncertainly up at him. ''Outside?''

He snapped his fingers in an earth-to-Rachel motion and smiled. ''You know, like outside in the yard? To sit on that little bench you have under that arbor? Come on, you're working too hard and we aren't going to get any further with this list tonight.''

She laughed a little, a very nervous sound.

He stared into her eyes. Any lightness, any teasing he felt was abruptly replaced by something else. The simmering tension made him feel utterly serious. ''I don't have much time,'' he whispered. ''I may be back in prison in a couple of weeks. While I can, I want to be outside.''

Her eyes clouded with worry.

Before she could say anything, offer any platitudes, he said, ''Listen to me. I'm doing everything I can to stay out of prison. And even if I go back,

I'm not staying there. I'm clearing my name and I'm coming out. I have a future. I really believe that now.''

The hallway clock ticked. It was so loud, he could hear it way out here in the kitchen. She just looked at him, a sheen of tears in her eyes, her lips parted.

He took a deep breath. "I didn't think I had a future to offer you ten years ago. Some would say I don't have a future to offer you now, but I do. I'm getting out sooner or later and everybody will know I'm innocent.''

He gathered her into his arms. He could hear sounds of the evening. Some teenagers going by on the walk out front. A car. The cicadas in some strange kind of harmony with the ticking clock. She smelled so good. He held her loosely, when what he really wanted to do was crush her against him.

At first he felt resistance in her body. She even said, "Jake, we need to talk.''

He tipped up her chin. "We can talk. Later.'' He brought his lips down on hers.

The kiss was incendiary. It went so fast. The feel of her mouth on his kicked up immediate desire. Despite any intention to be gentle—and he was no longer certain that had been his intention—he couldn't be gentle. His lips just wouldn't move softly over hers. Instead, he pressed, demanded, devoured.

Her whole body sagged against him, and it seemed as if the press of her body was the most wonderful thing in the world. He put a rough cheek to her smooth hair and gathered her close. "I love you,'' he whispered. For a second he stiffened; he hadn't planned to tell her, not now, not with his life in the balance.

But then she whispered back, "I love you, too." He couldn't believe she felt that way, couldn't believe she'd said it. His whole being sang with the knowledge, and for a moment everything he'd gone through meant nothing. Everything he had to face meant nothing, because she loved him.

He touched his lips to her hair, almost overcome with emotion. Her cheek was to his chest, and he traced a finger along it, wanting to make love with her, to touch every inch of her. Her skin was wet.

"Hey, none of that," he said softly, setting her from him gently. "We love each other. At least for tonight, let's be happy."

She looked up at him and he could see her tears were in earnest. There wasn't just dampness there, a few tears of happiness. Rachel looked...sad. His heart lurched. "I'll do my best to make you happy—"

"Oh, Jake."

Her tone brought him up short. It was so bleak. He watched her take a deep breath and give a little, disgusted swipe at her eyes. "I don't cry all the time," she said. "Really, I don't."

"No, you don't," he said, wanting to soothe her.

She looked at him carefully, as if she'd never quite seen him before. She took his hand. "I have to tell you something."

He was struck with a vague sense of foreboding. But what could she tell him that would be worse than what he'd gone through? "Go ahead."

She swallowed. "I didn't intend to say I loved you. I only realized it tonight."

He said slowly, "That's good, isn't it? I still haven't gotten myself out of this mess, but—"

"I want you to know that, to remember I love you, because maybe it'll help you understand what I've done."

What she'd done? Jake went cold with unease. He knew Rachel so well. She was passionate; she always told the truth, and if she said she loved him, she did. For her to be hesitant now... Her lips were so pale. Lifeless.

"I...do you remember once asking how old Andy was?"

Andy? "Ah, yeah, I guess so."

She looked away. "I told you he was just going into fifth grade this fall. But I never told you how old he was."

She was going to confess how quickly she'd jumped into bed with Chris after Jake had gone to prison. He didn't want to hear it. "It's behind us now."

"No, it's not." She swiped at her eyes as if impatient with her own tears. But she didn't look him in the eye. "It can never be behind us. You see, I started Andy in kindergarten a year late. I was reading all these books on child development, and he didn't seem emotionally ready. Anyway, he should be in fifth grade. Andy's ten years old."

She looked at him then, and in her eyes he saw sadness and fear...

My God. Dear God, she couldn't mean... She was trying to say that Andy was older than Jake had thought, and she was telling him this because...

He reached out and grabbed her shoulders as all the implications sank in. He held her hard, whether to make her tell him the truth, or to hold on to the one person in the world he'd loved, he wasn't quite sure. "Andy isn't...isn't Chris's?" he finally got out.

The world was too bright. The kitchen light was too bright, too hot, and the walls seemed suddenly too close.

"No." She faced him squarely now. "Andy is your son."

Shock went along his veins. "My son?"

"Your son."

"But...you married Chris. I thought—"

"I know. I wanted you to think that. When I got pregnant, I didn't know what to do. You'd just gone to prison, and you wouldn't answer my letters. I didn't have a job, I didn't know how to do anything to support myself or my baby. My father wouldn't have let me stay with him, not with your baby."

Her words picked up speed, poured out. He heard them in a kind of daze. "I couldn't bear to have an abortion, and if I had him adopted, I'd never see him again, and I couldn't bear that, either. So I told Chris and he offered to marry me and raise Andy as his son. Chris loved and cared for Andy as his own..."

There was a kind of foggy noise in Jake's ears and he could hardly follow what she was saying. The busy pattern of the wallpaper overwhelmed him. He pushed away from her, threw open the screen door and headed out into the twilight.

Once outside, he took a couple of deep, calming breaths.

He had a son.

He had Andy. Andy was his, Jake's. His flesh and blood.

A child he already cared about. His son!

He heard her come out behind him. "Jake? Are you all right?"

"Yes," he said, suddenly, irrationally angry that she was always taking his emotional temperature. "No. I'm not okay, I'm..." He didn't know what he was. Except confused. Proud of his son. Aching, somehow, and angry somehow.

"I didn't have a choice." She was still behind him. She added, "You didn't answer my letters."

He had a son. This was today, and for some reason, she was talking about letters she'd sent ten years ago. "I know about the letters," he said impatiently. "I've explained about the letters. I was trying to give you a life."

"I know." She was closer now.

"If I'd only known..." Then what? He'd have answered those letters? He'd have tried to be a father from prison?

She put a hand on his shoulder. He reached up and put his hand over hers, holding it to him. The dark was falling in earnest now, fading the colors of the backyard. For a moment, he tried to picture his son as a baby, but the images wouldn't come. He wasn't really sure what a newborn baby looked like. It had been so long since he'd really looked at a baby, even seen a picture of one...

He'd missed so much in prison. *So damn much.* He was angry about that, and sad about it, and at the same time he felt a wash of something so protective toward Andy that it was stunning in its intensity. His legs started to shake.

"I'm sorry."

"Yeah."

For a moment, they just stood there, her hand on

his shoulder. He could sense her behind him, her tension. The fireflies were coming out. Sparks here and there.

She said, "I had no choice. I was trying to do right by Andy."

"Yeah." It was just another blow among many, another reminder of time lost. And then...it hit Jake. The growing anger. He was stunned to realize who he was so angry at. Rachel.

He took his hand from hers and turned slowly to face her. "Okay." He was surprised his voice was so even; he was shaking inside. "I was in prison, and you thought you had to marry Chris. I understand that." With his head, he could. But with his heart...with his heart, he really couldn't. And there was the rest of what she'd done. "But why didn't you tell me when I came home?"

Her eyes looked dark out here, her face very pale, almost ghostly. She didn't answer right away, and all of a sudden, real rage swept through Jake. An overgrown bush was by his side; he reached out and grabbed it, holding on. His fist clenched so hard over a forked branch that it broke off in his hand.

"You were my P.O. You sat across from me twice a week." He mimicked her P.O. voice, mocking her. "'How're things going, Jake? How're you *adjusting?*'" She flinched, but he said, "All that time, you kept this from me. Then we got to be friends. More than friends. I touched you. I kissed you. I...wanted to make love to you. Yet you kept this from me."

"I didn't make love with you!" she cried. "I wanted to! But I didn't because of...this."

"You think that makes it all right?"

She put her chin up. "I think it makes it better than if I had."

He fought to get a grip on his anger. His hands clenched harder on the twig he held. "Why didn't you tell me when I came home? Or, if not then, why didn't you tell me a month ago? Why didn't you tell me last week? Hell, why didn't you tell me this morning, this afternoon, or even when I first got here?"

"I had reasons—"

"Then—" he took a breath for control "—you'd better tell me what they were."

"Andy. He thinks Chris is his father. I had to protect him."

He took a couple of steps toward her. "Sure. You'd have to be careful. You and Chris undoubtedly kept your secret well. But couldn't you have told Andy when Chris died?"

She was silent, and Jake knew she couldn't have. What would she say? *Andy, your real father is a convicted murderer?*

A small, almost threadlike sympathy started to grow in Jake. But he pushed it down. She should have trusted him, damn it. "Why didn't you at least tell him after I came home?"

"I had some notion of protecting Andy."

"So I wasn't good enough for him."

Even in the night, he saw her wince.

"Go ahead. Say it. I wasn't good enough for Andy."

"You'd just gotten out of jail. Chris hadn't been gone long. I hadn't heard from you in ten years. Prison...does things to people." Her voice slowed. "I didn't know what you'd be like. I was afraid."

His chest hurt. "Afraid of me?"

"Yes," she said so softly he wasn't sure for a second if he'd heard her.

He swore and threw the twig he held and started to walk. Her backyard was big, but even at night it felt enclosed, the canopy of trees stifling.

She followed him. "Please, Jake," she said finally.

He turned around so fast she almost bumped into him. "There was no reason to be afraid of me. Not after I came home and you saw how I was. You were all for my coaching your son—*my* son. When Andy got hit by that bat, I was sick inside with worry. I should have been able to go back in that hospital room with my boy while they stitched his head. Damn it, I had that right, and you took it from me." The enormity of what she'd done hit him full force. "The system screwed me ten years ago, but you did this to me after I came back!"

"I didn't want you to hurt Andy!"

She was breathing hard, and so was he.

She said, "Oh, God, Jake, I was afraid you'd hate me."

He did. He did hate her suddenly. She'd had months since he came back to tell him, and she hadn't. "You've always got to be the one making decisions, don't you, Rachel? You decided what Andy could handle. You didn't tell me, and trust me to do the right thing with my son. You're in charge. You're always in charge."

She gasped.

"You didn't have the right to make decisions about me and Andy."

"He's my son!"

"He's mine, too!"

"That's just how I was afraid you'd react!"

Another wave of rage swept him. "How am I supposed to react? I thought you were an honest woman, a woman who couldn't lie, no matter what. But you're not too honest to lie to make things easier for yourself."

She put her hands on her hips. "That's all you know. Do you think this has been easy? Do you think I didn't agonize over this? I love you, Jake! Even when you first came home, I had...feelings. But I've made some decisions that were very hard, and yes, I've learned finally to be in charge of my life. I had to protect my son. Is that such a crime?"

"You'd always had it easy, and you took the easy way out. You married Chris because that was the easiest way."

"The easiest way?" She almost spat the words. "I loved you. I was carrying your baby. Don't you think an abortion or welfare wouldn't have been easier than to tie myself to a man I didn't love, to try to repay his generosity by being the best wife I could?"

He didn't want to think of her, alone and pregnant. He didn't want to think of her lying in another man's bed. Being a good wife. Touching her husband, and letting him touch her. "You loved him," he accused harshly. "Maybe not in the beginning, but you loved him soon enough. Didn't you?"

He didn't want to hear her say yes. But in a way he needed to hear it, to nurse and nurture his anger.

There was a long pause. Finally, she said softly, "Yes. He was a good man and I loved him."

So, he thought, Princess Rachel had had her fairy-tale life after all. He turned from her and headed back into the house. He'd loved her all his life. She was *Rachel,* and he'd trusted her.

When Jake went into the kitchen, the brightness was almost blinding. He went down the hallway toward the front door.

She followed him. Damn her, why couldn't she leave him alone?

"What are you going to do?" she asked fearfully as he pulled the front door open.

She was afraid of him, was she? Well, maybe it was time to give her something to fear. "Judge Randall has come to see things my way. Maybe I'll just file for custody."

She gasped.

At the sound, suddenly he couldn't make himself lie to her, no matter how she deserved it. He turned slowly to face her. "I won't file for custody."

She almost sagged against the wall in relief. "Will you tell Andy?"

He wanted to. He wanted his son, if not to live with him, then at least to be *his.* To be acknowledged. The love coursed through him. Rachel had betrayed him. But Andy... He wanted to say, *Son, I'm your father, and I love you so much.*

He couldn't, and at that knowledge he fisted both hands. No matter what progress had been made on his case, he was still a felon.

"Should I tell him?" he asked, wishing he didn't have to ask her anything.

"I don't know," she admitted. "I've gone over and over it in my mind, and I just don't know."

Well, at least she was finally admitting that she didn't have all the answers. But the sting of her betrayal wouldn't let him acknowledge that aloud. Now

Jake faced a bitter truth: his son couldn't be told unless Jake cleared his name. That was Jake's choice, because he'd never let his son think of him as a criminal.

She said slowly, "I've been wondering, if we could sort out what was between us, maybe—"

"No."

"I wish—"

"I don't believe in wishes," he said curtly. "I don't believe in miracles, either." He walked out the door, more bitter than he'd been in ten years.

CHAPTER FIFTEEN

WAS SHE all those things he'd said? Did she have a need to control everything? Six days after her confession to Jake, Rachel's throat felt dry and achy as she emptied the dishwasher. Upstairs, Andy was in the middle of what she and her son always jokingly called mega baths. There were days when he pretended to be half grown-up. Then there were days—like this evening—when he wanted to take a pile of Aquazone Legos into the tub with him and play in the water for hours, exactly as he'd done as a toddler.

Rachel reached over her head and put a couple of glasses in the cupboard above.

No wonder Jake was bitter; he'd missed all of Andy's babyhood, his son's first steps, Andy's first ride on training wheels, his first day of school, his first— Well, so much.

And, thanks to her, he was missing the here and now.

He was right. She should have told Jake the truth when he'd first come home. Or at least she should have told him when she'd realized he was a person of fine character; she should have trusted him to do the right thing.

Jake had made no move to talk to Andy. He hadn't called her to insist on seeing his son. He had an attorney now, but Rachel had heard nothing from the attorney, had received no call—as she'd half expected—demanding visitation rights.

Jake, as angry as he was at her, was bowing to her expertise as a mother, bowing to her opinion that keeping the secret was best for Andy. Now that she thought about it, she wouldn't have expected less from the man who, at age nineteen, hadn't opened her letters so that she could get on with her life.

Her hand closed tightly around a glass, and she put it on the counter to avoid breaking it. She looked out the window.

She would *not* cry!

Instead, she called to Andy that it was time to come out of the tub. He protested, and she called back that he could have ten more minutes.

She left the clean dishes and wandered into the den. Maybe some music would help.

She and Jake had never had a favorite song. They'd never been to a dance together, seldom even listened to music, because the radio in his truck had been broken.

Now she longed for those normal things. She wanted to let Jake love her. She wanted him to share her home and her life and the raising of their son.

But it would take a miracle for any of those things to happen.

The phone rang, and she rushed to answer it, glad of the distraction. "Hello?"

"Rachel, this is Barb Thomas."

"Oh, hello, Barb." Rachel put the receiver in the crook of her neck and went over to close the draperies over the sliding door.

"I've got something to tell you. I don't know if it means anything, but we were cleaning up, doing some work around the farm and I…I found something. An amber pendant.''

Rachel froze in the act of pulling on the drapery cord. "An amber pendant?''

"Yes." Barb laughed a little. "It's probably nothing, I probably shouldn't have called you, but it's such an unusual piece, and, well, I read in the newspaper that one of the pieces of evidence the police were looking for in Jake's case was an amber pendant.''

Rachel's heart pounded. "What does it look like?''

"It's really large, like a big teardrop. A very odd piece. There's quite a bit of a butterfly wing in it.''

Rachel sat down in a chair, hard. "Where did you find it?''

"You don't really think it's the one, do you?'' Barb's usually quiet voice got louder. "We found it under the floor of our porch. You know we're remodeling, and we tore off the floorboards today. They were half-rotten, and the spaces were so big between the boards you could lose your keys if you dropped them. Anyway, there was a whole bunch of junk under there. Lying on the dirt was that pendant. I know it's a long shot, I mean, how could that necklace be that Floutz woman's and be under my porch?''

"I don't know," Rachel said, trying to think over her rising excitement. "Are you going to be home in an hour?''

"Sure.''

Rachel hung up the phone a moment later, and called to Andy. "Andy? You've got to come out of that tub right now. You're going to Grandma's for a while.''

She grabbed her purse and headed up the stairs, calling again for Andy to hurry up. In his room, she pulled on the dresser drawer and yanked out clean jeans and a shirt. She was praying the whole time. Praying for Jake's miracle.

"WHAT DO YOU WANT?" Jake asked with deliberate rudeness when he saw Rachel on his doorstep.

He felt like hell. He'd been going over his list like a robot these days, trying to narrow the field of suspects. He couldn't sleep. His parole hearing was in a few days, and he knew he'd be on his way back to prison soon.

She said quickly, "Barb Thomas found an amber necklace." She went on in a few short sentences to explain where it had been found and that she was on her way to the farm to look at it. "Come on. Let's go."

Despite her excitement, it was a fool's errand. He knew that. How on earth could Joann's necklace be under the porch of that old farmhouse?

"Are you coming?" she asked impatiently.

Much as he didn't want to go anywhere with Rachel, he had to check out all leads. He went to get his wallet and joined her in the passenger seat of her car.

On the way to the farmhouse, she said, "I'm sorry it had to be me coming with this information. I know you don't want to see me."

"You got that right," he said with the sarcasm he'd used to get through his teenage years. She winced, and he was suddenly ashamed. She was trying to help him even now. He watched her out of the corner of his eye and felt a twinge of an old tenderness. He shook it off.

A half hour later, he looked down at the pendant Barb had placed in his hand. "It's hers," he said bluntly, shutting his eyes for a second. When he opened them again, it was still there. Joann's necklace.

Rachel, Barb, and Robert Thomas, Barb's husband, stared at him.

"It's hers," he repeated. "There's the butterfly wing." The wing was black, ragged-edged, trapped in a sea of shimmering, bubbly amber. He closed his hand over the first real piece of evidence in a decade, feeling the amber grow warm from the heat of his palm. "How did you find it?"

Barb explained about the remodeling. "Since we moved in, we've been renovating room by room. And the porch was half-rotten. It's been deteriorating for years."

"Show me," Jake directed, too deep in thought to be polite.

They all trooped to the back of the house. There, a garish spotlight lit the scene. Half the porch floorboards had been taken off. Jake walked gingerly on the remainder. The spaces between the boards were wide, wide enough in places for him to put his fingers between them.

"Someone must have dropped it," he said.

"That's what we thought. This was the way everyone came into the kitchen," Robert said. "You wouldn't believe all the junk we found down there—coins, keys, an old toy truck."

Rachel was smiling, a wide-open grin. He couldn't

stand it when she smiled at him that way, because even after what she'd done, that smile made him want to touch her.

He said quickly, "It doesn't prove I didn't do it. I could have dropped it."

"Were you ever at the farmhouse?" Rachel asked.

He shook his head. "I don't even remember who lived here then. An old couple, I think."

Barb said, "We bought it from some younger people who dreamed of making the apple orchard pay."

Jake shook his head. "They didn't own it then." But his memories of the owners were hazy. In those days, he'd been distracted by too much responsibility and too many thoughts of Rachel.

"What are you going to do?" Rachel asked.

His mind raced. "I'll give it to the police. It'll maybe be enough to get my parole hearing put off for a few days, until I can figure out what might have happened."

JAKE WENT to the police, and the chief agreed that for the moment they ought to keep the finding of the pendant a secret. That would give them time to track down the former owners of the farm.

Jake was grateful for the help, but he didn't trust the cops to go all out on the search. Which was why this morning, he was in a dusty alcove in the real-estate clerk's office of the courthouse. Grange still hadn't computerized the older transactions, so he was looking through huge books and handwritten entries.

"Well, that's it," he said to Rachel, stopping his finger at one of the entries showing yet another real-estate transfer for the old farm.

She was helping him search. He'd told her

brusquely to go back to her own work, but she hadn't said a word, just sat down next to him and pulled out a ledger.

They'd spent a couple of hours at the task. They didn't talk much, but Jake imagined he could smell her perfume, even from this distance. It was that new one she wore, the one that smelled of sandalwood and class. Her hair was a curve of shining silk. He longed to touch it.

He told himself she was helping him so that she could ease a guilty conscience.

But as time passed, he realized he was having trouble keeping up the silence. He was having trouble not talking to her, not sharing theories, hearing her think out loud. He was having trouble hanging on to his bitterness.

She'd done what she had to do ten years ago. She'd been worried about her son, *their* son, his flesh and blood. Of course she'd wanted to be a good wife, because that way there would be a happy family for her son to grow up in. He'd decided all this last night, when he'd tossed and turned in bed, and finally gotten up to spend the night hours outdoors. This much he understood...and truly forgave.

Reluctantly, he'd decided that she'd been right, too, in not telling him when he'd first come back. She was a parole officer—she'd seen criminals from the petty to the violent, and not one of them would be a proper role model for her son. Even though he was innocent, she didn't know what he'd be like after ten years in prison. Prison taught people how to be better criminals. Look how hard he'd had to fight against the bitterness, the sense of failure that prison bred.

As for why she didn't tell him later, when they'd gotten to know each other again—that was the part Jake couldn't forgive. Why not in Columbus, when they'd shared so much of their inner feelings? Why not when he'd kissed her and held her close? Why not any of a dozen times—like when he'd coached Andy's team to victory in the Little League?

She'd been afraid, she'd said. Afraid that Jake wouldn't do the right thing for Andy. That hurt—that she thought he'd be selfish. She'd also said she'd been afraid that Jake wouldn't care about her if he discovered her secret. So who was really being selfish?

But she'd sacrificed so much for Andy's happiness.

That was the part that kept nagging at him. How hard she'd tried to do the right thing for Andy.

Wasn't she allowed to worry, to make misjudgments in the name of caution, if those misjudgments were made to try to protect the child they both loved?

"Jake, I've got the real-estate transfer. The farm changed hands six weeks after Joann Floutz was murdered."

Brought abruptly back to the case, he said, "There's got to be something to that timing. It's so close to the date of her death." He felt that familiar rush of excitement. They were getting close.

She pushed a strand of hair behind her ear. "I think so, too." She smiled at him, not the strained smile of greeting she'd given him earlier, but a real smile. It lit her features.

He told himself he couldn't forgive her. But all he wanted to do in that moment was take her in his arms and say, *It's all right, love. Everything will work out.*

She tapped her pencil on the table, thinking. "I remember the people who sold the house. They were old. They sold to an older couple, too. At least to my eighteen-year-old eyes they seemed old. The Allens. They didn't live there long, but they bought insurance from my father, and I seem to remember him saying the farmhouse was in more disrepair than they'd thought, and they didn't want to tackle it. The farm changed hands pretty often. Finally it was sold to Barb Thomas and her husband. Let's see. The original sellers were old, and Mr. Allen was probably at least fifty. So neither of them is a real likely suspect in the robberies."

She looked at him so earnestly, and not for the first time, he was struck by how much she cared. She'd stuck by him, and that meant a lot. Enough to forgive her? Under his gaze, she colored a little and dropped her eyes. "Jake, when this is all over, I want to talk again. I've been thinking over why I did certain things, and I want to explain."

"Okay."

"Okay?" She looked up at him in surprise, and the hope in her eyes melted the last chilly spot in his heart.

"Okay," he confirmed, and that spot in his heart just got warmer and warmer.

She looked as if she still didn't quite believe in his ready acquiescence. "Oh, Jake, do you mean…?"

He smiled and said, "We've got to take this one step at a time. The case first. That's what I've decided. No matter what happens, Andy's got to know his father is no murderer."

She sobered. "Yes. We're so close. But neither

the seller nor Mr. Allen is likely to be the murderer. What if someone held on to the necklace, then came over and planted it years later?''

She paused. ''Or even dropped it accidentally.'' She shook her head. ''God, this crime will be so hard to solve if that's—''

''Wait.'' With stunning suddenness, her words made it all fall into place in Jake's mind.

The murderer dropped the pendant. The floor-boards were wide, and it fell between them to the floor, unnoticed, especially if the killer was nervous, rattled... Who would have a reason to be at the farm the night of the murder? He knew who. He *knew*. And the man was dark-haired and just a few years older than Jake.

''Rachel, who was the real-estate agent that handled the land sale? Who might have been showing the farm to the Allens that night?''

''Easy. Karl Bremmer. He was the only real-estate agent in town then.''

''*Karl* Bremmer?''

''Yes. Travis didn't take over until his father retired...'' There was a long pause. ''Jake!'' She almost squealed the word. A couple of clerks looked up and she lowered her voice. ''Jake, listen. Travis Bremmer took over his father's real-estate practice about ten years ago. Remember, he had a wife and a baby, so his father retired early and left the business to him. He hates you.'' She brought a fist down on the ledger. ''All along, I thought he was just grand-standing when he gave you all that grief. But now that I think about it, what better way to make sure no suspicion ever focused on him than by keeping the townspeople all stirred up about you? He was even on our list! How could we have been so blind?''

''We had a hundred and twenty names on that list,'' Jake reminded her, but he was smiling.

''Aren't you excited?''

''Yes. Oh, yes, I'm excited.'' He leaned over and planted a kiss right on her lips, not caring who was watching. When a long moment later he finally pulled his mouth from hers, he said, ''Want to find out where the Allens are living now and take a little ride to see them? Want to solve a ten-year-old mystery?''

JAKE AND RACHEL walked back to Rachel's house the next day from the police station, talking over Travis Bremmer's confession.

Jake said, ''The saddest thing of all was that killing Joann was an accident. He was angry and he pushed her, but I really don't think he intended her to fall. He was angry at hearing she was pregnant with his child, and I think he could have gotten a jury to understand. He would have spent some time in prison, but maybe not a lot.''

''But his career would have been ruined.''

''Yeah. His career.'' Jake said it with only a minimum of bitterness. He was going to move on, not dwell on the past.

''And his marriage.''

They stopped at the curb. It was officially fall; Andy had just gone back to school. But the landscape still carried the greens of high summer, and it was warm. The leaves wouldn't begin to turn for another month. Jake breathed deeply. All this space, and he would be free to enjoy it. Maybe make a garden of his own. If he had a family. If Andy...

Rachel went on, still deep in the mystery and Travis Bremmer's confession. "Joann Floutz was carrying his baby. He'd just been married, and he had a baby of his own. There'd been a bit of talk among the old-fashioned types already, because his wife had been pregnant before the marriage. I remember that part, even though Travis was a few years older than me. There was only one real-estate agency in town, but even then, Grange was growing. Travis and his father had to have been afraid of the competition. No way could he afford to have his reputation ruined by Joann."

"He was newly married, but he was having an affair with Joann Floutz." Jake made a sound of disgust as they crossed the street together. "A married woman. So they were arguing, and he pushed her. I believe his story. Otherwise, I don't think he'd have confessed so readily. That death has been on his pea-size conscience for ten years."

He thought about Bremmer's confession, which the chief had let him and Rachel watch through a one-way mirror. Bremmer had seemed almost... relieved that it was over. He'd readily admitted to pushing Joann. After he'd seen her fall, he'd tried to help her, but he could tell she was dead. In a panic, he'd staged a robbery, putting her television set and VCR in the trunk of his car, the pendant in his pocket. He was late for an appointment he'd made to show a farm to a potential buyer. He hadn't had time to get rid of the evidence, so he'd taken it with him. He'd apparently lost the pendant when he'd walked across the porch of the farm.

The Allens had told the police that Bremmer was nervous. Hell, no wonder he'd been nervous. They said he'd kept fingering the keys and loose change in his pockets as he was showing them the place. His behavior had been a little odd, but they'd put his nervousness down to inexperience and youth.

"What I can't forgive," Rachel said quietly, but with a fierce note in her voice, "is his framing you. Both ten years ago and this time with those fake robberies."

"When getting the parents stirred up didn't work, and I didn't end up back in prison as he'd hoped, he had to stage the robberies. He had too much invested by that time. But I don't think that in the beginning, the night of the murder, he intended to set me up."

It had just worked out that way, Jake thought now. "My being out at Joann's that day working on the gutters, then giving a false alibi to the police—which made me look suspicious—was just a fortunate coincidence for Bremmer. Then the police found that tape deck Joann had given me a few weeks before, and I never had a chance. After all, Bremmer hated me anyway, after I insisted he stop his bullying. He could have even rationalized it to himself. He had a business, responsibilities. I was just Little Jake Monroe. I wasn't ever going to be anybody."

She squeezed his hand. "You've always been somebody to me."

They were standing on her front walk.

He stopped and took both her hands in his and looked down into her eyes. "With you I feel like somebody. I always have." He paused. "I always will."

Her eyes misted. "I love you."

"I love you."

He looked into her eyes once more and said, "Let's go in the house. I want to kiss you."

They headed up the front walk together and Rachel got out her key and opened the door. Once inside, Jake shut the door and pressed her up against it. He held her there gently, the old oak against her back, and kissed her until he could hear her breathing become raspy. His own matched it. He could feel the warmth of her all along his body, and the sensation set him on fire.

She whispered, "Jake, stop. We have to talk."

He kissed her neck. "Do you really want to talk?"

"No," she got out on a moan. "Yes. We have to talk."

"I'm a free man, really free for the first time in ten years. How long are you going to make a free man wait?"

She said, "Not long. I want to make love with you. Oh, you have no idea how much. Every night, I lie in my bed and wish you were beside me."

His hands tightened on her upper arms. "I don't want to sneak around. I want the whole world to know I love you. But I don't want to hurt Andy."

"I know." Her mouth smiled but her eyes were strained. "I love that about you. But I've been thinking, I almost ruined things for us by not trusting you. By not giving you the information and letting you make your own decision. Now I wonder if I haven't been selling Andy short, too." She took a deep breath. "I think we should tell him. He's a special kid, and I know he loves you. We should give him a chance."

At her words, he wanted to grab her up into his

arms and spin her around. He knew she wasn't ashamed of him. But for her to be willing to tell Andy, to take a chance—

His euphoria fled abruptly. What if Andy wouldn't accept the news? Jake wanted to marry her. He wanted them to be his family. Rachel *and* their son. "When?" he whispered.

"We've waited a long time. I don't see the point in waiting any longer. We'll tell him when he comes home from school."

They both glanced at the grandfather clock in the hallway. "What time does he come home?" Jake asked.

"Three o'clock."

The clock had just struck one. Two hours. He had two hours to wait before he could find out if he had a life.

He looked into Rachel's eyes and saw the concern there.

"We don't have to tell him," he said gruffly. "We can wait."

She kissed him. "I'm scared, but my heart tells me this is the right thing to do. Maybe the experts wouldn't agree, but I feel it here." She touched the area of her heart lightly. She leaned in, and her breath feathered along his neck. "I'm worried, but I'm try-ing to trust our love. To trust my—*our*—son."

Jake loved how that sounded: *our son*. He liked how her breath shivered, cool along his neck. He grabbed her and kissed her again. "I need you. I need you to hold me and wait with me."

Her arms went around his neck. "Make love to me," she whispered.

He didn't think he'd ever heard sweeter words. He

lifted her into his arms. She said with a weak laugh, "I'm too heavy nowadays." For a second he just stood there. He had no trouble holding her, but he didn't want to take her upstairs to the bed she'd shared with Chris. He remembered the sofa in the den, and he carried her down the hallway.

"Here?" she asked, a little pink as he set her down gently by the sofa.

"Why not? We've made love in a pickup truck, we've made love in the grass by the creek, and I've thought about making love right in your office."

"In my office?" she squeaked.

"On your desk, or in your chair. Hey," he said softly, looking at her, "I've had a long time to hone my fantasies."

She laughed a little again as he guided her down onto the sofa. The laughter helped lighten the mood, but it died very quickly. It had been too long for there to be anything casual about their coming together.

He dropped to his knees, kneeling on the rug before her. She half sat, half lay on the soft honey-colored leather. As her lips parted and he saw the pulse jumping under the tender skin at her throat, he knew he just wanted to feel, not think. And he'd do his best to make sure she only felt, too.

His hands went to the buttons of her blouse. His fingers were shaking. It had been so long for him that he was nervous. He could feel his upper lip begin to sweat.

"It's okay," she whispered softly, her own hands helping him. But her hands quivered, too.

Between them somehow, they got her blouse off, and he unhooked her bra. He bent his head to take a nipple in his mouth, and she moaned. Emboldened by the sound, he stroked her with his tongue. He spent long moments at the task, until her nipple was stiff and wet.

"More," she whispered, running her hand down his chest. She got her hands up under his sweatshirt, and the feel of her hot palms on his hotter skin had him kissing and stroking her more frantically.

She sat up, pushing his sweatshirt over his head. He pulled it off. Her hands trailed down his bare chest to his belt. "Help me," she whispered.

He helped her, opening his belt, sliding down his jeans and underwear in one motion. She looked at him then, and the boldness of her gaze was very different from long ago.

"Unfair," he whispered. "If you get to look, so do I."

She blushed a little, but he didn't give her a chance to be shy for long. Her slacks and silky underthings landed next to his on the floor. She lay back on the smooth leather, holding out her arms, and the sight of her that way was the sexiest in the world, so much better than his fantasies that he had to close his eyes for a second.

When he opened them, she was smiling, and that smile sent more heat through him. Once, he'd lived for her acceptance, her smile. He guessed he still did. He felt for his jeans, and then extracted a condom from one of the pockets.

He got on the sofa with her, wedging her body between his and the sofa back. The leather was cool at first, then warmed to skin temperature, enveloping him in erotic warmth. He had to go slow, he reminded himself. But that was going to be devilishly hard. His body was alive and free and bare and craving the feel of being inside her.

He kissed her, he touched her. And he went so, so slowly, gritting his teeth when he had to get control again. She wriggled and moaned, her thighs and belly pressing against his shaft until he thought he'd die if he didn't have her. He touched her between her legs, feeling moist, tender flesh, and her moans got louder, more insistent. They were like a drumbeat in his head, in tune with the pounding of his pulse.

When finally, *finally,* she brought his body over hers, he held her face and kissed her. When she guided him into place, he felt her soft gasp on his neck and groaned.

A decade, he thought. *A decade until I could touch her this way again.* He thrust slowly inside her, willing it to last, willing himself to savor the moment.

He did savor it. He kissed the golden freckles of her nose, the freckles above the swell of her breasts. He savored it all—her skin, her breath, her scent, the lush curves and the strong bones underneath. As her arms went around his back, he felt her love, and that made him clutch her to him and thrust more quickly.

He lost it then, but she didn't seem to mind. In a hazy fog of sensation, he dimly realized she was meeting every thrust, that the leather beneath his knees had grown hot and slick, that her nails were raking his spine. The sounds she was making were full and rich. He thrust harder.

He felt her gather and quiver beneath him and cry out in climax, and he thought it would be worth waiting a hundred years just to hear that sound again.

He closed his eyes as his own climax began. He reached down blindly, took her hand in his and squeezed it hard as he groaned out her name. He shuddered. Against his eyelids, the warm golden light expanded, became limitless. No walls anywhere. He was free.

THEY MADE LOVE more slowly the second time. They lay together on the thick rug, but the floor was hard, and Jake pulled her on top of him. It was unbearably good to watch her move above him, joined with him. But inevitably, the clock ticked toward three, and Jake knew that freedom was still an illusion. He'd never be truly free, he realized, until Rachel was beside him as his wife. Until he had the family he'd lost ten years ago.

They got dressed in plenty of time. Rachel made a pot of tea and offered him a cup.

He said, "Tea? Ah, no." His body was replete but his mind was edgy. So much depended on the next few moments.

"I guess tea isn't a guy drink, is it?" She gave him a fleeting, strained smile, and a moment later, poured the tea from her own full cup down the drain. She was as nervous as he was, he realized, and that made him more uneasy still. He knew Rachel understood children better than he did; she was a trained professional. Besides, she'd had ten years with her child, while Jake's experience with Andy was limited to their connections on a ball field.

Finally, Andy came home. He paused in the yard, his backpack over his shoulder, as a gray cat streaked out of the garage to be petted. Rachel opened the door and then Peppy was all over Andy, squirming and jumping. The huge cat—who had to outweigh Peppy by at least ten pounds—gave the puppy a look of pure disdain before walking off, tail in the air like a flagpole.

Jake's throat was so tight he could hardly swallow. He wanted this. An ordinary day, being there when his son came home from school.

Andy skipped up the walk and burst into the house past Rachel. "Hey, Jake, you're here. Cool. And hi, Mom," he added a beat late. His footsteps stomped through the hall, and he slung his pack on the kitchen table.

Jake and Rachel followed him into the kitchen.

Jake said, "Hi." It was all he could manage.

Rachel said too brightly, "How was your day?"

"Okay. We're going to have a spelling bee this week and I already know all the words. They're only a measly third-grade review." He looked both pleased and disgusted.

Jake had the sudden urge to cut and run. This kid was happy. Who was Jake to screw that up?

"Good," Rachel said. She offered Andy a snack, then went through his backpack for notes from the teacher. Jake tried not to pace. He couldn't tell if she was putting off the moment that Andy must be told, or trying to make his day as normal as possible. Once, she gave Jake a small, nervous but somehow intimate smile.

That helped.

But when she said, "Andy, we need to talk to you about something," it was like being in the courtroom all over again, waiting for the jury to come back and decide his fate.

Andy headed for the den, but Rachel suggested the living room. Looking puzzled but not alarmed, Andy went into the room. Rachel sat next to Andy on the couch, Jake across from them in an armchair. The coffee table was between them.

Rachel tucked a lock of hair behind one ear in a

nervous gesture, then took Andy's hand. He looked up at her in surprise.

"Something's happened." He sounded a little anxious.

"Yes, but not bad things. Good things." Jake saw Rachel stroke her son's hand. "For one thing, the police caught the man who was breaking into houses. He was the one who pushed Joann Floutz ten years ago, so the police know Jake didn't do it."

Andy nodded. "So now everybody knows Jake is not a murdering person," he said matter-of-factly.

Perhaps it was his son's tone that suddenly squeezed Jake's chest. As if Andy had been expecting this news all along.

"No," Rachel said. "He's never been a murdering person."

"I knew that. I *always* knew that."

Jake cleared his throat. "Thanks, buddy."

Rachel took a deep, visible breath. Jake tensed as she said, "Remember how I told you Jake had a trial ten years ago, and these people on the jury said he did murder Mrs. Floutz?"

Andy nodded, but fidgeted. What was so important to the adults had little meaning to him, Jake realized. Andy had made up his mind about Jake and so the machinations of the legal system had little impact.

Rachel swallowed visibly. "In Jake's trial, your dad helped Jake with money for his lawyer. Your dad helped Jake as much as he could."

"My dad was nice."

Jake said, "Yes, he was." He'd always liked Chris until he'd found out the man's secret. But Chris and Rachel had done a fine job with Andy. How could Jake be anything but grateful for that?

"And when Jake went to prison, your dad…helped me." Rachel had gone pale.

"Mom, you're squeezing my hand too hard."

"Sorry. I was maybe squeezing too hard because telling you this is very difficult for me. I've been keeping a secret from you, and I'm afraid it's going to hurt you, so I wish I didn't have to tell you. But I do."

Andy stopped squirming.

Jake looked over at Rachel. It was hard to do, but he shook his head, trying to signal her that she could bail out now, not tell Andy. If Andy took this badly, if he was hurt by it, Jake suddenly didn't think he could bear it. Nothing was worth hurting Andy.

Rachel shook her own head. "Jake, it's time he knew." To Andy, she said, "Your dad…Chris, I mean, was really your adopted dad. You know what adoption means?"

"Sure. Kevin Hesper is adopted. That means—" He cut himself off as comprehension dawned. "I'm adopted?"

Rachel let go of Andy's hand and hugged him.

Rachel leaned her cheek against the top of Andy's head. "You're sort of adopted. I'm your real mom, but when I got pregnant, your real father couldn't be a dad, so Chris became your dad right from the beginning."

Andy was rigid. He said nothing.

The damn clock ticked, loud. *Ticktock. Ticktock.*

"Chris loved you," Rachel whispered.

"I know that." There was impatience in Andy's tone, but anxiety, too.

"Your real father has always loved you, too," Rachel said gently. "Your real father is Jake."

Andy's eyes flicked to Jake and got very round.

Through the tightness in his throat, Jake said, "It's true. I loved you but I couldn't take care of you because they sent me to jail, so your mom and Chris took care of you."

Andy had gone white.

Jake prayed for the first time in his life as he leaned forward, gazing across the table into the clear, anxious eyes of the son he loved. It was a short, fervent prayer, nothing like the way the congregation had prayed in church last Sunday, standing with hands folded, voices dignified. Jake prayed in his heart, seeking a direct link to a God he'd believed in for all of a week. *Dear God, please don't let my son be hurt. Please give me the right words.*

He drew courage from somewhere and gave up trying to rationalize what to say. Instead, he relied on instinct. He went over to the pair on the couch and sat next to Andy. Rachel had done the hard part. Now it was up to him.

"Your dad—Chris—loved you very much." The words were hard, but he let them come from his heart. "But I love you, too. Very much."

Andy said, "My dad liked you? You were friends?"

"Yes."

"So my dad kind of did a favor for you?" Andy cocked his head, as if thinking hard.

Over Andy's head, Jake's eyes met Rachel's. *Yes,* he thought. Then he spoke to his son. "Your dad did me the greatest favor of all—he took care of you and your mom. And he made you a wonderful kid."

Rachel smiled, and he could see the hint of relief in the depths of her eyes. He allowed himself to believe, then. Maybe it was going to be all right.

"Is it okay to love my dad?" Andy asked after a moment.

"Yes, it's okay to love your dad," Rachel said, and smiled again at Jake.

It really *was* okay, Jake realized. He'd spent so much of his life in bitterness. Now that was gone. He felt his son's warmth next to him, and Rachel beyond. His family. From now on. Jake cleared his throat again. "It's fine to love your dad. I hope you do. But someday—" he had to clear his throat one more time to get the words out "—I hope you can love me, too. See me as a father, too."

Andy studied the toe of one of his sneakers, new and still white. Finally, he said, "I don't know. You don't seem like a dad, but you're cool." There was a long pause. "But I don't think it would be that hard to love you, Jake. I mean, I already like you an awful lot."

Jake reached out then, and took both of them—Rachel and their son—in his arms. He could almost hear Rachel's cautionary voice. Andy hadn't called Jake "Dad." There would be adjustment ahead, and strained times as Jake learned to be part of a real family, and Andy learned to accept him in the role of father.

Andy's body was rigid, but he didn't pull away. He didn't pull away! Jake hugged harder. It was going to be all right, he realized suddenly. He felt the rightness of it in his soul.

In the future, he'd do everything he could to make sure Andy was happy. But for this moment, Jake knew he had everything he'd ever wanted, and he was going to hold on tight. He had his family. Rachel and Andy.

EPILOGUE

"THERE'S DAD! I see him!" Andy pointed excitedly to one of the first in a line of graduates in caps and gowns, filing onto the field-house arena.

Rachel and her family were sitting in the audience, in the front row. She shifted on the hard folding chair and waved to Jake. "Yep, that's Dad all right."

Although the graduating class numbered in the hundreds, Jake was near the front of the line because he was graduating first in his class. He wore the Order of the Coif over his gown and an insignia commemorating his year as editor of the law review.

"My, isn't he handsome," Leora murmured from her other side.

He was. He wasn't only first in his class, Rachel thought, but with his dark good looks, he was the handsomest man there. Most important of all, he was a person of extraordinary character, a good man who had defied so many odds. Her eyes stung. She blinked and studied her program. This wasn't a day for weeping, even with joy.

She clapped when the dean was announced. As his speech droned on, though, her mind wandered. She and Jake had so many memories now. New memories. Good memories, built over the last four years of their marriage.

As soon as Judge Randall had formally exonerated

Jake and he was accepted into law school, they'd moved to Columbus, where Rachel had found a rewarding job as a social worker for the county child welfare agency.

In the city, no strangers knew of his past. Jake didn't try to hide what had happened to him, but not having to confront the issue every day had been a relief. It had allowed them both to relax, to concentrate on being an ordinary family.

Andy had thrived. He was on a baseball league here and had discovered soccer in the off-season. Rachel smiled ruefully every time she realized she was raising a jock. Andy had inherited Jake's athletic prowess.

Jake had found time to coach in the summers. He and Rachel had bought a big, old house. Rachel had acquired two more cats in addition to the seven that had moved with them. Peppy was still impossibly long and lean, but now he was sedate, a mature dog who never ran away, even if Andy left the gate open.

Last year, Leora had finally sold Drewers. She continued to refer to the new owner as "that hippie girl from the city." The woman had opened a floral and gift shop full of incense and aromatherapy products, mood rings and lava lamps, with a Yanni CD always playing in the background. Leora might complain, but Rachel rather liked the idea of a fun, frivolous shop in place of the dusty, dying department store. Things changed, and it seemed that even Grange was going New Age these days.

"Dad's getting up to talk." Andy's voice abruptly changed pitch, then cracked on the last syllable. He colored. At fourteen, his voice was changing, and he hated that.

For a long time, he'd referred to Chris as his "old dad" and Jake as his "new dad." There had been some tears, some resistance to Jake taking over the role of father. Jake had persevered. It had taken a while, but these days, Andy just called Jake "Dad."

She clasped her hands tightly together as her husband got up to speak.

It was a good speech, articulate and moving and triumphant. When it was over, Rachel clapped until her hands hurt.

Then the ceremony was over, and the graduates mingled with family and friends. Jake hugged them all, and Leora got a camera out of her purse. "Stand with Andy and Rachel," she ordered Jake, and Jake complied with a smile.

Then Leora had him stand with his friend, Hank Cauffield. Both older students with families, they'd found a lot in common. Jake's class rank meant that he'd had plenty of job offers with prestigious private firms, but he and Hank were starting work next week at the public defender's office. Jake wanted to continue with the criminal law he'd come to love. But they were talking about setting up their own practice eventually.

Finally, Leora called for a picture of just Rachel and Jake. "Get a little closer, Rachel," she instructed as somebody jostled Rachel.

"Yeah, come a little closer, Rachel," Jake whispered suggestively, his dark eyes alight.

After Leora snapped her picture, Jake passed the camera to Hank who took a portrait of the entire family—Leora, Rachel, Jake and Andy. Then as Leora turned to Hank to take back her camera and dab at her eyes, Jake tipped Rachel's face up for a kiss. Then he put his lips to her ear. Amid the tumult of celebration all around them, nobody heard Jake's words but her.

"I love you," he said softly. "I've got everything I ever wanted, but I know what's really important. You and Andy, a home. We'll always be together, no matter what."

Rachel's eyes stung with tears again, but this time she didn't try as hard to control them. Today, it felt good to shed a tear for Jake's miracle.

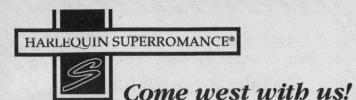

HARLEQUIN SUPERROMANCE®

Come west with us!

Start in January 1999 with *Twilight, Texas,* the next installment in our popular "West Texans" series by Ginger Chambers. West Texas—home of the Parker Ranch. And there's nobody Karen Latham loathes more than a Parker.... Then Lee Parker, her ex-fiancé's brother, shows up in the small town of Twilight—*Karen's town*.

Then in February 1999, come to Wyoming and find out *What a Man's Got To Do*. In this dramatic and emotional book by Lynnette Kent, you'll meet rancher Dex Hightower. He has to get custody of his young daughter—and get Claire Cavanaugh to help him win his case. Then he discovers he wants more from Claire.... He wants her love.

Available wherever Harlequin books are sold.

HARLEQUIN®
Makes any time special™

If you enjoyed what you just read,
then we've got an offer you can't resist!

Take 2 bestselling love stories FREE!
Plus get a FREE surprise gift!

IN UNIFORM

There's something special about a man in uniform. Maybe because he's a man who takes charge, a man you can count on, and yes, maybe even love....

Superromance presents *In Uniform*, an occasional series that features men who live up to your every fantasy—and then some!

Look for:
Mad About the Major
by Roz Denny Fox
Superromance #821
Coming in January 1999

An Officer and a Gentleman
by Elizabeth Ashtree
Superromance #828
Coming in March 1999

SEAL It with a Kiss
by Rogenna Brewer
Superromance #833
Coming in April 1999

Available wherever Harlequin books are sold.

HARLEQUIN®
Makes any time special ™

HARLEQUIN SUPERROMANCE®

COMING NEXT MONTH

#822 THE MAINE MAN • Ellen James
By the Year 2000: Marriage
The last thing on Meg Danley's mind is marriage. For one
thing, there's no fiancé in sight; for another, her demanding
career leaves no time to plan a wedding. Both good reasons for
Meg to regret the vow she made ten years ago with her two
best friends—they'd all be married by the year 2000. Meg is
quite prepared to miss the deadline...until she meets
Jack Elliott. Suddenly marriage is a definite possibility.

#823 ARE YOU MY MOMMY? • Kay David
Count on a Cop
Ray Menendez is a cop. A good cop. He knows the standard
procedure for dealing with a lost kid—turn him over to the
proper authorities. When his ex-wife, Abbie, asks him to help
the little boy she found, he knows that *not* getting involved is
also the smart thing to do. But even though their marriage is
over, he doesn't want Abbie to get hurt. Sometimes the smart
thing isn't the *right* thing....

#824 WHAT A MAN'S GOT TO DO • Lynnette Kent
Home on the Ranch
Rancher Dex Hightower wants custody of his six-year-old
daughter. So he needs to hire the best lawyer in town. And that
means Claire Cavanaugh. But Claire grew up on a ranch and
she isn't convinced that kind of life is best for a little girl. But
Dex isn't like the cowboys she's known. Maybe life on a ranch
with *him* wouldn't be too bad—even for a grown woman.

#825 FIRST BORN SON • Muriel Jensen
The Delancey Brothers
Tate Delancey and his brothers have inherited a winery in
Oregon, and Tate sees it as the perfect opportunity to start a
new life. He never expected things to be easy, and that was
before he found out the winery came with a beautiful but
prickly field manager named Colette. She fights him at every
turn—but he soon realizes fighting's the last thing he wants to
do with her!